BLOOD ORCHID

NIGHT FLOWER BOOK TWO

CLAIRE WARNER

Published by Raven Press

ISBN: 978-0-9954631-0-3

This is a work of fiction. Any similarity to any persons, living, dead or undead, is purely *coincidental.*

<u>Also by Claire Warner:</u>

Night Flower:

The Black Lotus

Blood Orchid

Faded Rose (in progress)

Coils of Copper and Brass:

Amber Sky (in progress)

Crimson:

Short Story collection (in progress)

To my family and friends,
thanks for encouraging my writing madness.
And my best thanks go to my editor.
Without you, my books would be
a mass of petty errors.

1752

CHAPTER 1

"You need to get these seen to," Justin murmured as he stared down at the wounds that crisscrossed Melissa's hands. Blood flowed steadily from the cuts and dripped onto the rough stone floor. "Or you'll bleed to death," He reached out and bound her hands with well-practised movements, trying not to look at her face, and the betrayed hatred he fancied was there.

"You mean I find someone?" She spoke for the first time since leaving her home, and he was surprised at how calm her voice seemed. "Find a donor for my life?" He looked up into her pale face and knew that her calmness was a charade. Her green eyes bored into his, and he felt himself grow cold at the bitterness, pain and grief he saw there.

"Exactly," He finished the last bandage and turned away, unable to hold her gaze much longer. That recrimination laden stare tore at his conscience and reminded him all too clearly of his sins.

"Like Montjoy did to my mother?" Brittle tones echoed in the still air of the parlour, and he bowed his head.

"Yes," What she had witnessed that night preyed on his mind and if he could have turned back the clock, he would have. "You will have to find someone to take your wounds and keep you alive," He coughed once more, and he suspected that blood had begun to fill his lungs, yet he did not allow it to worry him. After a couple of hundred years, he had become used to the feeling of teetering on the edge of life. Horror and panic were clearly visible in Melissa's face and voice. Unlike most of the others, she would find her first donor with the full knowledge of what she was.

"I'll be a monster," And there it was, the reaction he dreaded. He stared at the flagstone floor and made no answer. What could he say? He had condemned her to this life. Emily may have gifted her with the brooch, yet his selfishness had brought her into his orbit. "My mother is dead," Her voice broke, and he looked up in shame. Melissa's face was streaked with tears, and her arms were clasped tight across her chest. "I won't ever… can't ever," She struggled for words, the shock and terror of the evening had finally caught up with her. Choked, desperate sobs ripped through her body, and she sank to the floor. "I'll never see her again,"

Ignoring the pain that radiated from his ribs, Justin knelt down and drew her into his arms. Shudders raced through her as she cried against his chest. Tears were expected, for the pain and the hurt, demanded nothing less. He said nothing as he held her but the shame and guilt flooded through him at each wretched sob.

"And my brother," Muffled words as well as tears now soaked into his shirt. "I don't even know if he's alright," Justin continued to hold her. "I was awful to him…and now I may never see him again," Emotion choked her words, clouded her mind and she lapsed once more into silence.

"Marcus will be fine," He spoke softly into her hair. "I guarantee it,"

"And what if Montjoy goes back to finish him off?" She pulled away from him and stared into his face, anger as well as fear in her gaze. "He's got a locket as well. What if he does to my brother what he did to my mother?"

"He doesn't have his locket at the moment…" Justin reminded her gently. "Remember I threw it into the fireplace at your house,"

"He could retrieve it,"

"He will need help to retrieve it," Justin responded calmly. "He also has to dig himself out of the ground. It'll be a few years before he can manage his decaying limbs well enough," That was certainly true enough; the amount of will needed to keep dead limbs in motion was beyond most individuals. It had even taken John several years to master the skill, and his strength of will was almost as prodigious as his hatred for Justin.

"But one of the maids could retrieve it," Melissa persisted, another thought occurring to her. "When they sweep out the grate in the morning, they could find Montjoy's locket," She remembered the pages she had read from Justin's journals and how they had discussed the hardy nature of the brooch. "What if they pick it up?"

Justin thought for a moment, his mind helpfully providing images of maids toppling over senseless before joining him in eternity. With that thought firmly ensconced in his mind, he pulled away from her. "I see what you mean," He murmured as he pulled himself upright, favouring his bruised limbs as he did so. "I'll go and retrieve it and check on your brother,"

"But what if my father catches you?" Melissa argued, suddenly afraid for him and what could happen. Justin had already been suspected once of murder and assault and though Marcus had discovered the truth, her father had not. Images of her father attempting to hang the already damaged Justin were at the forefront of her mind.

Justin pressed his fingers to her lips and shushed her gently, thankful that she still showed some degree of care for him. Selfish though it was, he could not bear the thought that she would hate him too. Romantic notions aside, he wanted at least one ally he could trust. Her gaze softened as his fingers brushed her lips and relief swept through him.

"Don't borrow trouble," He cautioned as he leant forward and brushed his lips across her cheek. He pulled back from her and reached for his coat. "I'll sort out that brooch and make sure that Marcus is alright," With slow, pained movements he pulled the coat about himself and reached for his hat.

"But what if…" She changed tack, looking at his still battered form. "You still have injuries from the beating my brother gave you,"

"It may be difficult to get there but not impossible," He answered as he moved across the floor, favouring the broken ribs that screamed at any motion. "John still has my locket but I have a great deal of experience with working through crippling pain," He smiled weakly at her. "I can walk myself there,"

"And getting into the house?" Melissa argued, finding new things to worry about as she watched him limp to the door.

"That too is something I can handle," And with that, he walked through the parlour door and out into the night.

CHAPTER 2

"So what do you intend to do?" Hugh asked as he sank into the soft cushioned chair with a sigh of gratitude. After the events of the evening, they had returned to Emily's current residence and were now sat in comfort within a large parlour. "Now you've openly declared your colours," A quiet servant brought a tray of drinks and pastries into the room, and Hugh fell silent as she crossed the floor.

"Thank you Anna," Emily said in a dismissive tone as the woman set the tray down on a small side table. "I can take over from here," The maid nodded once and retreated quietly from view.

Emily waited until the parlour door shut before she sat opposite Hugh, rearranging her skirts as she did so. "I fancy I shall have to watch out for John," She answered in a flippant tone as she smoothed the wrinkles from the rich brocade fabric of her dress with the palm of her hand.

"Well that is rather obvious," Hugh replied as he picked up his quizzing glass and began to polish it with a finely embroidered handkerchief. "But I'm more interested in your immediate concerns and plans," He breathed lightly on the lens and regarded the blonde steadily. "Your actions this night will not have found you favour with Justin. I fancy he will be upset with you,"

"As I've already said Hugh," She reached out and picked up a pastry from the table beside her. "I don't care if I have made friends or not," Biting into the flaky confection, she chewed carefully, ignoring Hugh's exasperated tut. "Justin needed the De Vire girl," She explained as she brushed crumbs from her skirt. "And not just for companionship, if it were only sex I wouldn't be going to the trouble,"

"Would that be because you serve as his lover from time to time?" Hugh returned the handkerchief to his pocket and flourished his quizzing glass with the other hand.

"Don't be a bore Hugh," Emily replied with a petulant twist to her lips. "Yes, Justin and I have been lovers over the years. We are not in love," She stood and walked over to the fireplace. The flickering embers lent a reddish cast to her skin as she picked up the poker and prodded the glowing coals. A flurry of sparks escaped up the chimney as the cinders briefly flamed back into life and she watched them fly with a faraway look on her face.

"Then what is it between you two?" Hugh leant forward

as he tried to decipher her expression. "Don't forget how long I've known you," He reached out for a glass of brandy and took a small sip. "If you aren't in love with him, then why are you so bitter towards the De Vire girl?" Tension rippled through her body at his words. Emily liked to think that people could not read her emotions, but he could. With all the years they had spent together, he could sense her mood as clearly as if she had spoken. The silence lengthened as she stared deep into the fire and tried to avoid answering his questions. With a sigh, he pulled himself from the chair and walked over to her. The flames were higher now, and he felt the heat caress his skin as he reached her side. With a gentle touch, he caught hold of her arm and slowly turned her to face him. "And why would you change her if you would prefer to keep Justin for yourself?" Hugh watched her expressive blue eyes carefully as he waited for her to speak.

"Don't make this out to be something it isn't," She pulled her arm free and straightened the sleeve. "I'm not jealous of the De Vire girl,"

"Then what is it?" He stopped her started protest by pressing his fingers to her lips. "No I mean it Emily. This is first addition to our little family since fifteen forty, and I need to know what is behind it,"

"Why do you need to know so badly?" Her voice hissed out from between clenched teeth. "It isn't important,"

"I disagree," He leant forward and spoke carefully, enunciating each word as slowly as he could. He wanted to be sure that no misunderstanding could arise. "We have two, possibly three ongoing feuds within our merry band," He counted them off on his fingers. "John against most of us; Alistair versus Justin and I think after tonight, Alistair versus you," He gave a small snort. "I think we can also count Katherine in that merry little band. Henry may not have been heard from for a while, but I would fancy that his feud with Abbott still stands," Emily nodded slowly as he reeled off the names, aligning each of the alliances in her head as he mentioned each name. Realising he had her attention, Hugh moved back slightly. "I believe three blood feuds is more than enough trouble to be going on with," A note of warning entered his voice and countered the almost lecturing tone he had adopted. "If your actions could set off another one, I would like to know now,"

"Very well," Emily snapped, allowing frustration and anger to finally spill into her voice. "But it's not that drastic,"

"Let me be the judge of that," Hugh answered as he leant back against the mantle. "Just tell me,"

"Alright," Emily replied, her voice sharp. "I am jealous, but not in the way you think," Picking up her skirts, she returned to her chair and settled back into it. "Justin is trying to find a cure, has been for years but," She rubbed her forehead, dislodging some of the white powder that was caked to her skin. "He won't work as hard for me as he would for her," Hugh started at her announcement but said nothing, unwilling to distract her from what she would impart. "I don't want his love, but I want to know that our struggle, that my struggle, spurs him on,"

"You think he isn't working hard enough for us?"

"Yes," She pushed herself upright; agitation prevented her from sitting calmly. "But, I think she'll provide the impetus for him to continue. He'll care more,"

"And that's why you did it?" Emily nodded, and Hugh bowed his head. "Because you feel that he will make more of an effort to find a cure for her?" He had to admit that she had a point., Justin had spent a good portion of the last few years half-heartedly researching a cure, bowed down no doubt by the enormity of the task. Perhaps he would apply more of his energy to the cure now that he had a deeper reason to succeed.

"I suppose," She reached for one of the glasses and took a long drink. "I'm not enough for him," The glass clinked as she placed it upon the table with more force than was necessary. "I don't matter enough," Her gaze fixed onto the flickering fire. "It shouldn't bother me, but…" She rested her head in her hands. "It does. He won't fight hard enough for his oldest friends, but this girl smiles at him, and he'll move heaven and earth to save her,"

"You could have let John kill her," Hugh suggested gently.

"And earn Justin's hatred? Not a chance," She snorted and shook off the melancholy that was threatening to overwhelm her. "Besides, I didn't want John to claim another victim; I'm not that much of a bitch," She reached out for the second glass of brandy and finished it in one swallow. "Did that answer your question?"

"Yes I suppose it did," Hugh replied, looking down at

her with some sympathy. "So what are your plans?"

"I'm going to visit Katherine," A raised eyebrow greeted her pronouncement, but Hugh said nothing as she continued to speak. "I'm going to try to convince her to switch to our side…" A smile touched her lips at Hugh's small sniff of scepticism. "Or at the very least, to give Justin's brooch back to him,"

"Were his injuries that bad?"

"Life-threatening," She replied in an almost flippant tone. "If his life could be threatened, that is. He had at least two broken ribs and a punctured lung," With those words, she stood and rang the bell for the maid. "I'll pay a call on her tomorrow,"

"Does she still have a home in Highgate?" Hugh questioned as Emily leant against the back of the chair.

"Yes," The maid walked into the room as she spoke and Emily beckoned her over. "Mr Tarlington will be leaving now, please fetch his outdoor clothing,"

"Yes Madam," The maid bobbed a curtsey and left the room.

"You're kicking me out?" Hugh said with mock offence. "You could at least offer me a bed for what remains of the night," He nodded at the clock on the mantel. "It is two thirty in the morning,"

"Well I would, but my new husband should be back any moment, and I doubt he would appreciate it," A look of utter derision and disgust flooded her features as she spoke of her new partner.

"Ah yes, I'd forgotten," Hugh replied, glancing down at

her hand where the fresh wedding ring glimmered in the firelight. "What are you called now?"

"Lady Morton and despite having to put up with him, I am quite glad I managed to save some poor innocent from his attentions," She sneered. "He is an odious man,"

"I thought he was your…" Hugh waved vaguely, unwilling to put a name to those that they drained.

"He's going to be," Absently she reached for her choker and the smooth surface of the lotus attached to it. With slow movements, she traced the enamel bloom as she spoke. "I unfortunately still have the old one. I'm just making sure I'm prepared,"

"Very well, I'll bid you goodnight," Hugh stood and picked up his hat from the sideboard. "Have a pleasant sleep and try not to hurt Katherine tomorrow, I'm fond of her, despite her alliances,"

"I'm not a monster Hugh," Emily protested as a broad smile settled on Hugh's face.

"Yes, so you've said in the past," He chuckled as he reached forward and took hold of her hand. "I'm serious though; don't provoke her," He gently brushed his lips across her fingers.

"Good night Hugh," Emily said dismissively as he released her hand. "Don't concern yourself with me," He almost smiled at the ease at which she dismissed his concerns. Emily was many things, but stupid was not one of them. As he placed his hat upon his head, she reached forward and kissed him on the cheek. "Have a pleasant ride back home,"

CHAPTER 3

Marcus woke to dim light and the sensation of bandages wrapped securely about his body and head. A dull ache radiated along his left side, and his skull throbbed. Groaning slightly with the discomfort, he pushed himself upright and stared about his empty room in confusion. After several moments, the memories of Montjoy's attack on the manor returned to the fore and panic rushed through his mind. Rolling to the side of the bed, he struggled to his feet and reached for the robe draped across his chair. With jerky hurried movements, he dragged the fabric across his naked, bandaged body and made for the door. As he pulled the door open, he almost fell into the arms of his valet.

"You must stay abed sir," The man uttered as he steadied

his master. "The doctor said you should rest and heal,"

"Damn that," Anger ran through Marcus' voice. "I'm not staying here after Montjoy..." He took a breath and tried to calm down. "After Montjoy hurt my mother," Concern flickered in his valet's eyes, and Marcus felt the icy fingers of fear caress his spine. "Is my mother alright?" The quaver in his voice betrayed the dread that was racing through his mind as he regarded his valet's concerned face. "What happened?" The desire to know outstripped the fear of knowledge. "What has he done to my sister?"

"I think you should rest..." His valet protested weakly as he tried to usher Marcus back to his room. "Your father..."

"Let go," Marcus shoved the other man out of the way and headed to Melissa's room. "Melissa!" He shouted as he reached the open door to her chamber. Apprehension settled on his mind, and his stomach clenched with fear as he approached the ominously silent portal, "Melly?" He softened his voice as he walked through the door and into an empty room. The wriggling sensation of fear burst into full blown life as he stared at the deserted space.

"Melissa?" He turned on his heel and left her chambers, heading for the staircase. One of the servants hurried past as he reached the landing. The sound of blood rang in his ears as he raced down the steps, taking them two at a time, despite the screaming pain from his body. At the bottom of the stairs, he turned left and ran across the hallway towards the closed study door. He stopped outside, desperately hoping that he would find a tidy room and his mother smiling. Swallowing his fear, he depressed the door handle and pushed open the door.

The once warm, friendly room was cold. The fire was unlit and the shutters drawn down across the windows lent a darkly forlorn aspect to the room. With his heart in his mouth, he picked up a candle and ventured into the dimly lit space. Shattered glass littered the floor beneath the window, and broken remnants of furniture and ornamentation littered the floor. He moved deeper into the room, dread sending chill shudders over his skin. He reached the desk and stopped, his gaze caught by the dark stain which obscured the pattern on the carpet.

"Oh God," He whispered as he raised his hand to his mouth. Gingerly, he knelt down and touched his fingers to the discolouration, scraping a few flakes of the dark stain with his nails. A careful sniff confirmed the telltale odour of blood and his heart sank at the size of the stain. "Oh dear God no," The desk bruised his hip as he backed away from the mess and the knowledge that either his mother or sister had died.

"Marcus," His head snapped towards the door and the sight of his father walking slowly into the room. The older man had not shaved, and a bleak, desolate look lay in his eyes. "I see you're awake," His voice was hollow, a ghost of its former vitality and Marcus felt the fear rise once more to choke him. "I hoped that you would wake today."

"What happened?" Marcus stepped forward, noting the sorrow on his father's face. "Please just tell me?"

Edward said nothing as he stared past his son and at the ruins of the study. As Edward drew level with him, Marcus thought he heard a choked sob leave his father's lips, but a glance at his face revealed that his eyes were dry.

"Father?" He prodded, wanting to know what had occurred, even though he dreaded the answer.

"Your mother is dead," Edward delivered the ill news with a bleak calmness that Marcus found as upsetting as the information he imparted. "And your sister is missing."

For a long moment, Marcus felt unable to speak. His father's words reverberated through his mind and stopped his thoughts in their tracks. Grief swamped him yet he choked back the cry of anguish. He would not cry, not here, not before his father. He bit down hard on his lower lip and tasted blood. His mother was dead, and Melissa was missing. Thoughts of never seeing them again raced through his mind and rendered him incapable of coherent thought. He rested a hand against the wall and closed his eyes, trying to still the tumult of emotion that threatened to drown him.

"What happened?" Distantly he heard his father speak and the words prompted dark memories of that night. The shattered remnants of the room mocked as he opened his eyes and began to reconstruct the horror of Montjoy's invasion.

"I told her to run," A whisper escaped his lips, and he squeezed his eyes shut again as he tried to force himself to remain calm. Melissa had shot Montjoy twice, but he had kept coming, shrugging off blows that would have crippled or killed others. He did not recall the blow that had sent him into darkness and he did not know what had happened to Melissa.

"It was Montjoy," He uttered finally, dragging his mind back from dark memories and looking up at his father. "He did this," He glanced back down at the bloody floor and a flame of anger began to displace the shocked grief from his mind. "He attacked mother and Melissa,"

"Montjoy has my daughter?" Edward started, the bleak expression of despair on his face altered to blazing anger in one stunned moment of revelation. "That abhorrent rake killed my wife and took my daughter?" Marcus nodded in assent, watching his father's eyes fill with an equal mixture of rage and determination. Edward glanced about the ruined study, the devastation fuelling the anger that was beginning to burn within. "How dare he?" His fist slammed into the wall, grazing the knuckle. "I'll have his guts for this," Beads of blood began to ooze from the graze yet Edward paid it no mind. "What possible reason would he have for this outrage?"

Marcus didn't trust himself to speak. His anger matched his father's and his thoughts provided him with disturbing reminders of that night. He remembered the older man's sneering confidence, his comments directed at Melissa and his anger grew.

"He was upset that I had bested him," Marcus mused aloud as he fed the anger that burned within him. "Melissa had rejected his advances," He stopped speaking, unwilling to give voice to his fears for his sister. Tearing his mind away from images of Melissa in Montjoy's custody, he came up with an answer to another problem. "Montjoy must have assaulted her that night, not Justin," He felt it was right to end the dark cloud that they had laid on the young man. With a pang, he remembered the man's urgent plea for Marcus to ensure that Melissa's reputation would be spared and he clenched his hands into fists. "I believe Justin truly cared for her," Stepping back into the hall away from the scene of devastation, he held back his guilt and frustration. "Montjoy can't be allowed to get away with this," He headed for the main door.

"Where are you going?" Edward reached his side and caught hold of his arm. "You're far too injured to go after him,"

"I'll be fine," Marcus insisted as he shook his father's hand from his arm. "My wounds won't stop me,"

"Marcus," The anger that Marcus' words had triggered in Edward was still there, but fear for his son had taken over from that emotion. "I know that you're angry but if you go after him now, you may be hurt," He reached out and seized Marcus for the second time, turning him round so that he could look directly into his face. "Or killed," He continued, his voice breaking with emotion as he spoke. "I have lost my daughter and my wife, I will not lose my son," Marcus took a deep breath as his father's heartfelt plea tugged at him. "Please Marcus, go back upstairs and heal," Marcus wanted to push away, to head away from the blood stained study and find Montjoy but his father's words sent stabs of guilt through him and he nodded reluctantly.

"Alright," He uttered as he turned away from the front. "But I won't rest for long. As soon as I am able, I will find

Montjoy and my sister," He turned and began to head up the stairs.

CHAPTER 4

Melissa fell into a deep, dream haunted sleep, full of faceless beings that chased her through endless dark alleys as the lotus bloom in her hand greedily drank her blood. Pursued through the shadowy landscape, she hunted for a way out. A door loomed out of the darkness and she ran toward it, desperate to escape the shadowy beings that clamoured and snapped at her heels. Something sharp tore into her leg and she stumbled, her hands slapping into the door with bruising force as she fell forward. The door opened and she threw herself through the aperture. Beyond the door lay the corridor that had haunted her dreams for the past few months. Dust rose in choking clouds about her as she ran past the pictures on the walls.

The faces of the dead leered down at her, spitting curses she could not hear or understand as she rushed headlong towards the waiting maw of the lotus and the warning that she belatedly recognised for the hell she had found herself in.

With a stifled scream she jolted awake and stared about in shock at the strange parlour. The parlour was lit by the dying light of the fire. Shadows danced in every corner of the room and across the ruined and mouldered furniture. She listened carefully, but could hear no other sound from within the cavernous house. Pain screamed from her hands as she pulled herself from the makeshift bed. The bandages that covered her wounds were drenched with blood and rich drops fell from the saturated fabric to land in small spots on the floor. Wincing with the pain that did not seem to lessen, she undid the bindings and stared at the cuts. They were as fresh as they had been earlier and showed no sign of clotting or healing. She sucked in a deep breath and reached for the fresh set of bandages that had been laid on the side table and clumsily applied them. That done, she settled back down in Justin's chair and stared blankly at the wall opposite as she tried to come to terms with the horror that had suddenly engulfed her.

The fire in the hearth had burned down to embers yet she sat in the same place, her mind focused on the pain in her hands and the inescapable truth of her current situation. She had cried more than once, the tears had dripped down her face to mingle with the blood that continued to ooze from her hands. Through the long hours of the night, she had pondered one definitive truth. Her hands would never heal again and they wouldn't until she found someone to take her pain. Intellectually she understood the need, but her mind recoiled at the thought. How could she place somebody under this spell? How could she ask, no, insist that someone give her their life? She would be a monster. Even if she tried to find those who deserved such a fate, how could she live with that knowledge? She dragged herself to her feet and finally left the parlour. Following the route she had traversed all those weeks ago, she headed for the library and hopefully some answers.

She reached the book-laden room and walked inside. The room had not altered since the last time she had visited. The same books were messily piled on the shelves, and the papers on the table lay in haphazard piles. Blood spattered on the stone floor and drew her from her reverie. Much as she needed to read, she could not touch the pages with her hands as bloody as this, and she left the library to fix the problem. Rebound in fresh cotton and free of blood for the moment, she returned to the room and began to sift through the stack of parchment. She seized hold of the first piece of paper in Justin's looping script, sat down on the cold stone floor and began to read.

Hours passed, the sun finally sending fingers of pale yellow light to supplement the meagre glow provided by the lamps yet she paid it no mind. Engrossed in the notes that Justin had painstakingly produced, she failed to hear his return

"Melissa," She started at her name and stared up at

Justin. In the pale light of day, his bruises were clearer, the pallor of his skin more pronounced and he looked as though death had already taken him.

"I'm sorry," She uttered, her words soft and miserable. The truth of his research hitting her harder than she thought it would. What ensnared her had no cure and death was no escape.

"Don't be," He settled into the chair next to her and stared at the paperwork before him. "I understand," He reached out a hand and rested it on her shoulder. "Your life has been altered beyond expectation," She stared back at him, at the understanding she saw in his gaze. "I don't wish you to accept it without question,"

She nodded and glanced down once again at her hands, at the blood that still seeped through the fabric. He followed the direction of her eyes and reached forward. His fingers skilfully rebound her cuts and she gave him a watery smile in gratitude.

"Did you manage it?" She asked, dragging herself free of introspection. "Did you retrieve the locket?"

"Yes," Justin responded, reaching into his pocket and drawing forth the enamelled flower. "It was easy, no one had woken and I was in and out in a moment," He opened the box beside them and placed the brooch within.

"And my brother?" Melissa demanded, impatience thrumming through her as she spoke. "Is he well?"

"Yes," Melissa closed her eyes and breathed a huge sigh of relief at the words. "He was fairly badly beaten but nothing he won't heal from,"

"Thank God," Melissa whispered, tears once again beginning to spill from her eyes. Unlike the tears she had shed throughout the night, these were tears of relief. Justin reached forward and drew her into his arms, wincing as his ribs screeched in protest. Her head lay on his chest, and her bloody hands reached about his back. For a long time, he held her, saying nothing as she cried.

"Come on," He muttered finally as her sobs began to cease. "I'll put you to bed," He stood and drew her with him. Moving out of the library, he led her back to the main staircase and up to the first floor. They walked past walls damp with mildew and mould as he led her along the upper gallery. The door at the end opened into a lit bedchamber. The room was dry and fairly clean but simply furnished. A large four poster dominated the room, and a stunted set of drawer stood against one wall. Melissa climbed onto the bed and settled back against the pillows. As Justin drew the blankets about her, she could smell the lingering scent of his cologne on the sheets, and she closed her eyes, torn between anger and care.

"Get some sleep," Justin muttered, he wished he could tell her that this was only a bad dream. Her dark hair fanned out over the pillows as she drifted toward sleep. Several stray strands of hair fell across her face and he brushed them away with a gentle touch. "You need some rest.

"I rested earlier," She whispered, her voice hoarse from crying. "I had nightmares," Melissa looked directly at him and tried not to blame him. She knew that he had tried to prevent the tragedy that had befallen her and his eyes spoke volumes of guilt and sorrow. The gentleness of his touch told her his feelings; she had felt concern and what could be described as love as his fingers lightly traced over her skin. "Could you stay with me?" The terror of the previous hours infused her words, and his hand stilled. "I don't want to be alone,"

"Of course," He settled himself as comfortably as he could and watched as she drifted off to sleep. He coughed into his handkerchief and stared down at the bright bloom of blood on the white cotton with a wry smile. It was getting worse; he had indeed punctured a lung which didn't bode well for the future. He needed to retrieve his brooch from John. That was one of his first priorities. He had 'died' at least once before, but he didn't relish repeating the experience. Bars of golden sunlight fell through the gap in the curtains and pierced the gloom. The pale light fell across Melissa's sleeping face, and guilt gnawed at his insides. If he had not approached her, she would have been free of this joke of life. If she did not hate him now, she would. The first time she had to kill would drive that wedge of anger into her mind, and he would pay the price. In this instance, he could not even claim ignorance of the curse's power. His own selfish desires had drawn her into this web and had it not been for him. He closed his eyes and attempted to banish the dark thoughts that were gathering inside his head. For now he had to make sure she was well, there would be time later to worry about things he could not change. The sun climbed higher into the sky as he stayed by her side, kept alert by his injuries and his guilt.

CHAPTER 5

Emily knocked sharply on the door of Katherine's home in Highgate. As the blonde waited, she regarded the poorly kept columns at the porch and the weed-choked drive with a sniff of derision. Katherine seemed not to care about her accommodation or means. Even given the fact that she was linked to John's purpose, she should not be so careless of her living space. As she pondered the cracked paintwork on the door it swung open. To her surprise, a butler stood behind the portal. She would not have thought that Katherine would have employed help with the limited means she seemed to have.

"I need to see your mistress," Emily said with a bright smile, dismissing the idle speculation with the urgency of her task.

"And who should I announce?" The butler asked after a moment's hesitation. He did not recognise the woman before him, and it was rare for his mistress to receive guests.

"Just say Emily," The blonde replied. "She'll know who I am," The butler nodded and showed her into the hallway. Like the garden outside, the house showed signs of neglect and abandonment. The hall was oppressive, its peeling walls and air of neglect made her cringe, yet she suppressed the feeling and used the time to take in the details around her. It was clean and smelt of beeswax, but the rugs that lay on the flagstoned floor were threadbare and the paper that lined the walls was peeling. A mirror hung at the end of the hallway sported a long crack through its silvered surface and added to the general feel of neglect. A set of battered wooden drawers stood by the front door, and she wondered if Katherine had been foolish enough to keep Justin's brooch there.

"May I take your coat Madam?" She shook her head and stopped at the bottom of the staircase.

"No thank you," Her eyes darted quickly towards the upper landing before returning to the butler's solid face. "I won't be here long,"

"Very good madam," He walked down to the end of the hallway and disappeared from sight. As she waited for him to return, Emily moved across the hallway and quickly checked the drawers. As she had anticipated, she did not find any sign of Justin's brooch. Hearing the returning footsteps of the butler, she slid the drawer shut and returned to the centre of the hall.

"The mistress will see you now," The butler nodded and led her through a door at the end of the hallway. Emily walked into the room and waited for the butler to leave. As soon as she was alone, she began to examine the room. Like the hallway, the parlour screamed of neglect. The furniture was several decades out of date, shabby and well worn. A vase on the bookcase held a selection of late summer blooms, yet they too seemed faded, as though affected by the melancholy that exuded from every facet of the faded house. Above the mantel, a portrait of a young woman in a cream and red dress smiled down at her. Emily averted her gaze from the image of Katherine's long dead sister as she continued to look around. In the corner, a small desk with a small pile of paper stacked on top gave her some measure of hope. With several light steps, she crossed the room and began to rifle through the stack. Many of the letters appeared to be recent, bills and the like but as she dove rapidly through the pile, one partially buried letter caught her attention. Quickly, she drew it free and shoved it into her dress pocket.

"What are you doing here?" Katherine's voice echoed round the parlour, and she whirled about, hoping that the other woman had not seen her pilferage. Katherine had stopped in the doorway, her glorious chestnut hair half hidden by a mob cap. "I thought you weren't going to talk to me," She moved into the room, her steps brisk and businesslike.

"We all say things we don't mean sometimes," Emily

replied. She crossed the room towards one of the chairs, making sure that the letter was hidden out of sight. Katherine's dress was plain and unadorned and her once sweet face was creased into an expression of contempt. With a pang of worry, Emily noted bruising beneath the choker that encircled the woman's throat.

"Oh you meant it," Katherine retorted as she sat down in the other chair and delicately folded her hands on her lap. "You weren't joking when you said it,"

"Am I not allowed to change my mind?" Emily sat down and directed a friendly smile at the other woman. "People can change you know,"

"Not when that person is you," Katherine rang a small bell and ordered tea. They remained silent until the butler brought in the tray of refreshments and as he exited the room, Katherine turned back to face Emily with a grim, unfriendly look on her face. "What do you want?"

"Straight to the point," Emily muttered in appreciation. "No, how have the last one hundred years gone Emily?" She picked up a cup and took a small sip. Setting the cup back in its saucer, she continued. "Simply what do you want?"

"If you wanted small talk, you would have started with small talk," Katherine replied, "I don't want to know what you've been up to for the past century. I'm certain it's been far more entertaining than mine," Her voice was brittle with barely contained pain and anger. "You haven't shown any sign of wanting to be sociable in the past, so obviously, you want something," She leant forward and fixed Emily with a piercing stare. "What is it?"

Emily paused for a moment; Katherine's tirade was distinctly out of character, and she stared across at the woman for a long moment before answering. Had she become John's creature? The silence stretched between them and as Emily wrestled with that frightening and upsetting thought.

"Well?" Katherine's brittle tones shattered the stillness and Emily took a deep breath. "Very well," The question needed an answer and despite Emily's concerns, she had never retreated from difficulty in the past. "I want Justin's brooch,"

"Ah," Katherine breathed with some satisfaction. "And what makes you think I have it?"

"I don't think you have it," Emily replied with a small sigh of derision as she picked up her cup again. "I know John has it,"

"And you want me to go against John?" Katherine had been in the process of picking up a cup of tea, yet she drew back in order to stare at Emily in disbelief. "Do you know what he'll do to me?"

"I have an idea," Emily retorted, looking at Katherine with a mixture of pity and exasperation. "Why do you still stay with him?"

"Because I can't leave," Katherine snapped back, She caught the look on Emily's face and her anger flared anew. "You've never understood," She blinked, her brown eyes filled with tears of anger. "None of you have ever understood. I can't go against him,"

"Is it because he has your brooch?" Katherine started at her words and in answer, Emily pointed at the bruises which were just visible above the choker she wore. "You haven't healed,"

"Yes. He has mine and Justin's," Katherine rubbed her bruises absently as she replied. "I can't do anything, or he'll do so much damage to me that I won't be able to move," Staring down at her skirts, she continued. "Do you think I like doing this for him? Do you know what I did?" An angry, bitter note entered her voice. "On his orders I gave this," She shrugged helplessly. "Gift to one who should never have had it," A look of horror crossed her face. "I promised that I would never curse anyone," Her voice cracked with anger. "That I would never bring someone into this and what did I do?" A mocking bitter laugh flowed from her mouth. "I cursed that bastard Montjoy and sent him after the De Vire girl,"

Emily froze and stared at Katherine in disbelief. "You cursed that monster? John's bad enough," Her voice snapped out like a whip. "If he gave you the damn brooch back, then why did you follow his instructions?"

"You don't understand anything Emily!" Katherine shouted, the volume of her voice bringing the butler in a dead run to the door of the parlour. "I can't disobey him!"

"Are you alright Miss?" He asked, staring across at Emily with deep suspicion.

"Yes I'm fine," Katherine's voice settled back to a more even tone. "I was explaining something to my friend. Please leave us,"

"Very good Miss," The butler nodded reluctantly as he turned and slowly left the room. Emily had paid no attention to the butler's interruption; she was watching Katherine's face as her head began working through numerous scenarios.

"When you say you can't disobey?" Her voice was low and touched with intrigue. "In what context do you mean?"

"I mean I can't disobey," Katherine said carefully, distinctly, as though she were talking to a simpleton. "I physically cannot disobey. I may want to but I can't,"

"How?" This was news to Emily, she quickly began wracking her brains to work out if Justin had mentioned anything of this in the past. If Katherine could not actually go against John, then it changed a good deal. If she achieved nothing else from this meeting, the information she had gained would be worth the trip.

"I don't know," Katherine replied in a voice close to tears. "I don't know how he does it, but it's more than threats and violence," She glanced over her shoulder as though she feared that he was stood right behind her. "I wish I'd gone with you when you'd asked," Emily started at the change in Katherine's tone. She sounded wistful and scared. Not for the first time, Emily's heart reached out to the woman. "He may not have discovered the way if I hadn't been there," Emily stood and walked over to the other woman's side. "I want to help but I don't know how," Katherine looked up as Emily reached her side. "And if you ask me to help, I'll betray you," A sparkling tear spilled from her eye and ran down her cheek. Emily's face clouded with sympathy and she opened her arms. Katherine fell against her and began to weep. Emily stroked her hair as her mind travelled back a hundred years or more and the last time that Katherine had wept in her embrace. If she had known then what John was fully capable of, she would have never let the other girl go.

"Just tell me where he's currently staying?" She murmured into the woman's shoulder. "I'll do the rest," Katherine's arms were around her back and she could feel the tears sliding into her shoulder "I don't care if you tell him. John has never scared me. If anything, he should be afraid of what I can do to him,"

"You don't know what he's like, not really," Katherine muttered into her ear. "You have never felt his anger,"

"No?" Emily pulled away and looked at her calmly. "I tussled with John for several years before you joined us," Carefully she brushed the tears from Katherine's face. "Now tell me Kat, where does he live?"

CHAPTER 6

Hugh was at Whites when the first streams of gossip regarding the De Vire family reached his ears. He had just returned from the bar when the conversation from a nearby table seized his attention.

"I heard De Vire lost his wife and daughter in the same night," Hugh came to an abrupt halt, the carafe of burgundy swung loosely from his hand the liquid sloshed over his fingers as he turned to face the group. The speaker, a middle-aged gentleman continued, his voice divulging the choice gossip with relish. "Apparently Edward De Vire arrived home to find his wife with a cut throat and blood everywhere,"

"You exaggerate Davenport," One of the others

announced with equal relish. "My information is that she was shot," Hugh moved closer and watched as the man knocked back a brandy in one swallow. "It's not as salacious as you make it seem,"

"Excuse me?" The four men glanced up as Hugh interrupted. "I couldn't help but overhear," He addressed the second speaker, "What has happened to the De Vires?" The group shifted slightly to let him in.

"Well, I don't know the full details," One started, eager to spill the news. "All I know is that Edward De Vire returned home to find his wife dead, daughter missing and his son unconscious,"

"Do you know who did it?" Hugh projected the right level of excited curiosity as he listened with a growing sense of horror.

"I heard it was Montjoy," A white-haired gentleman volunteered from one of the other tables. Hugh glanced over at him, and his heart sank. This was not the news he wanted to bring to Justin. He was already dreading having to inform him of her current state, but this news shocked him to the core.

"Wasn't she the one that slapped him at the Palace?" One of the other patrons interjected and the conversation continued. At any other time, he would be gossiping along with the rest but, this news needed relaying to Justin. Making his apologies, Hugh excused himself from the table. With a heavy heart, he left Whites as quickly as he could without drawing suspicion. Once outside, he collected his carriage and directed the driver to head for Justin's manor house. This wasn't the news he wanted to deliver, but he felt he had to.

The journey from London to Justin's ancestral home took several hours, and it was late afternoon by the time the carriage finally rolled down the weed-choked drive. The coachmen drew to a stop, and Hugh opened the door without waiting for the coachman to perform the service. Stepping onto the moss covered gravel, he told his driver to wait before he walked swiftly towards the main door. A maelstrom of nervous energy and emotion whirled within his head as he raised his cane and rapped loudly against the door.

Several moments passed as he waited on the doorstep, impatiently tapping the ground with his cane. Despite not knowing how to broach the difficult subject, he still did not wish to wait too long before bringing the news to Justin's attention. A chill breeze tugged at his clothing and he stopped the agitated tapping to listen for any sounds from beyond the door. The sound of slow shuffling footsteps reached his ears and he gave a sigh of understanding for the delay. Emily had said that Justin was injured. The footsteps reached the door and there was the sound of bolts being drawn back. Hugh drew a breath and composed himself as the door finally opened to reveal the dishevelled and very badly injured form of Justin Lestrade. For a moment Hugh stared at the young man, shocked by the state of him. He had thought that Emily had been exaggerating but one glance at Justin dispelled that notion. In that moment, he very much wished he did not have to give such bad tidings.

"Hugh, what in the blazes are you doing out here?" Justin asked, bemusement in his face and voice.

"I've heard some troubling news," Hugh announced as he walked towards the door. "And this conversation will be better conducted indoors," He wondered at his understatement, but decided that the news was sufficiently unpleasant to not need any further drama.

"Of course," Justin stood aside and let Hugh walk past him into the hallway. "What's the matter?" He shut the door and began to shuffle slowly towards the ruined parlour.

"It's about Melissa De Vire," Hugh started as he followed the younger man's laboured gait. "Perhaps you'd better sit down," He glanced about the room as Justin sank into his favourite chair with a look of bemused concern on his face. The room was almost as he remembered it and he gave a sigh at the state of the once grand room. Justin coughed, drawing his attention. Hugh waited patiently as bright blood sprayed into the handkerchief that Justin held to his mouth.

"Go on Hugh," Justin uttered in a husky groan as he finally managed to get the cough under control. "What about Melissa?"

"She's been abducted," Hugh said it fast, trying hard not to drag out the torment any further. Justin's eyes widened and he continued, hoping to finish the news before the questions started. "Montjoy killed her mother and dragged her away," He watched Justin carefully, hoping that the boy would not break down. "I'm so sorry my boy,"

Justin opened his mouth to speak, and Hugh braced himself for the storm, but at that moment, a female voice interrupted from the doorway.

"Hugh?"

Tarlington turned and gaped as Melissa De Vire walked into view. The young woman was safe. Her clothes were ripped and shabby, and her bandaged hands dripped blood, but she was safe and well. Relief rushed through him as he took in her appearance.

"Oh my dear girl," Hugh exclaimed as he reached forward and caught hold of her forearms. "My dear, dear girl," he repeated, joy in his tone "I was so concerned for you," He nearly embraced her, but thought better of it as he stared down at her face. She may have been kept from Montjoy's clutches but, grief and pain were etched into her face and not for the first time, he cursed Justin for the trouble the lotus flower had brought them.

"I take it the news of my disappearance is out?" She asked. Her voice was subdued, the events of the other night clearly preying on her mind. He had to remind himself that it had only been two nights since she had joined their little group and with Montjoy's assault happening on the same night, he wondered if she would recover.

"Yes," He bent his head. "I'm so sorry to hear about your mother,"

Melissa did not answer, and he could not blame her. The pain was too new, too raw. Not only did she have the loss of her own mortality to deal with but the death of her mother. It had taken them several decades to come to terms with the horror that they were forced to live with, but she had been dragged directly into the middle of it all.

"So it was Montjoy?" He asked, looking across at the still wounded Justin. He didn't really need the man to answer. He could see the anger in his face.

"Yes," Justin replied, wincing with each word, "There is worse news than that however," Hugh felt a cold shiver run down his spine as the other man spoke. "Montjoy is now one of us,"

"What?" Hugh took a step back, "How did that happen?" A sick feeling settled over him and he glanced down at Melissa. The woman's face was immobile, but he could see ice cold hatred deep within her gaze.

"Not me," Justin replied shortly. "It appears that John has got involved again," He coughed again and blood trickled from the corner of his mouth. Weakly, he raised the handkerchief and mopped up the red fluid with an irritated gesture.

"John made another?" Hugh was startled, part of John's hatred revolved around the curse that Justin had unleashed upon them. It did not make any sense for him to have cursed another one this far along in the game. "Why?"

"I wouldn't know," Justin shifted uncomfortably in his chair and coughed again.

"Does it matter why?" Melissa spoke and her voice sounded dead and hopeless. "He killed my mother," He thought for a moment that she was about to cry, yet she held back, controlling the impulse with a supreme effort. "He used my mother to heal," She dragged her locket free from a pocket and stared at it. "He used one of these and made her look at it," Hugh could hear anger building in her voice and he glanced across at Justin. "I watched him do it and I could do nothing," There was rage in her tones and Hugh finally caught hold of her shoulders. "I couldn't save her," He could feel tremors of anger running through her as she continued to speak. "He gloated when he did it," She bowed her head and angrily pushed the tears from her eyes.

"There is nothing I can say that will help," Hugh said softly, carefully as he lifted her chin so that she could meet his eyes. He could see the rage boiling within her coupled with a bleak violence that he had never wanted to see in her face. "Don't chase this question, it will drive you insane,"

"He has to pay," She ignored his words, lost in her own anger. "I will make him pay,"

Hugh looked at Justin as the young man dragged himself from the chair. He did not know whether Justin could talk to her, but it was worth a try

"Don't go down this road Melissa," Justin whispered as he reached her side.

"Why?" She stared up at him, bright spots of anger in her face, "Why should he feel that he has gotten away with it? Why should he be able to do that and smile?"

"Because you are better than this," Justin murmured, reaching out and holding her arms. "It won't make you feel any better and to best him, you will become worse than he is," His fingers seized hold of the hand that held the brooch and he raised it to her eye line. "You would have to use that brooch and risk your physical wellbeing," She tried to pull her hand back, but he kept hold of it and continued. "But you won't just risk yourself, the person who lives for you will also have to suffer for your vengeance," She stiffened in his arms and looked up at him, the anger freezing in her eyes as what he was saying made her think. "Are you willing to do that?"

Silence settled over the parlour. There was only the sound of the fire crackling in the hearth as the echoes of his words died. Violence twisted and died as his words penetrated her thoughts and she wept. The emotional storm raged through her as he held her tenderly and waited. He glanced over at Hugh and hoped that his words had done something to forestall a blind quest for revenge. After a few moments of quiet tears she pulled away and he looked down at her face. The bleak look was gone, yet the anger remained. Troubled, he sat back down and watched as she settled in one of the other chairs. The tears had dried and a grim determination began to settle over her features. He hoped she had taken some of their advice.

"Perhaps John didn't do it," He returned to the earlier conversation, occasionally glancing at Melissa as he spoke. He shifted in the chair as he tried to move to a more comfortable position, but the pain in his ribs froze him in place. Focusing through the pain, he continued to speak. "I don't think he's above getting someone else to do it. He can then claim that his hands are clean,"

"Kat then," Hugh sighed and stared down at the younger man. "Well we'll soon find out," Justin looked at him quizzically. "Emily's gone to talk to her," He explained as Justin's mouth formed the question.

"Really?" Justin raised an eyebrow. "I thought they weren't speaking,"

"They weren't" Hugh replied, sitting down on the edge of the chest of drawers. "But Emily wanted to retrieve your brooch; she should be there now trying to convince her to help,"

"Who is this Kat?" Melissa asked and they both started at the brusque note to her voice. Her face was still red and though the tears had ceased, anger still simmered in her gaze and they shared a worried look. "Hugh?" She glanced at the older man, who sighed and began to speak.

"Katherine is John's creature. She does whatever he asks, without question,"

"So you think she made Montjoy?" A hard note entered her tone. "She's the reason he's like this?"

"She wouldn't do it on her own," Justin responded quickly, trying to head off the inevitable conclusion of her reasoning. "John would have forced her,"

"But she still did it," Melissa argued as she leant forward and gestured with her bloody, bandaged hands. "If she hadn't, Montjoy would have died when I shot him and my mother would still be alive," Her voice rose and both Hugh and Justin winced at the sound.

"If is the cruellest word," Hugh uttered. "It can drive you crazy," Hugh felt his heart sink as he stared at her. He had seen others at this same point, almost broken by anger and regret. "I can give you one piece of advice here and now and

I advise you to heed it," She looked at him, drawn by the intensity of his gaze. "Never use the word if," He fixed his eyes on hers, hoping that she would hear and understand his words. "It will bring you nothing but pain and anger," He leant forward and caught her hands. "Please Melissa, I know it's difficult and I know you're angry, but don't do this to yourself," Melissa pulled her hands back yet Hugh held tightly to her fingers as he continued to speak in a sharper tone than he had been. "I would listen, because I have stood where you are now,"

Melissa pulled her hands free and stood up. "Yes," Her voice was quiet, leeched of all emotion as she stared at him. "You stood by and let Emily do this to me," Hugh winced at the condemnation in her words and backed away. Straightening up she whirled round and began to stride out of the room.

"Melissa," Justin pulled himself to his feet and began to walk after her, only for Hugh to stop him.

"Leave her," Hugh cautioned, "Let her deal with her anger alone,"

"But?"

"No buts," Hugh continued. "Your own guilt will make this worse. She needs time to think and she can't do that if you're stood by her," He pushed Justin back to his chair. "We have other things to discuss, leave her to work this out for herself,"

CHAPTER 7

Melissa stalked from the parlour, her anger carrying her from the mild platitudes that Hugh dared to speak. How dare they tell her how to feel? Did they not understand? If this Katherine had not cursed Montjoy, her mother would still be alive, and her brother would be well. She reached the stairs and raced up them, taking them two at a time, her anger driving her up the uneven steps until she reached the top. Without a pause, she ran along the landing to Justin's room, threw open the door and flung herself onto the bed. Laid prone on the sagging bed frame, she pressed her face into the damask pillows and listened to the sound of the blood pounding in her ears. Katherine was responsible for her mother's death. The thought reverberated round her mind as she curled her fingers into claws. How could Hugh try to say that Katherine wasn't responsible? Without her interference, Montjoy may not have been well enough to even invade their home. She rolled over onto her side and curled up into a ball. This Katherine must have known what Montjoy was like; yet she had let him loose. As she gave free reign to her anger, her mind began to conjure a picture of Katherine. She pictured a woman much like Emily, a mocking blonde with cruel eyes. Screwing her eyes shut, she imagined the sound of Katherine's laughter as she handed the lotus to Montjoy and her rage increased. Montjoy would have taken it with that vicious smirk and chuckled as the curse took him. Melissa clenched her hands into fists, ignoring the pain from the cuts as she pictured the scene.

"I hate her," She breathed into the pillow beside. "God I hate her," Tears of pain and anger dripped onto the fabric as her nails dug into the wounds on her palms. Blood dripped onto the counterpane through the makeshift bandages.

"It's all her fault," Her voice mumbled into the cool darkness of the room as her mind began to focus on thoughts of revenge. "If she hadn't…" She couldn't finish the sentence as white hot rage began to smoulder within her. Once again, her mind returned to Montjoy, to the look of triumph he had given as he killed her mother. "It's all her fault…" Her bloody fist slammed into the pillow as she took out her rage on the only target available. Blood stained the pillowslip as her fist slammed down into its yielding surface. "I'll kill her…" Her fist struck again as her rage built again. "I'll kill him…" Her anger filled cries were muffled by the bedding as her hands punched into the soft target again and again. With each bloody punch, with each rapid breath, her thoughts vanished, obliterated by all-encompassing fury.

She did not know how long the rage took her, did not know how long before the pain in her hands finally brought her back. Through deep, ragged breaths of utter exhaustion, she stared down at the blood-stained pillow. The cuts in her hands had opened wider as her fingers had pressed into the bloody creases. As her rage began to subside, the wounds began to sing in pain, and she gritted her teeth. For a long moment she stared at the makeshift bandages, feeling the pain across her fingers. Pushing the bloody pillow aside, she flopped onto her back and stared up at the ancient canopy above her. The wood was black with dirt and age, yet she could not manage to care. All that remained in her thoughts was a desire to hurt Montjoy and the one she would hold responsible for him.

For a long time she lay there. Her green eyes stared into space as she waited for the oblivion of sleep. In the cool stillness of Justin's bedroom her senses seemed sharper. The wood above her was pitted and cracked, she could see old evidence of woodworm, yet the bed seemed solid. Pain radiated from her hands and she tried to ignore the oozing wounds as she listened to the sounds about her. Wind whistled through cracks in the shutters and raced along ruined corridors. From the direction of the landing, something creaked and her eyes flicked to the door. She drew a breath, waiting to see if Hugh or Justin would open the heavy wooden portal. Moments passed with no further noise, and she slowly relaxed, she did not want to see either of them, did not want to listen to anything they had to say. As sleep stole closer, she tried to remember her mother. Closing her eyes, she pictured Lydia reaching out for her with a smile on her face. Lost in the memory, she finally drifted off to sleep.

The dream hallway stretched out ahead of her. She moved along it, her eyes everywhere. Along the wall, blank rectangles showed where paintings had once hung, and cobwebs crowded in every corner. Slowly and noiselessly her feet carried her through the dust-choked hallway. The silence was deafening before she had been suffocated by sound but now... She shuddered and continued towards the opening at the end of the corridor. The lotus was still there. Its dark glossy surfaces dripped dark blood. Shadows draped this room like lace and she looked away from the lotus into the dim corners, nerves jangling with fear. People stood within the shadows, their eyes fixed on her as she backed away. From the other side of the room, more figures stepped forward, the lotus design standing out on their clothing in cream and gold. As they reached the dim light in the centre of the room, she choked at the grim determination in their unfriendly faces. Stepping back from the centre of the room, she turned away from them and fled into the corridor. Almost tripping in her haste, she raced past the blank walls, struggling to get away from the ominous group that followed her. Panic pulsed through her as she fled, sending up clouds of dust from the filth choked floor.

She choked and woke up, her breath coming in sharp gasps as a cold sweat clung to her body. Disorientated in the darkness of Justin's bedroom, it took a few moments for her memory to return. The wind had died and she could hear distant conversation, Unwilling to fall back into the nightmare, she got up and headed for the door. With careful, quiet steps, she walked along the upper corridor and headed down the stairs. The conversation from the parlour grew louder as she approached and she stopped outside the door to listen.

"Will you find him?" Hugh was saying, his tones echoing through the heavy wood.

"I'm going to have to find him," Justin replied with irritation dulled by the husky notes to his voice. "What kills me is that he was here at the house," Melissa started at the news and moved closer to the door.

"John was here?"

"Oh please Hugh, don't start repeating what I say," Justin retorted, a ghost of his former humour rippling through his voice. "John was stood in that hallway," With a start, Melissa glanced involuntarily about the hall and chided herself for being jumpy. "He had killed Coll," His voice was calm, yet she could hear the anger beneath the stillness "It was all I could do in the circumstances not to beat him into a bloody pulp," He coughed again, a wheezing pained cough and she pictured the blood smeared across the back of his hand.

"So why didn't you?" Hugh's voice was mildly curious. "He was here; you could have solved several problems at once,"

"I couldn't waste the time to stop him," Justin continued in a tired voice. "He said something about Melissa and I knew he was targeting her,"

"So you left him here and ran off," Hugh sighed and there was a creak from what Melissa took to be his weight as it settled on the table. "I still think you should have punched him,"

"He wouldn't have kept my brooch on him,"

"Not for your brooch dear boy," Hugh replied. "For the sheer pleasure of pummelling him,"

"Well that may have to wait until another day," He coughed again and his voice grew weaker.

"Such patience…"

"No, not patience," Justin said, his voice sounded thick and somewhat liquid. "The unfortunate matter of dying has a tendency to slow me down,"

Melissa heard him sink heavily onto a chair and she edged closer to the door, fear suddenly thrumming through her as she processed his words.

"Are you that close?" Hugh's voice was hushed and sympathetic.

"I've a punctured lung; it's been filling with blood for the past day," Justin coughed again and Melissa shrank back against the wall, trying hard not to listen to the ragged breathing that was now issuing from Justin's mouth. "I've been here before Hugh, I possibly have a couple of hours left until I'm a corpse. Though I will say that I've lasted longer than the last time this happened,"

Hugh chuckled bleakly "You make a habit of this? I would have said that it was most uncomfortable,"

Justin did not answer yet his coughs echoed through the room. Melissa clasped her hands to her mouth and tried not to panic at the rattling breaths that Justin was now taking.

"Justin?"

Justin's breath grew shallower and slower, and she stepped forward, pushing open the door and walking into the room. Justin lay slumped in his favourite chair, blood trickling over his chin as though he had been drinking the stuff. He skin was a ghostly grey, and his eyes were closed. With a sinking heart, she raced to his side.

"Justin?" She uttered, clasping his hand and drawing it to her chest. The blood from her damaged fingers mixed with his and she felt her stomach twist. "Justin?"

"It's alright my dear," Hugh's fingers settled reassuringly on her shoulder. "He'll be fine,"

"He's dying," She whispered,

"Indeed he is," Hugh turned her away from the other man. "But give it till morning and he will be walking around," He tilted his head and continued. "Well, after rigor has eased. But yes he will be dead,"

"Will he know me?"

"Of course, he just won't be as manoeuvrable," Gently he pulled her away from the dying form of Justin and drew her over to the fire. "It's not pleasant, you don't need to watch," Melissa took one look at the pale still form of Justin before she flung her arms about Hugh and hugged him tight, horrified by the world she had fallen into.

CHAPTER 8

Emily returned to her London home in a state of deep thought. Her talk with Katherine had been illuminating yet troubling. She pushed open the door of the large mansion she now inhabited and walked inside. Heavy dark wood panelling on the walls seemed to absorb the light from the candles laid on the sideboard. She sighed a little at the heavy, oppressive decoration of her new home. Closing the door she began to untie the ribbons on her bonnet as her mind continued to churn. What kind of hold did John have over Katherine? Could she break it without him knowing? Deep in thought, she removed her bonnet and placed it on a hall table.

"Glad to see you finally," A deep voice interrupted her

thoughts and she stared up as her new 'husband' walked into the hall. As always, she resisted the urge to laugh at his rotund figure and blustering red face. She removed her cape and handed it to the butler without response. Morton was far too fond of his own voice for interruption, and one look at his small eyes revealed a darkness that she didn't wish to wake. His anger had been shown to her already, and he did not yet know how much she despised him.

"Well?" He walked forward, a dangerous gleam in his eyes.

"I'm sorry," She affected a meek tone and dropped her eyes submissively, wondering if he was free with his fists. "I was delayed at the home of a friend," Stepping forward, she caught hold of his hand, noting the white knuckles on his clenched fist as she did so. "Will you forgive me?" The meek and mild apology sometimes worked, it all depended on the man she was talking to. Silence followed her remarks and for one moment she thought she had talked him out of violence. She saw his muscles tense in his shoulders, and she readied herself for the blow. His fist connected with her face, and she fell to the floor, rolling with the punch so that she landed with little pain.

"You're forgiven," He stepped over her and poured himself a whisky. "Now go upstairs. I'll be with you shortly,"

Emily nodded silently; affecting tears as she rushed to the stairs yet rage boiled within her. It took every scrap of patience from the last hundred years to stop herself from returning to the hall and castrating the cruel bastard she had married. As her feet touched the landing floor, she had begun to longingly think of the day when she would no longer play the simpering victim and teach her 'husband' the true meaning of fear. She reached her room and pushed open the door. The maids had already lit the candles and warm, ruddy light spilled over the dark, heavy furniture that crowded the bedroom. On top of being a violent pig, her 'husband' had the taste of a gnat and Emily couldn't wait for the day when she would have her own home and money once more. As she let her maid remove her clothing, she decided that her next incarnation would see her tied to one of the others and not stuck in hellish matrimony. The nightgown settled over her pale skin as she watched the maid turn down the bed.

"Could you bring the master a glass of brandy?" She asked as the woman finished the bed and walked to the door. The maid nodded once and left the room. Emily waited for the door to close before she reached into the pouch hanging from her dress and removed a small phial from the depths of the pocket. She slid it out of sight beneath the mattress before she climbed into the bed. She did not have long to wait. In seemingly no time at all, Anna had placed a large glass of brandy beside the bed before quietly leaving the room. Emily quickly uncorked the phial of laudanum and laced his drink liberally. Tossing the empty phial into the fireplace, she lay back on the bed and waited for her 'beloved' to arrive. She did not wish to suffer his attentions further this evening and the drugged brandy would ensure that.

Her fingers briefly stroked the tender skin of her cheek as she pondered the mystery of Katherine and John. Kat's words to her had been a revelation. She had often wondered why John had managed to keep the woman shackled to his will. If what Kat said was true, she could not even attempt to leave his control. Her mind drifted back to the conversation that had followed that admission. Katherine had finally drawn back from her embrace and dried her eyes. In the conversation that followed, she had spoken freely about the restraints she was held under. Emily closed her eyes as she focused on what Katherine had said. It seemed as though John had discovered a method of controlling those he had cursed. Emily sighed and nibbled her lip. She would have to speak to Justin about this. If there were any truth to this theory, then Justin would have to be appraised of it. Opening her eyes, she stared up at the ceiling as she thought of Katherine's plight. John was cut from the same cloth as her new paramour. Controlling and far too willing to use violence to achieve his ends. The only difference between them was mortality. Not for the first time, Emily considered the benefits of removing John from the world. She was not above murder to escape untenable situations, and it would at least have a positive effect. It was such a pity that death eluded their little group or she would have attempted to kill him many years ago. She rubbed her top lip. If she could only convince Kat to find John's brooch, the possibilities would be intriguing and even temporary death would be something.

"I'm glad to see you're waiting for me," Emily's thoughts

vanished as Morton entered the bedroom. Pushing herself into a sitting position, she hid her feelings of contempt behind a well rehearsed smile.

"Of course," She replied in the sweet, mild tones that would have warned anyone who knew her well of trouble. She reached down to the side table and picked up the glass of brandy.

"I got you a night cap," With a bland, vacuous smile, she handed over the glass and mentally crossed her fingers. "I thought you could do with a drink," Morton gave an indulgently smug smile as he reached down and stroked his fingers across her neck.

"Thank you," He seized hold of the glass and took a long swallow of the warming liquid. "You understand that it is my painful duty to ensure that you know what I expect of you," He sat on the bed and reached down; the fingers on his other hand reaching for her skin.

"Of course," She moved obligingly as he began to push her nightgown free from her shoulders. "I am your wife," She leant back and watched him take another swallow of the doped brandy.

"And don't forget it," He pulled her gown free and his fingers began to move across her skin. "What would you have done without my direction?" He moved his face closer to hers and his alcohol soaked breath almost made her gag. At least the laudanum would work faster. His tongue invaded her mouth and she almost choked. It took all of her self control not to bite down on the slippery appendage. He pulled back and began to drag the fabric from her skin.

He took another measure of brandy as he reached down and roughly caressed her breasts. She moved to one side, and he lay next to her, his hands and lips moving across her skin. Emily closed her eyes and drifted, trying not to think about his skin against hers.

He mumbled something against her thigh and she looked down, elated at the sight of his clumsy movements and sleep filled eyes.

"Are you alright?" She pitched her voice at just the right note to indicate concern. It would not do for her to appear happy at his descent into sleep.

"I'm just a little tired," He murmured, his eyelids drooped as sleep began to descend on him. A heavy hand pawed at her body once more before he finally succumbed to the laudanum and alcohol. Before he could land on top of her, Emily rolled swiftly to one side and watched as he landed heavily on the bed.

"Sleep well," She whispered; keeping up the pretence in case he had not fully succumbed. For several moments, she lay in fraught silence and waited for him to begin snoring. Staring up at the ceiling, she wondered if this life was worth all the hassle. When bone rattling snores filled the room, she got up, seized hold of a robe and left the bed chamber. She walked across the landing, dragging the robe about her shoulders as her feet made little noise on the rug strewn floor. She made her way downstairs, startling the maid who was in the process of dousing the hall candles.

"It's alright Anna," She waved the woman aside as she moved past her into the study. "I'll put out the lights myself, you can go to bed,"

"Thank you ma'am," Anna bobbed a curtsey and headed back along the corridor, leaving Emily alone in the hall. With a sigh, she sank into one of the chairs that lined the hall and waited for the house to go still. Candlelight flickered over the panelled walls and cast long shadows over the paintings that lined the walls. The ancestors of the man she had married stared down at her as though in silent judgement. Closing her bright blue eyes, she turned away from them and rested her head against the wall. The rhythmic tick from the grandfather clock echoed through the empty hallway and allowed her thoughts to drift. To her mind, that heavy and expensive piece of furniture was the only decent thing about this house. Tucking her feet beneath her, she settled into a meditative pose and allowed the measured beats of the timepiece sooth her.

Not for the first time, she wondered why she had decided to marry Morton before tying him to her. Saint-Clair had been her donor from the moment she had married him, as had any of her other husbands in the past. She reached into the pocket of her robe and drew the locket from its depths. Flipping the enamel bloom open, she stared at the two pictures within and gave a sigh of exasperation. Saint-Clair's piggy eyes still stared back at her when she glanced within and that was why she couldn't take Morton as a donor. Saint-Clair should have died two years ago. He had displayed all the signs and her tame doctor had certainly thought he was heading for the hereafter. Looking down at the picture, she felt her lips curl into a snarl. Damn Saint-

Clair for living longer than he should. Forced to announce his death prematurely, she was now stuck in this frustrating and painful situation. She closed the locket and stared at the flickering lights of the candle as she pondered her options. She could kill Saint-Clair, people thought he was dead already but without him giving her life, she would need to enslave Morton which would present its own problems. Leaving Saint-Clair alive would keep her ticking over, but then she would be left to deal with Morton on a daily basis. The thought of having to pretend to be someone else for that bastard made her feel ill.

"With any luck, Saint-Clair will die on his own," She mused, looking forward to the day when she could teach Morton just who she really was. The clock chimed the quarter hour and she glanced up, she could make it to Lestrade's by morning if she left now. However, er eyes flickered to the staircase and she was forced to squash that idea. If she left before Morton woke, it would certainly draw down his wrath. Tapping her fingers against her thighs in time to the ticking of the clock, she turned once again to the problem of Katherine and John.

Her thoughts ran round in circles as they replayed her earlier meeting. The clock had chimed the half hour before she finally remembered the paper she had taken from Katherine's desk. She rifled through the pockets of her coat and pulled the dog eared scrap of paper free. The scrawled address might not have meant anything significant but it could also be John's new abode. Tapping the piece of paper thoughtfully against her chin, she contemplated her options. Justin needed his brooch back and he certainly couldn't get it himself. It would be simplicity itself to visit the address on the form and try and retrieve the locket, assuming that the address did in fact belong to John. If it did then the outcome of her visit would almost certainly end in her name on his revenge list as he would not take the intrusion lightly. Despite all she had told Alistair, she did not truly wish to anger John as his version of revenge would make her life unpleasant.

"Why am I even considering this?" She whispered softly to herself as she leant back and bumped her head on the wall behind her. "I don't need that aggravation," The thought of being chased from every safe harbour did not appeal to her and it was a problem she could avoid. She stared at the crack in the ceiling plaster as she pondered her choices. The line she had straddled for over a century had kept her free from John's agenda but she was not going to leave Justin without his brooch. A hiss of impatience left her lips at her cowardly thoughts. John's displeasure had not troubled her before and it would not scare her now. The clock chimed the half hour as the thought raced round her head. Peering back at the clock, she calculated carefully. She could return to bed for a few scant hours and leave the house just after breakfast. As the clock ticked closer to quarter to, she returned to the staircase and walked back upstairs.

CHAPTER 9

"Marcus," James' voice echoed from the hallway and drew him from contemplation of the dark red stain. His mother had lain there, breathing her last as her blood soaked into the fibres of the rug. Montjoy had watched her die, he was sure of that. Marcus clenched his fists as sorrow and anger threatened to swamp him. He could not tear his eyes away from the floor. The stain obliterated the rug's simple design and dappled the legs of surrounding furniture with dried red drops. There was a sharp sting as he bit his lip and tried to contain his rising anger.

"Marcus," James called again and Marcus finally dragged his eyes away from the wreckage.

"I'm in here," He called back, as he looked over his

shoulder towards the door.

James entered the room and froze at the devastation he saw. Signs of violence lay in every shattered item of furniture, and a low gasp of horror escaped his lips as his gaze fell on the blood-spattered area of floor.

"Your father said you may be in here," James reached his side, studiously avoiding the large stain in the middle of the room. "I heard what had happened,"

"I daresay," Marcus' voice was terse and James could see the fury burning in his eyes.

"I'm so…" The standard apology dwindled from his lips as he took in the pain on his friend's face. Words could not salve this wound, and he dropped his gaze back to the wreckage before him. The window had broken, and blood was smeared over the jagged points of glass left in the frame. His gaze moved downwards and focused on the small, smudged and bloody handprints that marred the floor. Thoughts of Melissa crawling, helpless before Montjoy's advances, scored through his mind and he clenched his fists. Abandoning polite platitudes, he continued. "What's being done?"

"Not a lot," Marcus retorted savagely as he strode toward the fire. "My father has kept me abed these last two days," His fingers trailed across the mantle as he spoke. "From what I can gather, he sent people to investigate Montjoy's estate, but the place is empty," A bitter laugh broke free from his lips and echoed through the room. "And beyond that…" He picked up an ornament from the mantle. "I don't think he's done anything further," Closing his hand tightly about the ornament he stared into the fire. "I do not think father is particularly concerned with getting her back alive," James stared at him, noting how Marcus' knuckles whitened as his fingers tightened on the china figurine,

"Marcus, I don't think your father would…"

"What?" Marcus whirled round to face his friend. "You don't think my father would abandon my sister?"

"I would have thought,"

"Well I can assure you that my sister's wellbeing is not particularly high on Father's list of priorities," The fingers gripping the ornament squeezed and there was a crack as the china broke in his hand. "After all, think of the scandal," His voice, mocking and bitter, stretched across the room. "He may even make her marry the bastard if we do ever find her," At those words, he threw the ornament into the grate where it shattered into several pieces.

"Marcus," James stepped forward and placed a hand on his friend's shoulder. "I'm certain your father would not be as callous as all that," His voice was calm, belying the anger that he felt. "And I'm sure that he will be doing everything he can,"

"Whatever he's doing, it's not good enough," Marcus replied. "He wouldn't let me go after him," A deep sigh escaped his lips. "He kept me here," James heard the lost sound in his voice and pity mingled with rage that surged through him. "I was kept here while Melissa could be…" He choked then and staggered back from the grate, his feet crunching the pieces of china into powder as he did so. "My sister could be dead or worse," With visible effort he controlled his emotions, clamping down on his rage as he marched from the study, trying not to think of the blood that covered the floor. Rays of pale sunlight flooded the hallway and he stopped to watch the dust motes dance as he tried to still his thoughts. Worry for his sister and rage for his mother's death warred within him, leaving an empty hollow sensation. He tried to think clearly, tried to find something solid to cling to, something that would stop this helpless feeling. Stood in the familiar hallway, he forgot about James as his thoughts and emotions boiled within him. Even if they found Melissa, her reputation would be beyond ruined. Montjoy would only have to say that they were married and that would be that. Gritting his teeth, he tried to force those unwelcome thoughts from his head.

"Melissa will not be tied to that man," James assured as though he could read Marcus' thoughts. "After all, he did kill your mother. That's enough for him to be hanged," Taking some comfort from James' words; Marcus raised his head and nodded gratefully at his old friend. "We'll find her," James' voice reassured as he left the cold horror of the study behind him.

"Will we?" Marcus reached forward and picked up his hat from the stand that lay in the corner by the front door. "I can't wait around and hope that happens," He opened the door and made to step through. "I have to do something about it,"

"Wait," James rushed forward, worried by Marcus' sudden move to action. "Don't do anything rash," He caught hold of his friend's shoulder. "You're not fully healed,"

"I can't stay here and do nothing," Marcus shrugged off the restraining touch of James' hand. "I'm well enough now," Pulling his coat about his shoulders he strode out of the hallway and into the grey sky of a cloudy morning.

"But where are you going to look?" James followed his friend out onto the front porch. Weak sunlight shone through the heavy clouds and a brisk breeze rippled the grass of the meadow.

"I'll start at Montjoy's and work my way back from there," Marcus shouted back as he strode across the drive, heading for the stables. "Someone must know where he has gone,"

"But your injuries?" Gravel crunched beneath his feet as he hurried after the other man.

"Are healed," Marcus did not moderate his tone and James winced as the anger battered against his ears. Moments passed and rustling leaves filled the silence between them as James shifted uncomfortably, unsure of how to calm the other man down "God curse it James," Marcus breathed; his voice softer, a plea for understanding thrumming through his tones as apology shone in his eyes. Pushing a distracted hand through his hair, he stared at his friend. "I can't stay and do nothing. I know what you're trying to say, but she's my younger sister. I'm supposed to look after her," Once again, James heard the pain in his voice and sympathy swelled within him. "I can't just stay here and hope that someone else makes the effort,"

"Alright then," James nodded, "I'll come with you..."

"James..."

"No," Small clouds of dust rose from the stony driveway as he walked forward. "What kind of friend would I be to either of you if I let you go alone?"

Marcus gave a short huff of gratitude and nodded. "Alright," He turned and led the way to the stables.

CHAPTER 10

"There doesn't appear to be anyone here," James said as they stood before the closed door to the Montjoy family home. "In fact," He nodded at the shuttered windows. "It doesn't look as though anyone's been here for a while," Montjoy's home in the city was a large affair situated in the more fashionable areas of the city. Built from white stone at some point during the last century, the house fitted neatly and invisibly into the surrounding area. Casting a look back to the main road, James watched the citizens of London move about their business, seemingly uncaring of their presence. Tired by the trip from the De Vire family home, he felt nervous and exposed as they waited on the steps of the shuttered mansion.

"I can see that," Marcus replied. He glanced up at the house and grimaced. "That doesn't mean that he isn't here,"

"Come on Marcus," James continued, anxious to leave Montjoy's doorstep. "Do you honestly think that he's hiding in the dark?" He pressed his hand against the window and tried once again to see through the crack in the shutter.

"I think he could be," Marcus backed away from the door and began to examine the upper windows of the property. "That's exactly what he could be doing," A determined look settled on his face as he turned from the front door and began to walk toward the back of the house.

"That seems unlikely," James protested as he followed his friend with some reluctance. Casting a look back to the main road, James checked to see if any of the people on the street had taken notice of the two men. Satisfied that they had been ignored by the populace, he followed Marcus down the side of the house. Stepping into the small courtyard at the back, he stared up at the building in trepidation. The windows here were also shuttered and the house had a distinctly closed and abandoned feeling. He tore his eyes away from the structure, unnerved by the closed and unwelcoming feel of the place.

"Marcus," He watched with alarm as Marcus reached down to pick up a large rock. "What the devil do you think you're doing?"

"Checking the place out," Marcus' fingers closed on the large stone as he glanced at the ground floor windows. "I want to see if he's keeping her here," He strode forward, fist clenched about the large stone in readiness.

"Marcus wait," James caught hold of his friends arm and pulled him to a stop. "This is breaking the law; you can't just enter a man's home,"

Marcus glared at James as though he could not believe what he had just heard. He took a step forward, the intensity in his gaze making James take a backwards step.

"He broke into mine and killed my mother," The words were soft but venomous. "Not only that, he took my sister," He peered down at the hand that James had on his arm. "Do you think I care about breaking into his house?"

James looked at the bleak look on his friend's face and slowly released his arm. Much as he wanted to dissuade Marcus from this path, he recognised the determination on his face and knew that he would not be able to dissuade him. The only thing he could do was keep him from getting too deeply into trouble.

"Thank you," Marcus whispered as he walked forward. He reached the window and let the stone fly. They noise of breaking glass seemed extremely loud to James' nervous ears. He shot a look over his shoulder, half expecting an irate citizen to come rushing from the street and discover them. His eyes swept the alley as Marcus continued to break the window behind him.

"Hurry up," James shrank back against the wall of the house; the thought of being caught lending a squeak to his voice. Marcus reached up and began to unhinge the sash window.

"Nearly got it…" There was a click and Marcus pushed

up the broken sash window. Wrapping his coat over his hands, he brushed the shards of glass from the sill before reaching inside to push at the shutters. "Give me a hand,"

James took another nervous look over his shoulder before moving in to stand beside Marcus. He bent forward and placed his hands on the closed shutters, adding his strength to Marcus'.

"With me..." Marcus muttered, "One...two..." As he called three, there was a loud crunch as both men pushed at the same time. James fell forward as the shutter burst open. He gave a huff of pain as his midsection slammed into the windowsill.

"You alright?" Marcus reached down and pulled him upright.

"Fine," He ran his hands over his body, checking for any damage from leftover pieces of glass. Satisfied that he hadn't cut himself, he turned back to Marcus. "Well, aren't you going in?"

Marcus turned back to the window and vaulted himself into the room beyond. After checking once again for any onlookers, James followed.

They stood in a dimly lit parlour. The weak rays of sunlight from the window served only to lighten the deep shadows that crowded the room. Marcus walked deeper into the room, staring at the shadow shrouded scene before him. The room was cold and the musty smell of damp lingered in the air. It felt as though no one had lived there for days. Shrouded beneath heavy damask sheets, the room's furniture remained concealed from view. Dust lay on every surface and cobwebs hung in the corners of the room. An inquisitive mouse raced across the floor and fled into a hole in the skirting. The air was thick with neglect and abandonment.

"See," James called as he ran a finger over the cold mantle. "I'd say it hasn't been lived in for about a month," He dusted his fingers as Marcus reached the door to the hall. "Where are you going?"

"I have to check the rest of the house," Marcus spoke softly as he walked through the door and into the hallway. His footsteps sent small clouds of dust into the air.

"Why?" James followed, his voice as soft as his friend's. "It's clear that he's not here, that nobody is here," He glanced around the dark hall and towards the stairs. "Not even the servants. Montjoy probably moved out after your duel,"

"I have to make sure," Marcus knew it was a long shot, knew that the state of the house would indicate that his sister could not have been there, but he couldn't just leave. This shuttered and abandoned building could hold some clues to Montjoy's whereabouts or information on holdings that no one knew of. He turned back to the dark hallway and headed down, the shadows deepening the further he went. The light afforded by that one open shutter did not reach far enough into the house and soon he could barely see.

"This is stupid," James reached his side and took hold of his arm. "We can barely see and I don't think it's a good idea to open a shutter," Turning Marcus to face him, he continued. "You don't even know what you're looking for," In the dull light of the hallway, Marcus' face was drawn and ghostlike, loss etched deeply in the normally laughing lines of his face.

"Then I'll find a candle," Marcus shook his arm free and kept walking. James watched him move deeper into the darkness, his left hand reaching out to hold the wall next to him.

"Sometimes Marcus…" James hissed in exasperation as he followed him along the ever darkening hall. "Ow," He grunted in pain as his knee slammed into a small table. "Goddamn it Marcus," His voice rose as he clapped a hand to his throbbing knee. "We're not getting anywhere like this," He stared out across the quiet hall, searching the darkness for Marcus' body. "Marcus," He called again as he straightened up and moved ahead, his fears once again clamouring in his head. In a burst of panic, he rushed through the hall after Marcus, bumping into walls and furniture as he hurried further in. The darkness and silence from the other end of the corridor troubled him, and he moved faster, searching for Marcus in the shadowed gloom of the hall. There was the sound of metal striking tinder from up ahead and he stopped. The noise sounded once more, and light finally flared in the darkness.

"What?" Marcus stepped out of a doorway, a candle held before him. The candle cast an orange glow across the hallway and illuminated furniture shrouded in dust sheets Marcus felt his heart sink as he stared across the piled and stored furniture.

"You're a bastard," James muttered as he walked

forward, staring at the illuminated scene with curiosity. "Next time you want to break into someone's house, count me out," He walked past his friend and into the main room.

"James…" Marcus began as he followed his friend.

James glanced back at his friend and gave a weak smile. "No I'm serious," James continued. "If you're going to convince me to take up burglary, at least stay within earshot," He playfully thumped Marcus on the arm. "That way I know you haven't died," He walked through the parlour door and stopped on the threshold. The dim light of the candle partially illuminated the dusty, echoing space. He reached the fireplace and knelt down. The grate was cold, and it was clear that no fire had burnt there recently. The whole room felt musty and damp, clear signs that habitation had ceased.

"There's no sign that she's here," James stood and glanced over his shoulder at Marcus. "And no indication that she's ever been here," His fingers tracked a line in the dust on the mantle, and he showed the dirty thumb to his friend. "I think we should go,"

"But there might be…"

"What?" James asked as he stepped forward. "What do you think you can find?" He reached Marcus' side and caught hold of his friend's arm. "This was a long shot, there was no real evidence that she would be here. We gave it a try and there's nothing,"

"He must have papers…" Marcus pushed past James and moved to the shrouded desk in the corner of the room. "There must be something that could tell us where he's gone," With a flourish, he pulled the dust sheet free and began to wrench open the drawers in the desk. James watched in stunned disbelief as Marcus heaved open drawer after empty drawer. "There must be something," Despair ran through his words as in vain hope, he moved onto a small bureau, yanking at each drawer in frustration. Foiled in his attempt to discover anything of interest, he crumpled to his knees in anguish.

James walked forward and reached Marcus' side, pity thrumming through him as he stared at his friend's broken expression.

"There's nothing here, James whispered.

"But there must be…" Marcus insisted as he turned to the rest of the furniture, throwing the heavy sheeting to the floor as he searched frantically for anything that would lead him to his sister.

"Marcus, James seized hold of his friend's shoulders and forced him to stop moving. "There's nothing here, nothing of any use,"

"Help me look?"

"No," James replied. "It'll do no good," Marcus tried to pull away but James held him still. "This place has been abandoned," He spoke clearly, deliberately, ensuring that Marcus could clearly hear each word. "He must not plan to return to England,"

"There must be something here," Marcus insisted again, desperation obvious in his gaze. "Papers, bills; anything that could tell me where he's gone," James kept hold of Marcus as he slowly shook his head.

"There's nothing here my friend," His voice was softer and full of regret "It's time to try something else,"

"Like what?" James removed his arms as Marcus slumped back against the desk behind him, the fight leaving him as he looked about the dusty, shrouded room.

"Someone must know where he's gone," James replied, stepping back and pulling the sheets back over the furniture. "He does have friends,"

"Father already tried," Marcus sounded hopeless and lost as he stared into space. "No one seems to know anything and I don't know who to ask,"

"Just think," James encouraged as he finally stepped back to face Marcus. "There must be somebody who can help,"

"No there…" He stopped speaking as a thought flickered through his mind like summer lightning.

James raised an eyebrow and wondered at the reason for Marcus' break in conversation. The dim light from the guttering candle, illuminate his friend's face, frozen in revelation.

"Well?" Marcus' head twitched in his direction. "What is it?"

Marcus looked at James, wondering just what he could say to his old friend. He wasn't even sure that his idea would bear fruit. Calm settled over him as he pulled the sheet back over the desk.

"I might see Justin Lestrade," And with that, he turned on his heel and left the parlour, leaving James to stare after him in curiosity.

"Why Lestrade?" With several quick steps, James caught up with Marcus as he reached the kitchen.

"He knows people that I do not," Marcus hedged slightly, unsure of the wisdom of informing James about Justin's interest. "It's as good a plan as any," A quick puff of breath ended the warm light of the candle and Marcus returned it to the table. "Let's go,"

James watched Marcus carefully climb out of the window and shrugged, wondering why the young rake had entered Marcus' mind as a contact. Clambering out of the window he almost bumped into Marcus' frozen form. A complaint stuttered to a halt as his eyes fell on the woman that was stood before them. The shards of glass crunched beneath his feet and his stomach sank.

Marcus landed awkwardly as his feet hit the ground and he almost fell. As he regained his balance, the hem of a dress drifted across his vision. Fear jolted through him as he straightened up before the curious eyes of the woman before them. Blonde ringlets were pinned up beneath a cap and she wore a sturdy looking yet good quality dress. A small twinge of remembrance made him search the depths of his memory as he tried to place the woman before him. As James scrabbled out of the window behind him, his mind went blank as he tried to figure out some excuse for leaving a house in such an unconventional manner.

CHAPTER 11

After a stilted breakfast in the morning room of Morton's overly ornate mansion, Emily had pleaded several engagements and left the stifling environment of her new home with a sigh of relief. Knowing that Morton would probably check up on her visits, she ensured that she conducted her morning calls, albeit in a shorter time frame, before instructing her driver to drive close to the address that had been given on the paper. As the town house came into view, she descended from the carriage to take a 'walk'. She approached the front of the house, noted the abandoned look to the property and walked past. From past experiences, she knew that John tended to remain anonymous. Taking a left turn, she walked towards the back of the property. As she reached the rear of the house, she stopped at the sight of the broken window and open shutters. Wondering if one of the others had made a visit, she walked closer to the opening, only to stop as a figure began to scramble through. The man stumbled as he cleared the window and that left her time to get a good look at him before he stood up. After a moment and a spark of recognition, her mind began to work quickly as Marcus De Vire froze at the sight of her.

The small scrap of paper in her pocket had clearly given this address and she could not see why Marcus would be at John's house, assuming of course, that this was John's house. As she tried to work out what to say, another man climbed out of the window. For a moment, they both stared at her, both displaying identical expressions of guilt and panic.

"Ma'am, I err..." Marcus started to speak first, clearly floundering at coming up with a good story. It took all her self control not to laugh at the guilty look on his face. "I err..." and she placed the letter back into her pocket.

"Mr De Vire?" She raised her face and stared at the house behind him. "What are you doing?" She thought she had better begin the conversation in a way that he would expect.

"I err, I..." Beads of sweat began to dot Marcus' forehead as he tried to formulate an answer to her question. "I was..." He was definitely sweating now. "We were..."

"We saw the broken window," James interjected, coming to the aid of his friend. "And we had to investigate,"

"Oh?" She managed to control the mirth that threatened to spill over at the rushed and obvious lie. The two men looked so incredibly guilty that she could have recognised the untruth even in the dark. "Whose house is it?" Still, coming across them wasn't a total loss, it were entirely possible they knew whose house they had broken into. The chances of the home belonging to John were extremely rare, but any information was useful. "Maybe we should tell them about the broken window?" Even to her ears she sounded naïve and ludicrous, yet it was a pose that could prove useful. These two would be grateful for any way out of trouble. If it meant sounding like a half-wit to gain information, then that's what she would do.

"I don't think that's an option," Marcus finally spoke coherently as his brain kicked into gear, relieved by the apparent gullibility of the blonde before him. The longer he had spoken to her, the more he had remembered. The woman was the young widow Saint-Clair, not that he knew anything beyond that. "This house belongs to Lord Montjoy, and I believe he's left the country,"

Emily nearly choked as she recognised the name of the man who had just joined her little 'family'. Her fingers brushed the note in her pocket as she recalled Katherine's words. Yes it would have made sense that Kat would have Montjoy's address on her dresser. The woman may be unfortunate in her choice of allies but she wasn't stupid, she would have John's location memorised, not written down.

"Yes, the place is covered in dustsheets," James

interjected, breaking her train of thought. She looked at him, wishing she could tell him that the desperate attempts to lie were pointless. There was no way that she would bring them to the attention of the magistrate.

"I see," She glanced back to the street, "Well I'm glad to see that we have such upstanding gentlemen as you to keep an eye on things,"

"Quite," Marcus managed to speak through the overwhelming urge to laugh at the woman's credulity. He was still surprised that they had managed to convince her with such a paper thin lie. Despite her obvious beauty, she seemed insanely simple. Astonished at her reactions, he glanced up into her blue eyes. For the briefest instant, calculating intelligence stared back at him before her gaze clouded and a smile of dazzling vapidity lit her features. In that moment, he revised his opinion of the woman before him, that glimmer in her gaze was far too sharp for how she appeared and she could easily be pretending to swallow their flimsy lie.

"Well, it's about time that I was going," Emily stepped back, breaking the stare and interrupting his chain of thought. "I have errands to run and I'm sure you have things to do,"

"Wait," James interjected as he walked forward. "We'll accompany you,"

Emily glanced at the man and repressed a smile at his chivalry. "Why thank you," With a delicate lift of an eyebrow she glanced up at Marcus, noting the quizzical twist to his sensual lips. He did not seem fully convinced by her performance and she resisted the urge to applaud his intelligence. James, on the other hand, did not look too far beyond the obvious. Maybe the desire to be believed had swamped him. In any case, she dismissed further thought into the matter as they reached her side.

"It's the least we can do," Marcus called as James fell into step at her other arm. "I wouldn't want to leave such a delicate flower as you to walk alone," He said the phrase, yet he somehow knew that delicate was not a word to be associated with her but he still managed to tone down the mockery.

"Thank you," The laughter was there, buried beneath the surface and she struggled to hold the giggles in as she heard the sarcasm hidden beneath Marcus' cultured tones. For one wild moment, she wanted to drop the charade and see how he reacted. As a group, they turned and walked towards the alley at the side of the house.

"So what brought you to Montjoy's house?" Emily asked as they walked through the alley and headed towards the street.

"Nothing really," James started, trying to play it cool. On the other side of Emily, Marcus suppressed a snort. Despite her apparent idiocy, when Emily heard of the attack on his sister by Montjoy, she would realise that they had broken into the house, though it was clear that she probably already knew.

"We were looking for Montjoy," Marcus announced, deciding that some honesty would help their cause. "We received no answer on arrival and when we checked the back of the house, we found the broken window,"

Emily glanced at Marcus, realising that he was attempting to placate future questions with half-truths, the question was why? What could have happened for Marcus to come to Montjoy's home? Katherine had said that she had sent Montjoy after the De Vire girl. None of the people she had spoken to that morning had mentioned the De Vires but that meant nothing as she had spent little time socialising. It made it even more imperative for her to meet with Justin. It was only a shame that she could not bring his brooch with her.

"I see," They reached the main street and she came to a stop. "Thank you for walking with me," It was a dismissal, both men could see that. Emily wanted, no needed, to leave their company so she could ponder on this meeting.

"It was a pleasure," Marcus replied, glad to be given the excuse to leave her company and further awkwardness.

"Likewise," She gifted the pair with a dazzling smile, "Good day gentlemen,"

James and Marcus called their goodbyes and watched her walk back along the road towards her waiting carriage.

"That was close," James muttered as they watched her carriage drive away from the scene. "When I saw her outside, I thought we'd had it,"

"Hmm," Marcus kept his eyes on the coach until it finally drove out of his sight. "I don't know if we got away with it," Despite her seeming vacuity it was more than possible that Emily had not swallowed the rapidly constructed lie. The calculating flash of intelligence he had seen in those blue eyes had suggested that she had seen straight through their faltering attempts at subterfuge.

"I can only hope," James turned and began to head back down the road. "Come on let's get out of here,"

"I'll take you back home," Marcus fell into step beside his friend as they hurried to where they had left their transport. "I'm heading to Lestrade's,"

"Why?" James asked his friend as they clambered into the phaeton and Marcus took up the reins. "As far as I know, the Lestrade boy isn't even connected to Montjoy,"

"No," Marcus clicked to the horses, and they set off along the cobbled streets. "But I think he can give me some help,"

"After you threw him out with that beating?" James chanced a look at his friends face as he spoke. "I doubt he'd be amenable to the suggestion,"

"You'd be surprised," Marcus did not take his eyes from the road as he continued to speak. "I'll drop you off and head out there now,"

"Marcus?"

"I've dragged you into enough this morning," Marcus replied, forestalling further argument. "She's my sister…"

"I said I wouldn't let you do this by yourself," James insisted. "Granted, I did not particularly appreciate breaking into Montjoy's but…"

Marcus drew the phaeton to a halt and stared across at his friend. "I understand that you want to help and I know that you care for Melissa, but I also know that you have an appointment with the woman you're going to marry," James looked away from Marcus' green eyes and stared down at the slightly worn upholstery. "Even if I find her alive, your father would not let you marry her. Save yourself the heartache and go now,"

"Marcus,"

"No, I mean it," Marcus relaxed his grip on the reins as he stared across at his friend. "I've dragged you into too much," Looking back to the road; he clicked to the horses and moved out into the London traffic. "I'll drop you off at Whites,"

CHAPTER 12

Several loud bangs on his front door drew Alistair from a deep dreamless sleep. Stretching lightly, he pulled himself upright and reached for the robe on the chair. The knocking increased in volume as he dragged the fabric across his body.

"Alright..." He muttered as he opened his bedroom door and headed onto the landing. Unlike the others, Alistair did not keep staff at his city home. Despite his occasional foray into society, he did not play the role of bored nobleman and his house, while fine, was not staffed to the degree it should be. He staggered down the stairs and pulled open the front door.

"Morning Alistair," John pushed past him as the door swung open. "May I?" Without waiting for an invitation, he strode into the hall, glancing at the furnishing with a sneer on his lips. "I thought you were living frugally?" He placed his cane in the stand by the door, his hat on one of the cabinets and then turned to the mirror. Alistair rolled his eyes at the presumption as he turned to face his unwanted guest.

"What are you doing here?" He affected a bored, slightly annoyed tone yet he watched John preen in the mirror with a growing sense of apprehension.

"Did you do as I asked?" John did not turn from the mirror as he spoke. His fingers played with his cravat as his eyes flickered sideways, observing Alistair's features. He exuded confidence and Alistair shuffled awkwardly at the note of command in his voice. John's insistence at treating him like a lackey grated on his nerves, but he kept silent at the treatment.

The silence lengthened and John finished tying his cravat. With a huff of impatience, he whirled about and walked straight towards Alistair.

"Well?" He stopped a pace away from the younger Lestrade and stared directly into his eyes. "Did you do as I asked?" Soft and menacing, John's voice jangled unpleasantly on Alistair's ears, and he swallowed nervously. "Must I treat you as I would my daughter?"

"I spoke to them," He offered finally, the cold gaze in John's eyes sending a spike of fear through him.

"Good," John did not move away. "And what did they say?" He was barely blinking, and his eyes bored into Alistair's, like a snake hypnotising its prey.

"They said no,"

"Did they?" John's voice grew colder and Alistair had to force himself to stay still. "Did you make my feelings on the matter clear?"

"I did," Alistair felt a trickle of cold sweat slide down his neck. He knew he should not fear John, but he could not help it. There was a crazed intensity to the other man that made him nervous. In many ways, Alistair's goals linked with John's yet the man made him cringe.

"I see," John's expression did not change. "Are you certain you applied yourself diligently to the task?" Alistair winced at the almost friendly note to John's voice. The friendliness was even more unnerving than outright threats.

"I tried…" Fear seemed to freeze his vocal chords and he spoke in a husky whisper.

"Don't mumble Alistair," John's hand shot out and seized hold of him by the nose. Alistair gave a shocked yelp and staggered as John applied pressure. "I despise mumbling and excuses," Alistair's hands reached up and gained a hold on John's forearm. The pain was excruciating despite the healing applied by his donor. John's fingers pulled on his nostrils forcing him to his knees. Alistair's fingers scrabbled uselessly against John's rock solid forearm and he resorted to blind punches. John shrugged off the blows as though they were nothing. With torturously slow movements, he continued to draw Alistair's head back, the healing failing to keep pace with the pain. After a few moments of unrelenting pressure, John released his hold and Alistair slumped to the floor. Several shuddering breaths were cut short as John's foot slammed into his kidneys causing him to bite his tongue with the pain. From somewhere in the house, the answering scream of his donor echoed along the quiet halls. Alistair tried to draw breath as the white hot pain in his kidneys obliterated all thought.

"Now you know not to mumble," John reached down and drew a dagger from his belt. Leaving Alistair on the floor, he crossed to the mantel and ran his gaze over the knick knacks that covered the top. He gave a snort of laughter as he picked Alistair's dagger from its hiding place in a jar. He returned to Alistair's rocking form and with an almost bored sneer, he opened the locket and shredded the picture within, watching as Alistair took the loss of connection like a punch to the gut.

"You Lestrade boys are so easy," John palmed the dagger and walked into the parlour. "You should really learn to keep these somewhere safe. It takes away any challenge," He reached one of the high backed chairs before the fire and settled down into it.

"Now if you want this back," He waved the dagger before Alistair's blurry gaze. "You will report coherently and accurately," Leaning back against the fabric, he smiled. "I am sorry for having to teach you this way, but I really don't like people to mumble," He flicked shut the locket and began to clean his nails with the dagger. "And besides, I don't want to have to order you. After all, you have the same aim I do,"

"And what's that?" Alistair staggered through the door,

flecks of blood frothing from his nose. It took all his self will not to launch himself at the man on the chair. John held cards that he did not understand, and if he played the game correctly, he could gain an advantage over his brother. He did not relish having to deal with John, but sometimes a deal with the devil was necessary. With painful steps, he reached the chair opposite John and sank into it.

"Your brother," He answered. "You hate him as much as I," Leaning forward, he rested his chin on his hands and continued. "We can help each other,"

"Can we?" Short of breath, it was all Alistair could do to speak, even though his eyes followed the movements of the dagger in John's fingers.

"Of course, but first I need to know what transpired,"

"Emily said that she was already your," Another shuddering breath racked through him and he tried to calm his breathing. Not for the first time, he wished that he had not been the younger of the brothers. Justin would not have taken such a beating.

"And?" John urged him to continue, using the knife as though it was a conductor's baton.

"Hugh said that if you felt the need to threaten him, then his sympathies may lie elsewhere,"

"So Hugh still claims neutrality?" John leant back in the chair tapping the end of the knife against his thigh as he did so. Alistair followed the movement of the blade with narrowed eyes.

"It would seem so," He answered simply, quietly, his gaze preoccupied with the rhythmic tapping of the blade.

Visions of that knife slicing into John's thigh began to burn excitedly through his mind.

"Hmm…" John looked straight at him and smiled slightly. "Do you want this back?" The knife stopped moving and he held it up, offering it back to Alistair with a knowing twist to the lips.

"Yes," Lying to John was the fastest way to earn his enmity and as he seemed to know when people were lying, it was pointless to do so.

"You want to kill me?" The smirk grew wider as he ran the tip of his finger along the knife edge.

"Isn't that obvious?" Alistair took another breath, trying to dispel the burning pain left by John's boot.

"Indeed it is," John pushed himself upright and walked forward. He reached Alistair's chair and reversed the dagger, holding the hilt end towards the other man. "Well why don't you?"

Alistair reached out for the blade, wondering at John's motives. As his fingers closed around the handle, he glanced up and looked at the other man's face. John was smiling at him, almost as though he expected him not to strike. White hot anger flowed through him, and Alistair thrust forwards, stabbing John in the stomach. Still wearing the smirk, John staggered back and landed in the chair. He pressed a hand to the rapidly healing wound and spoke.

"Feel better?"

"A little," Alistair wiped the blood from the blade and sat back in the chair. He flipped open the locket and stared in consternation at the empty space where his donor should have been.

"Good, that means we're even," John stood up and headed for the door. "I don't expect any further unpleasantness between us," Alistair stared after his departing guest with some confusion. Much as he understood John, it seemed strange that the man was preparing to bury the hatchet so clearly.

"That's it?" Disbelief swelled every syllable from his lips. "You attack me, remove my link and expect me to let it go?"

"Of course not," John reached the door and turned around. "But I do expect you at my home from tomorrow," He smiled at the mystification on Alistair's face. "After all, we can't deal with your brother as enemies," He walked into the hall, his voice drifting back as he did so. "And I think that as you've had a chance at retaliation, you're sensible enough to deal with me fairly,"

"Wait," Alistair pulled himself out of the chair and followed John. "You honestly believe that I will work with you?"

"No," John stopped opening the door and stared at Alistair. "You are working for me," He reached for the door handle once more. "Unless…" Alistair felt his stomach twist. "You wish to be my enemy," Leaving the door slightly open, he walked back into the hallway and stopped just before Alistair. "In which case, let me know now,"

A heartbeat of silence stretched between them and Alistair felt sweat begin to gather on his brow. In those few moments, his thoughts buzzed about his head like angry flies on meat. John as an enemy was not something he wished. The discomfort he had felt in the last few moments was nothing compared to what John could serve up. Besides, he glanced at the other man's smirking face; there was always the chance that he could learn more about the curse. If he stayed at John's side, perhaps he would learn secrets that Justin did not know yet.

"Well?"

"Where are you living now?" He asked finally, unwilling to formerly declare his new found allegiance, even if it had already been decided.

"Blackfriars," John replied as he picked up the hat he had left by the door. He returned to the door and glanced back over his shoulder at Alistair. "Same place I stayed a hundred years ago," He pulled open the door and placed the hat on his head. "I'll see you there,"

CHAPTER 13

It had been the longest three hours of Melissa's life. Waiting and watching for signs of life within Justin's corpse, for corpse it clearly was, had taken its toll. She sat next to his body, her bloody hands wrapped around his cold fingers as she looked at the man who had changed her existence. Hugh had long given up on sending Melissa out of the room and he was sat at the dining room table when her gasp told him that Justin had finally returned to them. He returned to the main room to see Melissa sat beside Justin, tears running down her cheeks. He could not tell if they were of joy or horrified sorrow.

"God's teeth, I hate that," Justin muttered through a voice box that didn't work as well as it should. His eyelids flickered quickly as he tried to open them and his fingers squeezed Melissa's hand with troubling weakness.

"Justin?"

"The same," With a supreme effort he opened his eyes and stared at Melissa. "I wish you hadn't had to see that,"

Melissa took a shuddering breath and stared down at him through a veil of tears. His eyes were flat, the expression within them distant and difficult to read.

"Melissa?" Hugh reached her side and caught her shoulder. "I said he needed time,"

"You didn't say it would be like this," Anguish rippled through every syllable as she kept hold of his heavy, unresponsive fingers.

"I never said it wouldn't," Hugh knelt down beside her and rested a hand on her shoulder. "Give him time, he'll get control of the body soon,"

"It won't be pretty," Justin added in the same rough tone as before. "I do try not to get to this point;" He tried to move but his body still trapped him. "Usually I have someone by then," Melissa wondered how he could sound so flippant, given his condition. "Strange though?"

"What is?" Hugh leant forward, concern in his voice.

"I've had my throat cut and not been as lethargic as this," He tried to push himself upright but the strength of his arms failed him.

"Perhaps because you weren't sedentary during that encounter?" Hugh replied after a moment's thought.

"Maybe," He tried again to move and grunted with exasperation when he could not. "I'll have to get moving soon, I need to get that damn brooch back. Moving about like the walking dead is damned conspicuous,"

Melissa followed the conversation with a bewildered look; she could not understand how they could sound so calm about the dead body that Justin had now become. She took in deep gulps of air and tried to process the information that was almost crippling her.

"We need to sort out your hands," Justin's concern pulled her away from her thoughts and she stared down at the blood soaked bandages. In the welter of confusion, she had nearly forgotten the constant bleeding. Despite the frequent change of bindings, her lifeblood still dripped inexorably away. Justin managed to move his head and glance up at Hugh, who sighed and released her.

"Indeed we do," he echoed, a troubled expression crossing his features as he looked at her pale, clammy skin. "I know it's terrible but…" He took a glance at Justin before continuing. "But it has to be done before you bleed to death,"

"But I don't understand why,"

"You don't heal anymore," Justin explained gently, his words still not producing any corresponding facial expressions. "And that means even the mildest injury will not heal. A pinprick could eventually be fatal to us,"

"I'll find someone," Hugh said with deep regret to his tones. Standing up, he moved to the door. "I won't be long,"

"Hugh," Melissa left Justin's side and approached the older guy. "No,"

"Then you will die and become like Justin," Hugh caught hold of her upper arms and stared calmly into her face. "I won't pick anyone who doesn't deserve it,"

"Does anyone deserve this?" She whispered her voice tremulous and wavering.

"No," Hugh replied, his voice just as quiet. "But what else can we do?" His fingers gently pushed away strands of hair away from her face. "You won't kill whoever I choose," Melissa's eyebrows shot up and he continued. "They'll take your wounds but they can heal naturally,"

"But I thought…"

"I know," A shadow of his former vivacity entered his voice. "But believe me," Melissa followed his gaze to Justin's rigid form. "That is hell on earth and if you can avoid it, then you should,"

Silence descended on the hallway and Melissa bit her lip. She could feel the blood dripping from her fingers and pain danced across her hands every time she tried to close them. Hugh and Justin were watching her, the pain and regret etched so deeply in their faces that she was sure it would never lift. She glanced down at the weeping bandages and came to a decision, one that she knew would be irrevocable.

"Alright,"

"Very well," Hugh turned back to the door and reached out for his hat. "I'll be back soon,"

"Thank you for your help Hugh," A sad smile creased his feature at the listless quality to her voice,"

"Don't mention it," With that he picked up his hat and

cane from the stand. "I wish I did not have to and I am sorry this had to happen," Impulsively, Melissa reached up and kissed the older man on the cheek.

"I know," She whispered.

Hugh ruffled her hair and turned away. As he reached for the door handle, the sound of hooves thundering across the gravelled drive stopped him. With a frantic wave of his hand, Hugh directed Melissa towards the stairs. Panicked with the thought of discovery she tore up the stairs and ran out of sight.

Even as Melissa fled, several loud knocks hammered against the front door. Hugh held still as the door shuddered with the force of the blows as he waited for Melissa to disappear from view.

"Lestrade," Muffled by the heavy wood of the door, Marcus' voice echoed through the hall. Melissa started, stunned by the sound of her brother's voice. Hugh shot a look up the stairs, silently pleading with her to stay still as Marcus knocked again.

"Damn it Lestrade answer the door," Several loud blows hammered against the wood, and the door rattled against its frame. Marcus' voice was strained, anxious and she longed to tell him that she was alright. It took all her self-control not to rush down the stairs and push the door open.

"Please," Marcus' voice sounded again, a lost whisper of its former strength. "Please Lestrade, you have to help me," There was a soft thud, as though Marcus had bumped his head against the door. Tears of shame pricked Melissa's eyes at the broken sound of the brother's voice. "Melissa's missing and I don't know what to do," She was responsible for his pain and she couldn't bear to hear him suffer.

Hugh saw her step down the stairs, and he moved to intercept her. A pained expression crossed his face as he shook his head frantically.

"Don't," He whispered softly as his hand closed about her upper arms. His grip was soft, unwilling as he was to hurt her. She glanced up at him, and he almost took a step back at the grief on her face.

"I can't let him think that I'm…" Tears ran down her cheeks as she tugged her arms free. "I can't do that to him,"

Hugh stared at her for a long time, unwilling to seize hold of her again. Marcus knocked again. "Please Hugh," Hugh lowered his eyes and stood out of the way. Breathing a thank you, Melissa walked to the door and pulled it open. Marcus dropped his hand and stared at her in stunned silence.

"Melissa?" He whispered unbelievingly as he took in her wild-eyed, ragged form. His eyes travelled across her body from the messed hair to the blood dripping from her bandaged hands. "Oh dear God, Melissa," Something between a laugh and a sob escaped his lips as he reached forward and pulled her into his arms. Melissa closed her eyes as she fell against his warm body. The grief she carried began to ebb as Marcus embraced her.

"What the hell are you doing here?" Marcus spoke as he finally released her. "How?" He held her at arms reach and stared down at her dishevelled appearance. "Did Lestrade?"

His features hardened as he spoke the name.

"No," Melissa pulled back and stared straight at him. "He saved me from.," She almost choked on the name. "Montjoy,"

"Then why are you here?"

"I think," Hugh's voice sounded from the depths of the hall as he walked forward. "That this is not a conversation for the front step," He reached the door and stared at the pair of them. "You'd better come in," He pushed the door open and beckoned them inside.

"Who?" Marcus stared at the older man in some confusion.

"Marcus, this is Hugh Tarlington, he's a long time friend of Justin's,"

"Speaking of which," Marcus made no move to walk into the house. "Where is he?" There was a worrying note of anger in his voice and Melissa hoped that Marcus wouldn't blame Justin for her condition. The cuts on her hands still dripped rich blood to the dusty stone floor and from the way Marcus' eyes kept returning to them, she could tell that they worried him.

"He's, errm," What could she say? Marcus could not be told of their secret but there was no explanation that she could offer. As she tried to formulate something to say, the noise of an approaching horse and carriage interrupted the conversation.

"Get inside," Hugh ordered as he joined them on the steps. "Both of you,"

"I'm not going anywhere," Marcus replied, anger now

in his voice. "Who do you think you are to order me around?" Hugh sighed once and seized hold of Marcus' arm, making the younger man wince in discomfort as his fingers dug into the soft flesh of his lower arm.

"I'm the man keeping your sister safe," Tarlington spoke slowly but with some impatience as his eyes bored into Marcus' "I'm also older than you boy and when I say get in the house," He pushed Marcus closer to the door. "I want you to obey,"

Melissa felt the muscles in Marcus' arm tense and she pulled him away, halting the punch he was preparing to throw. "Come on Marcus," He glanced down, relenting at the plea in her eyes as he allowed her to pull him into the hallway. As they crossed the threshold, Hugh shut the door behind and waited on the steps for the approaching carriage.

"What the hell is going on?" As the door shut, Marcus turned to face his sister. "Why are you here?"

Melissa awkwardly shuffled her feet, unsure of how to respond. How could she tell him what she only barely knew? As the silence lengthened between them, they heard the carriage draw to a halt and both stared at the door, conversation briefly forgotten as they strained to listen.

"What the devil are you doing here?" Hugh's voice echoed from behind the door and both leaned forward to listen more clearly.

"What do you think I'm doing here?" Marcus started as Emily's voice snapped back. "I've just come from Montjoy's home and do you know who I ran into there?"

Marcus turned to face his sister. "Why is Emily Morton here?"

Melissa shook her head, unwilling to speculate. A hard knot of anger settled into her chest and she listened far more closely to the conversation outside.

"You met Marcus De Vire?" Melissa turned to face Marcus, raising her eyebrows at Hugh's pronouncement.

"Yes," The voice was closer to the door. "Is there something going on that I should know about?"

"Montjoy attacked Melissa,"

"What?!"

"Don't worry, she's safe," Hugh depressed the door handle and pushed open the door. "See," Emily walked into the hallway and stared at the siblings with a wry smile.

"I wondered whose horse that was," Stepping lightly across the floor, she came to a halt before the pair of them. "I did not expect to see you so soon," She spoke directly to Marcus, barely sparing a glance for Melissa.

"Lady Morton," Marcus bowed his head in greeting before he glanced at his sister in some confusion.

"I also didn't expect to see the pair of you here," Her eyes flickered to Melissa's and a hard line creased her forehead. "Care to explain?"

"It's..." Melissa looked helplessly at the blonde and Hugh. "I mean to say..."

"What your sister is trying to say," The blonde interjected with a small sneer, directing her words at a confused Marcus. "Is that she's an idiot," Emily shot an annoyed glance at Hugh. "And that Hugh's an idiot for letting you in to see her, thereby ruining years of hard work,"

"That's rich," Justin's voice sounded wearily from the doorway. "Particularly considering your part in the affair," He moved into the hallway, his limbs moving in slow, jerky motions. Marcus watched in shock as Justin reached the staircase and leant against the heavy wooden balustrade with a ragged sigh.

"Lestrade?"

Justin nodded to Marcus' question and rested his head back against the railings. The creak of his neck moving into place reverberated loudly across the hall and Melissa winced.

"Oh good god," Emily whispered into the silence as she walked to his side. "Not you as well?" She placed an arm around his shoulders.

"So much for keeping things quiet," Hugh muttered in a low undertone.

Marcus tore his eyes away from Justin's body with some difficulty and turned to face his sister. "Right that's it, you're coming home,"

"I'm afraid it's not that simple," Hugh began, yet Melissa's voice overrode his words.

"I can't go home," Marcus stopped dead and stared down at her face in utter disbelief.

"Melly, this place…" He gestured wildly at Justin. "These people, it's… they…" He swallowed quickly, trying hard to find words for the feelings that were running through his mind. "This doesn't feel right," Justin opened his eyes to stare at them and he stumbled at the sight of the milky pale surface. "I don't know what's happening here, and I don't want to know. I just want you home and safe. Now that I know Montjoy doesn't have you,"

"I'm afraid she can't go with you," Emily interrupted in a soft voice. "She doesn't belong there anymore,"

"Of course she…"

"No I don't," Melissa broke in, her voice full of misery. "I can't go back; people have to believe that I died,"

"Melissa," Marcus placed both hands on his sister's shoulders. "If this is because of Montjoy…"

"It's not," Taking a breath, Melissa tried to contain her feelings and speak rationally. "I can't explain, and I don't think you could understand,"

"Try me," Marcus pressed, his mind a welter of confusion. "If this is about the scandal?"

"Show him your hands," Justin interjected in his husky tones. "And tell him,"

"Justin?" Hugh shot a look at the young man, bewilderment mixed with warning in his voice.

"He won't let it go Hugh," Painfully, he pushed himself away from the staircase and slowly walked toward the pair. "He needs to see," Clumsy fingers reached out and lifted Melissa's left hand as he delivered an encouraging nod.

Slowly, Melissa reached out with numb fingers to unravel the wrappings on her left hand. One handed and clumsy, she slowly undid the blood soaked cloth. As her wounds were revealed, Marcus hissed with shock. Melissa let him stare at the wounds she had taken as she struggled to find the words to explain.

"These were done the night Montjoy attacked," Marcus leant forward and took hold of her hand to stare at the wounds, his fingers carefully turning her hand this way and that. "They haven't healed and they won't," She took a breath as she tried to find some way of telling him what had happened to her.

"I don't…" He stopped speaking as Emily reached their side.

"Let me explain," She leant past Melissa and smiled at Marcus. "Your sister will never heal another injury, she will also not die,," She reached up to her neck and undid the choker with the black lotus attached. "She has one of these…"

"Thanks to you," Melissa interjected with some animosity.

"Yes thanks to me," Emily did not even look abashed as she confirmed Melissa's words. "If she goes home, people will notice,"

"This is idiocy," Marcus announced as he stepped back away from the blonde, staring at her with something akin to hatred. "Lunacy," he caught hold of Melissa's wrist. "Let's go and listen to no more of this heresy,"

"It's the truth," Melissa pulled her arm free and stared up at him, tears glinting in her eyes. "Do you think I would give up the chance to come home on such a stupid lie?" A thin trail of blood followed her fingers as she gently stroked his cheek.. Marcus looked down at her face, his expression softening at the wretchedness he saw there.

"We can prove it," Emily continued.

"How?" Marcus snapped, not taking his eyes from the unshed tears and look of utter loss in his sister's eyes.

"There is a way of healing with these…"

"Emily," Confusion flooded Marcus at the note of warning in Hugh's voice.

"What do you mean?" Marcus was being forced to revise his opinion of Emily Morton in very short order. He had figured her for some level of calculation, but her coolness of speech lay outside of his expectations.

"Exactly what I say," Emily turned to face Melissa. "Do you have yours with you?" Melissa nodded and reached into the pocket of her skirt. As the brooch came into the light, Marcus reached out.

"No," Melissa drew it away from his fingers, "Don't touch it,"

"Melissa?"

"I'm afraid she's right," Emily answered as she slid her own locket out of sight. "I wouldn't touch it,"

"You said that you could heal with these?" The glossy black surface reflected the light and blood from her hands covered its petals. The sight provoked a profound feeling of unease.

"Yes," Emily stepped forward and placed the flat of her hand against his chest. Melissa started forward at her presumption, but Emily gave a derisive snort and ignored her.

"How?" Marcus whispered, staring down at the lotus with fascination. Despite the sense of horror it invoked, he could not help but stare at the perfectly formed item.

"It takes some of your life to heal her," A hushed voice answered his question and he glanced at Emily. "Her wounds will become yours,"

"You're not using him," Melissa stepped forward and dragged Emily away from Marcus.

"Then who else?" Emily rounded on her with a sneer, throwing Melissa's hand from her arm as though it were nothing. "It won't be permanent, you can detach the connection afterwards," She flicked a long strand of hair behind her ear and turned back to Marcus. "What do you say handsome? Do you want to heal your sister?"

"Yes," Melissa's blood was running down her hands and dripping onto the floor. She already looked pale, the slow drip of blood loss making its mark upon her. Unable to fully comprehend what Emily was saying, he focused on the chance to heal his sister. If there was any chance to heal his sister, he would take it, even if it meant a deal with the devil himself.

"You can heal her by taking the wound," Emily explained, her voice softer than it had been. "We will break the connection afterward," She smiled lightly and reached a hand to his cheek. "It's proof and healing in the same package," Turning back to face Melissa, she continued. "Or would you rather just kidnap someone?"

Melissa's anger finally reached breaking point and she reacted without thinking. Pain exploded across her palm as she slapped Emily hard across the face.

"Good blow," Was Emily's only comment as she cleaned the blood from her face. "Still doesn't invalidate my point,"

"Enough now Emily," Justin noted as he pushed himself from the stairs and walked forward. Reaching Melissa's side, he stopped and looked at her. "Emily has a point," A smug look slid over Emily's features as Justin continued. "She's being obnoxious about it but she's right. If you want to prove this to him and heal, then this is the best way to do it," He left Melissa's side and looked at Marcus.

"I'm sorry to have involved the pair of you in this,"

"I don't want to hurt him," Melissa said, her voice close to the edge of panic. "I don't…"

"He won't be your donor for long," Hugh added as he walked forward, casting a warning glance at Emily as he did so. "As soon as you're healed, we'll destroy his portrait,"

"Portrait?" Marcus felt as though he were drowning in information. Hugh gave him a sympathetic look as he indicated his own locket.

"In here there are two cameos, one of them shows an image of the one who owns the locket and the other depicts…" He gave a long sigh. "The one who gives their life," Marcus' gaze flickered to the locket in Hugh's hand. "Essentially, you will stare into your sister's locket and once your image appears you will take the damage that afflicts her,"

"And we will break the connection," Justin continued. "You can easily heal the damage to your hands after that,"

"And this will heal her?" Marcus pushed aside the explanations, they barely meant anything to him anyway, and focused on the one thing that he could understand.

"Yes," Justin replied.

"I don't believe...." Melissa cast her eyes about the room, her gaze falling on Hugh, Justin and Emily in turn. She could not believe that they were seriously suggesting this. How could any of them think that she wanted to drain her brother?

"It's alright Melly," Marcus assured, a ghost of a smile on his face. "Let's get on with it,"

"I don't want to hurt you," She looked down at her hands, at the wounds that Marcus was about to take and once again wished that she had never heard of Justin Lestrade.

"If not me then who else?" Marcus asked as he reached forward and took a careful hold of her hand. The skin was slick with blood and he could feel the tremors racing through her body. "If they are right," he nodded at Emily and Hugh. "I will heal naturally," Reaching up, he brushed several strands of hair away from her face and chucked her on the chin as though she were much younger. "If I can help you this way…" Melissa could not stop the tears from sliding down her face as she nodded. Glancing down, she slowly, gingerly lifted the locket to Marcus' eye line.

"How do I?" Her voice was a whisper and misery filled every syllable.

Emily touched Melissa's hand, making her jump. "Just open it," She murmured, her voice soft, even gentle. As Melissa gaped at the sudden change in her demeanour, the blonde continued. "And show him the inside, that's all there is to it,"

"Alright," Melissa fumbled with the clasp on the locket,

opening it to reveal the small portrait that lay within. Carefully, hesitantly, she reached over and showed the interior to her brother's curious gaze.

Marcus blinked at the strangely perfect portrait of his sister that lay within the small space. Confused by the nearly real depiction, he almost missed the formation of his own portrait on the other side of the locket. His wondering eyes took in the cloudy, slowly forming image. Hair and skin bloomed into existence on the minute canvas and as they did, a strange, unsettling cold began to twine around his body, threatening to swamp him with its chill. He shuddered uncontrollably as his limbs grew numb, the cold sapping the energy from his body as a dull ache began to build beneath his skin. The lines of his face began to trace across the locket and he watched the exact representation of his eyes flare into being. Pain scored across his hands drawing a ragged cry from his lips. Looking away from the locket, he stared down. Across the base of his fingers, the skin tore and broke, blood flowing freely from the wounds that had suddenly appeared. Next to him, Melissa gasped in surprise and he looked up in time to witness the cuts on her hands knit closed. Shocked by the sight and by the pain in his palms, he made no protest as Emily caught hold of his hands and began to bind the wounds.

"We'll need to stitch those," She advised in matter of fact tones. Glancing at Melissa's stunned features, she continued "Do you want me to?"

Melissa nodded, not able to take her eyes from the locket pictures and the bloody mess that were her brother's hands. Her hands were still slick with blood yet the pain had ceased the skin unbroken as though there had never been a wound.

"I think that's enough," Justin noted as he reached forward and sliced his fingernail neatly through Marcus' portrait. Melissa gasped as the cold hit her. Shudders racked her frame and she bent double, her stomach churning unpleasantly with nausea.

"Melly?" Marcus stopped staring at the wounds in his fingers as Melissa dry heaved, her shoulders shaking with each retch. He stepped forward, eyes wide as he took in her sickly pale features.

"She'll be alright," Justin noted calmly, reassuringly. "It's a normal reaction to the broken connection," He draped an arm about her shoulders and led her to the lounge. "Come on Melissa, take a seat,"

"This way," Emily tugged lightly on Marcus' arm and led him into the kitchen, where she settled him at the scrubbed wooden table. "She'll be fine," Emily murmured as she slowly and methodically began to dress his wounds. Stunned by the scene in the hall, Marcus offered no protest as Emily expertly cleaned the cuts on his hands. "Hold still," She ordered as she reached below the table and picked up a large brown bottle which she uncorked. A stream of acrid smelling liquid poured from the bottle and soaked a clean square of muslin cloth and with two swift motions, she drew the soaked cloth across his fingers. The liquid burned in the cuts and Marcus could not hold back the scream that passed his lips as Emily recorked the bottle and began to bandage his fingers. She bound his hands skilfully and he waited for the burning to subside before he dared to speak.

"So you're not the social butterfly everyone sees?"

"Far from it," She agreed as she tipped the bloody water down the sink and refilled the bowl. Sitting back at the simple table, she looked directly at him. "Whatever you may think of me, I don't care," With a damp, clean cloth, she washed off the blood that marred his face. "I am what I am," Her fingers left his skin, and clear blue eyes stared at him. "If I had known you were coming here…"

"Would you have warned me off?" The shivers from his encounter with the lotus brooch still rippled across his skin and his words were slightly slurred.

"I would not have wished you to know of our lot," She replied, returning the rag to his face, firmly cleansing the last of the blood from his skin. "Secrecy is how we have survived,"

"How did my sister get involved?" Her fingers froze against his face, and he stared at her. "You may as well say,"

Emily took a deep breath as she removed the cloth from his chin. "Justin has old enemies," Water dripped down his chin, yet he paid it no mind as he listened intently to her words. "They knew of her connection to him," A small derisive chuckle escaped her lips. "Tenuous though it may have been, it marked her,"

Placing the cloth back on the table, she stared straight into his eyes. "They would have killed her had I not cursed her," He jerked backwards at the matter of fact announcement and stared at her in horror.

"You?" He couldn't think of anything further to follow that statement.

"Yes," She pushed her chair backwards and stood. Placing the wet cloth on the table, she leant back against the wall and watched him carefully. If he were to attack her, she would see muscles twitch before he moved. Marcus' body was rigid in the chair, and he stared at her with dawning dislike. She sighed, "It wasn't from any ill will that I did this…"

"I fancy my sister would see it otherwise," Marcus finally found his voice, yet he made no move to stand. "I'm not sure that I see your good wishes in this act,"

"Do you need to?" Emily asked.

"She's my sister,"

"And she would have died if I had not acted," Emily did not move from her place by the wall, but she leant forward, holding his gaze. "The only reason she still stands is because of me,"

"I wish I could believe in your good intentions," Marcus stood up from the table and glanced down at his bandaged hands. "You have condemned her to a terrible existence,"

"As opposed to what?" She pushed away from the wall and walked closer. "Death or worse at Montjoy's hands?" A light derisive smile flashed across her lips. "At least this way, she has a chance,"

"A chance to do what?" Marcus stood and walked forward. "She can't heal, she can't die, she'll…," His shoulders sagged as he tried to visualise Melissa's future. "She'll be like this for…" He could not complete the sentence, could not envision the long years that stretched out before his sister.

Emily's fingers reached forward to squeeze his upper arm, a reassuring smile spreading across her face as she looked at him. "We will find a cure,"

"Have you so far?"

The door to the kitchen swung open, halting their conversation. Emily looked over Marcus' shoulder as Hugh entered the room. "Hugh?"

"Are you done?" His gaze fixed on Emily's hand as he spoke.

"Yes," Emily released her hold and moved back with a small smirk. "He can go home now,"

"Wait," Marcus looked at the two of them, anger coursing through him at the dismissal. "You can't expect me just to go home and forget about my sister,"

"That's exactly what we want you to do," Hugh continued. "There is nothing else for to do here, other than you already have," He saw the mutiny in Marcus' dark gaze but paid it no mind as he continued. "Accept your sister is dead to you,"

"Tarlington…"

"No my boy," Hugh stepped forward, hoping to forestall any rash decisions. "You've done enough," He reached Marcus' side and caught hold of his upper arm. "Please leave this alone,"

"I can't just leave her like this?" Anger thrummed through Marcus' voice as he pulled free from Hugh's grip.

"And what would you do instead?" Hugh's voice cracked

across the space like a whip, finished with the soft approach. "Take her home where people will notice?" Hugh circled him carefully, his words crisp with barely contained anger. "Stay here and hurt your family more?" Marcus hung his head and stared down at the dark flagstones and bit his lip. "Please elucidate your grand scheme to keep your sister's condition a secret,"

"There must be something I can do," Marcus agitatedly ran his fingers through his hair as he spoke. "Tarlington please let me help?"

Emily watched the two of them, ideas bubbling through her mind as she discarded scenario after scenario. Marcus was offering help, and if thwarted he could be a powerful enemy.. If left to his own devices, he could get into further trouble. Visions of disaster briefly played about her head as she watched Hugh argue with the determined young man.

Oh dear Hugh, you won't dissuade him

As Hugh began to shake his head for the second time, Emily came to a decision, one that she would possibly regret if she thought long and hard about it. "If you really want to do something," The effect of her voice was like dropping a weighty stone into a still pool. Both men turned to face her and broke off mid-sentence. Hugh glared at her, yet there was dawning hope in Marcus' eyes. Emily ignored Hugh's thunderous expression and continued to speak. "You can help me,"

Marcus glanced at her, hope burning wildly in his chest as he looked past the stunned Hugh to Emily. "How?"

Smiling sweetly, Emily turned from Hugh's forbidding

visage and rested a slender hand on Marcus' arm. "Retrieve Justin's brooch,"

Marcus and Hugh spoke together as they both stared at the woman before them.

"Of course…" Said Marcus.

"I don't think…" Started Hugh.

"Hugh," Emily held up her hand and forestalled any further words. "He wants to help and he should,"

"Are you trying to get him killed?" Hugh pressed, incredulous anger fuelling his words.

"No of course not," Emily leant against the wall and ran her finger across her bottom lip. "Why would you think that?"

"Because going up against John will get him killed," He stared at Emily in disbelief, and a long suffering sigh escaped his lips. "But you're not listening to me,"

"Hugh?" Emily asked as he picked up the cane that was resting against the wall.

"Still, I'm not up for any more argument, you do as you will," As he pulled open the door, he glanced back at Marcus. "I would be careful around her boy," He bobbed his head at the relaxed figure. "She may look like an angel, but…" Emily raised a querying eyebrow. "I would watch your back,"

"Hugh darling, you wound me,"

"I know you my dear," He walked into the hall and reached for the hat that was laid on the hall table. "And though I find you positively delightful," He placed the hat on his head and smiled. "I wouldn't trust you," He moved to the front door, leaving Emily to shake her head as his departing back. "Farewell Justin," He called into the quiet hallway. "Perhaps I'll see you again,"

"Hugh," Melissa walked into the hall, a concerned tremor running through her voice as she watched him prepare to leave. "Are you leaving?" With a small sigh, Hugh reached out and placed an arm around her shoulders.

"Yes," He watched the shock settle on her face, and his face softened. "It's alright," Tremors were racing through her frame as she huddled next to his body. Over the dark waves of her hair, he glared at Emily's unrepentant form. "You'll be fine," The whispered words soothed her and she took a breath, reining in her emotions as she did so. Releasing his hold Hugh tipped his hat at Marcus. "And so will you my friend," He gave a small chuckle. "If you stay clear of our disastrous lives,"

"So what do you intend to do?" Justin's ragged voice sounded as he leant against the frame of the parlour door.

"First, go to Whites and have a drink," Justin gave a huff of impatience and Hugh smiled at him. "And then I think I'll go and find Henry," Justin and Emily's faces fell as they stared at the older man. Hugh turned to the mirror and began to adjust the cravat that was messily tied about his throat.

"Henry?" Melissa asked, her eyes flickering between Justin and Emily's stunned expressions and Hugh's smiling face.

"Another one of us," Hugh answered brightly as he tied his cravat. "I haven't seen him for several years and…" He picked up his cane. "I suddenly feel the need to,"

"Last I heard, Henry had gone to the Americas," Justin interjected. "That's a lot of country to look through,"

"It'll keep me busy," Brushing several imaginary bits of dust from his coat, Hugh continued. "I think England is becoming problematic,"

"Because of me?" Justin asked, shuffling into the hallway.

"Oh no…" Hugh glanced over at Emily and directed his next words at her. "I'm afraid my dear that I can't keep up with your foolishness,"

"Hugh," Emily rushed forward, horror on her porcelain features. "I'm sorry for the De Vire girl, you know why I thought it was necessary…"

"I know and that's not why I'm taking my leave," He tweaked her nose and smiled. "You may not see it yet, but I know where you're going," He cast a glance at Marcus and sadness washed over his features. "And I don't want to watch,"

"Hugh?" For the first time since meeting Emily, Melissa heard tears in her usually calm voice.

"It won't be forever…" He brushed a tear away from her cheek. "When you've done what you intend, come and meet me," Reaching forward, he hugged her tightly. "I know you have your reasons, but they won't bring you peace," His voice whispered into her hair. "Maybe you will understand some day,"

Emily did not reply, she was trying to stifle tears. "Who am I going to talk to?"

"You'll find someone," He stepped back and nodded at

Justin. "Get your brooch back," He ordered. "And try not to bait John too much," Pushing open the door, he stepped out onto the gravelled drive. "See you in a few years," He called back as the door closed behind him.

Silence reigned as the portal closed on Hugh's departing back. In the wake of his departure, Melissa focused on her brother. He was staring at Emily's rigid figure, and she turned her head to stare also. The blonde was taking deep breaths, swallowing the emotion that was coursing through her. Melissa thought she understood. She had barely known Hugh, but he had been supportive, even caring. As she watched Emily drag her feelings under control, she wondered what she had felt for the man. Marcus stepped forward, and she returned to her scrutiny of his familiar face. His eyes were troubled as he looked at the blonde and Melissa could see pity in his gaze. Marcus took an involuntary step forward and gently squeezed Emily's shoulder, wincing as pain radiated from the expertly bandaged wounds. A flash of fury surged through Melissa as she remembered the reason for those bandages.

"Marcus," Her voice was sharper than she intended and he stared at her in surprise, releasing the grip he had on Emily's arm.

Emily recovered her wits as Melissa's outraged tones broke through the wall of emotion that surrounded her. Half turning, she looked down at Marcus' hand and then up into Melissa's mulish stare.

"Don't worry Melissa, I'm not going to seduce him," Covering her pain with sarcasm, she casually threw the barb across the room and was gratified to see Melissa wince. "Let's go," She caught hold of Marcus' arm and led him toward the door.

"Don't," He turned at his sister's voice and bowed his head.

"I can't just do nothing," He nodded towards Justin. "That man tried his best to keep you safe, I can't let him stay like this," Walking closer, he leaned forward and gave her a hug. Stepping back he turned back to face Emily.

"Let's go,"

They stepped through the door and turned to face Emily's carriage. Further along the drive they could see the departing back of Hugh's coach and Marcus heard the sudden intake of breath from Emily at the sight.

"You bring him back in one piece," Melissa reached the doorway behind them, her eyes burning into Emily's back. "If you get him killed, I'll make sure you regret it," Emily turned to face the other girl and gave a small smile at Melissa's threats.

"Of course," Emily replied mildly, forestalling any further outburst from Melissa. "He'll come back in one piece," Marcus helped her into the carriage before climbing the steps himself. As the door slammed shut behind him, Emily leaned out of the window. "So you don't need to make any empty threats," She gave the order to her driver as Melissa rushed through the door. Hurrying down the steps, she was too late to halt the departing coach and she stood on the drive watching the coach until it passed out of sight. Slowly she climbed the steps back to the house, a sense of doom whispering through her bones as she thought about her brother and Emily. She leant back against the door frame, wondering if she would ever see Marcus again.

CHAPTER 14

The sun was sinking as Emily's liveried coach pulled up outside the nondescript house and they stepped from its luxurious interior. It had been a strange ride into the city. Marcus and Emily had been too preoccupied with their own thoughts to attempt much conversation. Marcus in particular, wore the air of someone who expected to wake from the grip of some powerful nightmare. Emily glanced at his face and resisted the urge to squeeze his arm in reassurance, unsure of how he would receive the gesture.

"So is this Katherine willing to help you?" Marcus broached the uncomfortable silence as they both stared up at the house.

"No," Emily walked forward and approached the door.

The breeze picked up and tugged at the hat she had carefully pinned to her blonde tresses. "She said she wouldn't…"

"Then why are we here?"

Emily gave a small snort and reached for the door knocker. "If we get separated, meet at Hyde Park," Taking hold of the iron hoop, she angled her head at Marcus. "I'd hide if I were you," She called softly as she released the heavy ring, the deep note echoing about them and through the house. Marcus lost the retort on his lips as footsteps sounded from within the hall. And Emily shooed him away. Taking the hint, he almost ran to the side of the house and out of sight.

The butler opened the door and frowned down at her. "I'm afraid the lady does not wish to be disturbed,"

"I understand," Emily replied, her voice calm. "I don't need to enter," She took a step back. "Can you just inform her that Justin has retrieved his brooch," With a bland smile on her lips, Emily turned to walk away.

Footsteps dashed along the hallway and Katherine poked her head out into the street. "Justin couldn't have retrieved his brooch,"

"Oh?" Emily raised an eyebrow. "I don't think I mistook Justin's reaction to the discovery"

Katherine turned back to face the butler. "Get my carriage ready,"

Marcus, listening from his hiding place, felt his respect and wariness for Emily increase as he listened to her smooth lies. In contrast to Emily's polished tones, Katherine's voice was reedier and laced with panic.

"You'd better go," Katherine continued to speak, shooing Emily back to her carriage with a worried look on her face. "Now,"

"Can't I accompany you?" Emily questioned mildly as she opened the coach door.

"No," Katherine reached back into the hall for her hat and began to pin it in place. She looked at the still form before her and continued. "For pities sake Emily, if you have any regard for me at all you would just go and not follow me,"

"Of course," Emily replied as she mounted the steps. "I…" She stressed the word slightly. "Wouldn't dream of following you," Marcus rolled his eyes, picking up on the hint in Emily's voice as he backed away from the house. Hailing a hackney carriage, he watched the blonde's coach drive away from the residence.

"Where to?" The coachman asked, glancing over his shoulder to look at the other man.

"Nowhere yet," Marcus replied, "A coach is due to leave that house opposite; I want you to follow it,"

"Right you are," Marcus settled into the seat and waited. They did not have to wait long. Moments later, a small curricle left the property driven by a slight figure in a hood.

"Let's go," Marcus prompted. With a click of his tongue, the driver urged the horses away from the kerb and out into traffic. Lights were being lit as they moved through the increasing darkness. The breeze grew colder and it chilled him as he sat in the open carriage. He stuffed his hands into his sleeves as the brisk, foul air of the Thames blasted across his skin, making his eyes water. They travelled through darkening streets for at least half an hour until the small curricle halted. Motioning the driver to stop, Marcus watched the women climb from the curricle and approach a small terraced house. He waited for her to enter the property before he instructed the driver to return.

Hyde Park was shrouded in shadow as his cab finally reached the gates. Paying the driver, he leant back against the railings of the park, trying to warm his now frozen fingers. As the breeze rustled through the leaves behind him, he considered what had happened that day. Early today, he had been worried for Melissa's safety and now he was racing around London, looking for a magical item. Tilting his head back, he stared into space, trying to work out just how this had happened.

"De Vire," His head dropped back down, and he stared across at the hooded form of Emily Morton. She was hugging the shadows on the very edge of the park, her usual beauty shrouded by the darkness. Rolling his eyes at the poetic direction his mind was taking, he stepped to her side. "Did you follow?"

"Yes," Her arm slid through his, and they walked along the pavement, like any couple taking an evening stroll. "It's in a bad area…" He noted with some concern.

"I understand," Her voice was soft, and he glanced down at her, trying to gauge her emotions from her placid features. "Just tell me where and I'll deal with it?"

"Are you certain?" He muttered, nodding at the elderly couple that passed them. "I don't feel right about letting you go there alone,"

"Well you can't come with me," Emily retorted, her voice remaining at the same volume. "I've had more than enough experience with this," She removed her arm from his and smiled. "And besides, I think it's time you went home,"

"Lady Morton,"

"Emily," She replied gently, "Lady Morton is not my identity,"

"Emily," Marcus leant forward, "I can't just let you go there alone,"

A smile creased Emily's features, and she stopped walking. "And I fancy your sister would be most put out if anything happened to you," She moved into the shade of a large tree and beckoned him forward. "Personally I would be grateful of the company and…" She slowly reached her hand out and gently stroked his cheek. "I know that you need to be doing something," He caught his breath slightly as she leant closer, eyes fixed on his with a directness he found unerring.

"What are you up to?" Curious, whispered words fell from his lips as he followed her movements. Her fingers slid from his cheek and rested on the side of his neck and his pulse beat faster as she drew ever closer. She was beautiful; he would give her that. She stopped inches from his face and he could feel her breath drift across his cheeks.

"You're a good man," He started at the words, for one moment he had expected her to kiss him and he felt slightly disappointed that she hadn't. Hugh Tarlington's words echoed through his mind and he forced himself to focus.

"And?" Backing away, he removed her hand from his neck and stared down at her. Her eyes twinkled with amusement, and he sighed. "What are you playing at?"

"I'm not," She murmured as she stepped away from him. "Your sister will be furious if I tried to seduce you,"

"Are you?" He fell silent as another couple walked past them. Leaves blew against their legs, and he shivered in the chill night air as he waited.

"Not at the moment," Emily replied to his question with a grin. "Though if you're game?"

"Not at the moment," He replied, answering his flirtatious grin with one of his own. He held her gaze for a few moments more, before the reality of their situation intruded once again. "We're supposed to be getting Justin's brooch,"

"Much as I understand your desire to help," Emily's voice lost the soft notes she had adopted and added another piece to the puzzle of Emily Morton. "I'd have to live with her disapproval for a long time if anything happened to you,"

"I don't like feeling helpless," Marcus replied. "And I won't ask a woman to do a job in my place,"

Emily gave a tiny roll of her eyes. "That's immaterial," She continued. "I've experience of this and if things go wrong, I can survive it," She tapped a finger against his chest. "You on the other hand would not,"

"Then why did you bring me along?" He moved closer, focusing more closer on her. Despite her flirtatious manner of earlier, he doubted that she wished his company for anything less than business.

"I needed someone to follow Katherine," Emily responded. "She would have recognised my attempts to follow her but as you are unknown to her," She rested against the trunk of the tree and folded her arms. "You were the perfect choice," Marcus bowed his head.

"And now?" Marcus asked, eager to proceed further with the plan.

"You go home,"

"No," Marcus replied simply, rising to the dismissive tone in her voice with some heat.

"Marcus, do not make this difficult," Emily replied, her voice quiet, yet deathly serious. "It's too dangerous for you to go with me,"

"Use me as a distraction," Marcus argued. He fell silent as another couple walked past. The chill breeze ruffled his hair, but he paid it no mind. As the pair walked out of earshot, he continued, his words becoming more urgent as he spoke. "What if you can't get to him alone? What if he's carrying it on him?" Emily stared at Marcus for a long time, thinking through his words. "He knows you," Marcus pressed on, realising that he had a chance to convince her. "He'll be expecting you, he doesn't know me,"

"And what would you do?" Emily asked, finally as he finished his argument. "How would you distract him?"

"I'll knock on his door and improvise,"

Silence followed his pronouncement as Emily considered his words. A mournful breeze tugged at his hair and he felt himself growing more impatient.

"You know I'm right?"

"Alright," Emily finally conceded, looking at the man before her. "You can distract him by knocking on the front door and as he's answering it, I'll..."

"Go in the back," Marcus finished. "Either you'll hit him on the back of the head or I'll punch him,"

"Let's go then," Emily pushed away from the tree and linked arms with Marcus. "I'll let you lead the way,"

"Thank you," Marcus glanced down at her as her slender arm slid through his.

"Don't thank me," Emily interrupted. "This could be the worst mistake of your life,"

CHAPTER 15

A chill breeze stirred the pile of dead leaves that surrounded the fresh mound of earth. A vole raced across the moonlit ground, its little claws digging into the soft sod as it dashed through the undergrowth. Intrigued by the freshly turned earth, it stopped, nosing at the mound of damp brown soil for small insects. After a moment's digging, the vole stopped and glanced round, its nose twitching at the vibrations that rippled through the ground. It stared from left to right and above, looking for the source of the motion. The clearing was still, the vole was alone on the pile of earth. It returned its nose to the ground, crunching the small beetles with relish as the vibration came again, stronger this time and closer. Something beneath the soft mound of earth, something large, was clawing its way free. The vole took flight, its long claws digging into the loose soil as it ran from the mound and across the clearing. In the moonlight, the mound was moving; whatever lay beneath the loosely packed earth was slowly digging its way to the light.

CHAPTER 16

Melissa sat next to Justin and tried not to shake. With the house empty of all but her and Justin, she had more time to think about this morning. She remembered the deep shuddering breaths that Justin had drawn in his attempt to breathe, the slow rattle of the air as it left his lungs in his final moments. His subsequent resurrection was against all the laws of nature, yet she had witnessed it. Shivers raced up and down her back, echoes of the sickness she had felt when Marcus had healed her hands. Glancing down at the smooth skin, she recalled how the wounds vanished. Little by little, the pain had fled as the wounds had knit shut. Stunned, she had been unable to do anything save watch the tissue close until she had heard Marcus' cry.

"Melissa?" Justin was looking at her, his pale eyes revealing little, yet his voice radiated concern. She tried not to look at him with revulsion; after all, this was now her fate.

"Are you…" He began to ask, taking a hesitant half step forward.

"Don't ask if I'm alright?" She could barely voice the words as she stopped the hackneyed phrase from leaving his lips. "I will be…" Unable to honestly finish that sentence, she drew a deep shuddering breath and wondered if she were already half dead. "So…um.," She tried to be bright, unconcerned, yet she could not, the emotions were too raw. Justin turned to face her, his neck creaking unpleasantly as he did so. She winced at the sound and continued, trying to hide her growing fear and horror. "Now what?" She was pleased to note that her voice didn't shake.

"What do you mean?" Justin did not reach for her, his fingers stayed still and closed on his knee. In those rough, husky tones, she fancied she could hear sorrow.

"I mean, what do we do now?" Melissa pulled herself to her feet and stared down at the figure before her. Tension laced her voice, and she kept talking, trying to convince herself that things would, could be alright. "We get your brooch back and then what?"

Justin glanced down at the floor at her falsely bright and focused tones. He knew that voice. He had heard it from all of those he had cursed in the past. He had never wanted to hear it from her lips. "Now I find someone to kill," He did not attempt to soften his words. She would not be coddled and he would not hide anymore behind euphemisms. What they dealt in was death, and she needed the facts.

Melissa flinched at the self-loathing that she could hear in his voice and wished fervently that she could comfort him, but her skin crawled at the thought. "Is there any…"

"Other way?" His voice was mild, yet she could hear the despair behind it. "No," He rested his head back against the chair and attempted to close his eyes. "I've looked," He rubbed his forehead and stared at the candelabra. "Dear God, I've looked. I searched through occult tomes and books of myth and legend, as many as I could find, but none have mentioned this brooch," He waved towards the back of the room. "You've seen my library,"

Melissa nodded, remembering the stacks of books and notes that littered the room at the back of the building and something began to burn within her. A desperate ray of hope. "And you've found nothing?"

"No,"

"Not even in your family history?" Melissa remembered the tale he had told her, of the acquisition of the box from the crusades. "Anything about where the box had come from?"

"That's the first thing I investigated," Justin replied, "But nothing. All my family could tell me was that my ancestor got it from a witch who was decapitated somewhere in Persia,"

"Nothing else?" The flame was there, whispering in the background, suggesting that he had missed something, offering her a way free.

"No, nothing. I've gone through that box, read all of the engravings. I've studied every aspect of the legend, and I've learnt nothing new," Melissa walked forward and gingerly placed her hand on his, the cold flesh making her stomach lurch. "I just wish I could find something, anything that would help," He glanced up at Melissa and tried a tremulous smile. "I do keep looking, but sometimes it seems hopeless,"

Silence followed his words. The fire crackled in the background, and Melissa stared down at Justin's face. Despite the deathly cast to his features, she could still make out the expression of torment that dominated them. "I could take a look," She offered, watching his eyes snap to her. "You may have missed something,"

"I can almost quote the documentation but..." He pushed himself upright. "You can take a look if you wish," Melissa left his side as soon as the words fell from his lips and headed toward the door. "Do you want me to come with you?" A sense of dread settled over him as he watched her hurry to leave.

"No," Melissa replied, "I can work faster alone," With quick, almost running steps, she left the room. Justin settled back into the chair. He supposed he couldn't blame her for rushing away. With slow motions he ran his fingers over his face, wondering just how bad he looked. Clenching his fist, he brought it down against his thigh with a dull thud. Well, John had certainly scored a point this time. If only he had been faster… Shaking his head, he attempted to banish the negative thoughts that threatened to swamp him. John was so good at this. He did not even understand how he had become so strong. Through the film that had begun to cover his eyes, he stared up at the cracked ceiling. John had always been stronger; it was one of his greatest regrets that he had cursed him. That curse had borne so much bitter fruit, and he had now destroyed the life and hopes of a young woman. There was no turning back for either of them, and she would grow to hate him too. Sinking back into the cushions, he wallowed in his regret and anger.

Melissa left the parlour and hurried along the corridor, she couldn't bear staying in the room. Justin's limbs were stiff and unnatural and she fancied that the scent of death was about him. This morning she had grieved for his death and there he sat, talking still. She didn't know which was worse, her reaction to the thing he had become, or the knowledge that it could happen to her. Bile rose in her throat and she swallowed rapidly, trying to stop the panicked whimpers from escaping her lips. Rushing into the book lined room; she shut the door and leant against it, drawing deep breaths of air into her lungs as she tried to stave off panic. Justin was dead, she could accept that, but fear rushed through her veins like ice. Sinking to her knees, she lowered her face into her arms and tried to stop shaking. Would that happen to her? Would she lie twisted and broken like that? For a long moment, she gave in to the panic that was flooding her mind. What would her life be like from now on? Living through the centuries, stealing life from others to avoid becoming some crawling dead thing? Curling her arms about her head, she tried to stop the terrible visions flowing through her mind.

She did not know how long she sat there on the cold floor, letting the fear and horror rule her. Yet she eventually raised her head from her knees and stared about her. The library was as she remembered it, piled high with books and parchment. Picking herself up on unsteady legs, she reached the table and the first volume that came to hand.

CHAPTER 17

"Ready?" Marcus pulled the heavy coat about his body as he directed the question at Emily, looking with some appreciation at her new attire. They had returned to the coach and travelled the twisting route to what had to be John's house. Marcus had sat on the box with the coachman as the blonde changed her clothes within the carriage. His wondering eyes took in her form, and he gave a nod of appreciation at her transformation. Gone were the heavy dress and panniers that she had worn earlier, and she now stood before him in breeches and shirt, perfect, she said, for clambering through windows. Her blonde hair was tucked into a filthy scarf, and she had hitched up her corset and flattened her breasts. Despite the lithe figure, she now resembled an overly pretty youth. His concern for her welfare dwindled as he took in her almost masterful impersonation of a street urchin. She gave him a smug grin as she walked forward.

"Of course I'm ready," She answered as she tucked a pistol into her belt. Tearing his eyes from her figure, he focused on the scene around him. The street on which they stood was narrow and thick with grime. It was much later in the evening, but the streets were full. People in rough clothing bustled about them, and he grew conscious of his good quality garb. Pulling the cloak closer to his form in order to hide it from view, he kept a wary eye on the bustling crowds.

"Your man?" Marcus glanced up at the implacable driver in concern.

"He's fine," Emily dragged a rough woollen coat over her clothing; disguising herself even more. "He's my driver," She gave a small sign and the coach moved off, leaving them standing alone in the street. As the coach drifted from view, Marcus felt even more exposed, he wasn't in jewels or court dress, but his clothing was rich and completely out of step with what others wore about him. "I pay him very well for silence," Emily drew closer, and her voice dropped, so that only he could hear her. "Even my new husband can't command him,"

"I hope you're right," Marcus, suddenly concerned with the propriety of roaming through London with the wife of a Peer, despite how she was dressed.

"Are you sure?" Emily asked with some concern.

Marcus was watching the crowd, his agitation apparent.

"Yes," Marcus stopped fidgeting yet he did not look at her, too concerned with the press of the crowd. "I can't let you go in alone,"

"This isn't my first time doing this," Emily retorted with some exasperation. "Don't treat me like some fragile piece of glass," He did not answer, his eyes still roving up and down the street like some caged animal. Emily gave a deep sigh and caught hold of his upper arm. "You don't have to help, it's clear you're uncomfortable,"

"And leave you to this monster?" Marcus stopped his scrutiny of the street and finally stared at her face. "No,"

"Alright," Emily leant in and spoke rapidly. "Then do what we agreed, you knock on the front door. If he answers, badger him for some charity. Meanwhile I'll slip in round the back,"

"But what if he spots you?" Various scenarios were constructing themselves in his head, and none of them had a decent outcome. "What if he doesn't answer the door?"

"He'll answer it," Emily answered coolly, unconcern in her voice. For a moment, Marcus felt a flash of admiration for the young woman's bravery. She wasn't a fluttery young girl and had this been any other occasion… "Have you got that?" She interrupted that train of thought, and he floundered for a moment, trying to remember just what she had said. As her gaze hardened, he nodded, aware that her tolerance of him was running thin. "Good, then get going," Marcus moved past her, and she caught his arm. "One more thing…" Her voice was sharp, intense and he listened with greater care. "If things go wrong, get out of there. Don't help me I can take care of myself,"

"But,"

"No buts," She reached up and grabbed hold of his collar. "You will do as I say, if I get you killed, Melissa will be very upset, I will also be very annoyed. Do your bit and get out,"

Marcus gritted his teeth and nodded. "Fine..." he grunted as he walked past her. "I'll do what you say," He reached the end of the street and glanced back at her. "Good luck," He turned back to the narrow alley and began to walk down it. He turned once to look back at her, but she had gone, vanished into the crowd like a ghost. With confidence he did not quite feel, Marcus walked along the rubbish strewn road. Muck, horse manure and rotten vegetables sloshed in filthy puddles beneath his feet. He resisted the urge to rise up on tip toe and attempt to delicately make his way through the grime. People jostled into him, beggars, whores and possibly even thieves, but he did not stop. Straightening his shoulders, he pushed his way through the crowd, grateful that he had listened to Emily and had left his money and jewellery in her coach. In no time at all, he reached the house he had seen earlier, and he turned towards the peeling paint of the front door. A rusted iron ring was set into the door, and he knocked twice, hearing the sound echo within the house beyond. Before the noise died, he heard footsteps from within. Taking a deep breath, he waited for the door to be opened. There was the sound of several heavy bolts being drawn back and he reached into his pocket and drew out a leaflet. Once again he marvelled at the resourcefulness of the woman he had found himself with. With barely a blink of an eye, she had handed him this from a box beneath the coach seat and given him a credible story. As the door opened with a creak, he launched into the speech she had given him.

"Good evening," He modified his tones, trying to lose the accent of a nobleman. "My name is Robert Blakedon. I run the Whitechapel home for fallen women," He handed over the leaflet and looked up into the man's face. Cold, pitiless eyes stared back, and he suppressed a shudder.

"Yes?"

"Well as you know, moral decency is of concern to us all. It is therefore, incumbent on us all to help these lost souls," He continued his spiel, trying to suppress the feeling that he was failing horribly.

"And this concerns me?" The man's voice was calm and leeched of emotion.

"It should concern us all..." Marcus continued to speak, warming to his role as he waited for Emily to finish whatever she was doing.

The other man watched him in silence, his face revealing little of his thoughts. After a moment of listening to Marcus talk, he interrupted. "This sounds positively fascinating," Marcus stopped speaking and watched the man with interest. "Why don't you come in?" Marcus hesitated for a moment, yet he knew that he had to keep the man busy.

"Thank you,"

"Don't mention it," The man stood back and let Marcus walk past him into the hall. "I so rarely get visitors," Marcus barely heard him, struck dumb by the stench of rotting food that hit him full in the face. Struggling to get his stomach under control, he heard the door close behind him. "Come through," Breathing through his mouth, Marcus followed the man through the hall. Stepping into the parlour, he almost retched at the rotten and maggoty food that covered the table. He started as he heard the parlour door click shut behind him. He turned as the other man walked across the room toward him.

"Are you alright Mr De Vire?" Marcus felt his stomach clench with horror as he stared back at the other man. The expressionless mask on his face had fallen to reveal gloating amusement. "Oh yes I know you," He stopped just shy of Marcus and gloated. "I saw you when you came to the aid of your sister," He chuckled at Marcus' stunned face and continued. "Tell me, how is she?"

Marcus felt rage blaze into life and swamp the nervous horror at discovery. For a moment he was led back to the night of the assault, the night he had dealt the fatal wounds to Justin, wounds that had been precipitated by this man. Balling his hands into fists, he launched forward and solidly punched John on the nose.

John staggered back with the blow, his nose spraying blood as he continued to chuckle. "Beautifully done," He retorted as he dodged the next blow. Marcus kept moving, his fists flying faster than they ever had done before. He got in another hit before John seized him by the collar

face, concern in her blue eyes. He waved his hand and straightened up, trying to regain control.

"I'm fine," He uttered through short panting breaths. "Now what?"

"Now we find someone for Justin," She raised her hand and beckoned to her carriage that he belatedly realised was waiting on the corner. "And I know just where to find it," She clambered into the carriage and Marcus followed, wondering just who she meant to take.

CHAPTER 18

The carriage drew up outside of Lord Morton's London abode and Marcus watched Emily step down. She had changed in the carriage and was now back in the cumbersome garb she had worn earlier. For modesty's sake, he had closed his eyes, but he was still strangely in awe of the woman with him. Refreshingly immodest and remarkably adaptable, she was proving to be a very entertaining companion.

"I won't be long," She whispered as she stepped down. "Just keep yourself hidden," She stopped and felt into her pocket. "And you'd better take this with you," She drew out Justin's brooch. "Do you have a snuff box?" Marcus shook his head. "Damn," She whispered, "Alright, I'll put it between the cushions," She pressed it into place and stepped back. "Don't forget it's there and put your hand on it," Marcus looked down at the pinned flower and sat as far away from it as he could.

"What are you going to do?" He asked, tearing his eyes away from the seemingly innocuous brooch.

"Something I've wanted to do for a while," She muttered as she closed the carriage door and walked briskly to the front door of the house. It opened to her knock and she walked into the hallway with all the grace of a queen.

"Would it be too much trouble for you to inform me of your comings and goings?" Morton's words echoed across the vast space. As the footman hurried out of sight, Emily turned to face her husband with a bland smile. He marched toward her, anger rising off him in waves. "I don't know what Saint-Claire let you get away with, but my wife is at my beck and call,"

"Actually yes," Emily was tired and had no real desire to pander to the oaf she had married. Her voice was soft, yet full of a fire that he had never heard before. "It is too much trouble," Morton stopped walking as a somewhat comical look of shock spread across his face. "And I certainly won't be at your beck and call," She hung her cape on a hook and idly picked up a cane from the stand nearby. "I would feel much happier if you did not speak to me from now on,"

"What the blazes?" He strode forward, face like thunder. She could see the violence in his face and eyes and she moved to one side, swinging the cane as she did so. Shocked by her sudden move, he did not block the blow and the cane smashed into his temple stunning him.

Emily gave a small sigh and swung again, catching him between the legs. She watched without expression as he fell to the ground, unable to vocalise the pain he was in. Reaching into a pocket in her skirts, she drew a small bottle of Laudanum and unstoppered it. Calmly, she gripped his nostrils and poured the contents of the phial down his throat. As he collapsed back against the floor like a stuffed dummy, she stepped back, returned the phial to her pocket and set the cane back to its stand. Calmly, she walked back to the front door and opened it. She crooked her finger at the coachman, and he followed, heading for the hallway.

Emily waited for him to enter before she pointed down at Morton's body. Carefully, he lifted the body over his shoulder and began to carry it out of the building. Emily walked beside him, a twisted smile on her lips. She looked up at the coachman's face and gave a nod.

"I'll teach you to disobey me," He shouted in a voice that was uncannily similar to Morton's. They moved through the doorway as Emily slapped the semi-conscious form with all her might, the sound echoing through the large hall. She gave a shriek and threw herself against the wall before dropping to the floor. "Stop crying," The coachman shouted as he pushed the body onto the doorstep.

"I'm sorry… so sorry," Emily's voice came out muffled and tearful. Marcus glanced through the gap in the coach's curtains watching the proceedings with curiosity. The coachman noticed his interest and pointed down at the body. Marcus continued to stare as the coachman mimed lifting the body.

"Goddamn it woman," The coachman stopped his dumb show in order to continue the charade.

"I'm sorry, I won't disobey you ever again," Emily whimpered as the coachman beckoned at Marcus with more urgency. Finally getting the point, Marcus opened the carriage door and stepped carefully and quietly. A quick glance at the house showed that the shutters were fully closed, they were safe and unobserved. "Stop whining…" Marcus stared at the body before him for a long moment as the coachman continued his role. "I'm going out, I expect you to be properly contrite on my return," The coachman then slammed the door. Glancing at the static form of Marcus, the coachman cleared his throat. "Give us a hand," Marcus hesitated, knowing what Emily had in mind for the man at his feet. "Don't give a pig's fart for this bastard," The coachman whispered, correctly interpreting Marcus' wavering thoughts. "He beat his mistress to death," He spat down on the figure. "He deserves all that's going to happen to him," Marcus hesitated for one more moment before helping the coachman lift the heavy body into the carriage.

"What about Emily?" Marcus asked, taking a long look at the closed door and worrying about the blonde woman inside.

"She's got to play the role," The coachman responded as he mounted the box. Turning back in his seat, he tapped the side of the carriage to gain Marcus' attention. "Are you coming?" Marcus looked up, momentarily confused by the question. "To Lestrade's home?" The coachman clarified, patience clearly wearing thin.

Marcus nodded and climbed the rickety steps. As he sat beside the sleeping form, he tried not to think about what was awaiting the man in the carriage. If he was meant to heal Lestrade, then he was taking Morton to his death. The coachman clicked to the horses, and the coach rattled out of the drive. In the dark, curtained carriage, Marcus closed his eyes and tried to rest. The revelations of the last few hours had exhausted him, but he was too agitated to sleep. The presence of the lotus flower pressed between the cushions opposite weighed on his mind and the fear that Morton would wake before they reached their destination kept him alert and wary as the coachman drove quickly through the deserted countryside.

As the coach rattled away from the house, Emily heard the butler enter the hallway. Like most staff, he had not approached the fight and for that, she was immensely grateful. As she picked herself up from the floor she managed a very credible sob, and marvelled at her ability to do so. It was sometimes difficult to manifest tears on demand, but tonight was proving easier than usual. She only had to think of Hugh leaving and tears were not a problem. She certainly wasn't wasting precious emotion on the tub of lard she'd sent with her coachman.

"Are you alright Madam?" The butler was kind and solicitous as he helped her into the parlour. But then, she mused, he had to be. Good staff never upset their employers by making them mad.

"Yes I'm fine," She sobbed through dishonest tears.

"I made the master angry," She whimpered, hating the charade she had to play. "He went out…" She gave another fake sob and buried her face in her hands, hoping that her lies weren't written over her face. That was another problem she faced, she could never tell if her contempt for men like her husband was written on her features. "Can you fetch me a glass of canary and have the maid make up the library fire? I don't think I'll be able to sleep tonight,"

"Very good madam," The butler nodded and left the parlour. She waited until his footsteps moved away and down the hall before she stood. This wasn't the best turn for the evening, she had wanted to return to Justin's, and now she was stuck, having to play the worried submissive wife. And there was Marcus to consider. Sending him back alone with Justin's new donor was beyond the pale. She pressed her fingers against her temple, as she tried to salvage some good news from the situation. Her coachman would at least take Marcus and Morton to Justin, even if Marcus had an attack of conscience, but the experience would mark him. She had effectively sent him to witness murder, no matter how she may dress it up, Perhaps Hugh had been right to counsel against including Marcus in their workings?

Footsteps from the hall interrupted her chain of thought and she schooled her expression into one of appropriate woe and waited for the butler to bring in the glass of canary.

"The library is ready Madam," The butler said as he handed her the small glass and left the room. Taking small sips of the drink, she left the room and crossed the hall. The small library was well equipped thankfully and she sank into one of the chairs by the fire with some relief. Picking up the nearest leather bound tome, she began to read, trying not to think about the potential disaster she had just created.

CHAPTER 19

The sound of the front door banging woke Melissa from a dreamless sleep. She was curled up in the only armchair that graced the packed library. As she woke, the heavy tome that had been resting in her hands slipped to the ground and landed face up, its pages covered with the scrawl that she had come to associate with Justin. She had read late into the night, hoping to discover some lost gem in the pages of the books that were stacked about the room. Justin had let her be and she was grateful for that. She couldn't trust her feelings now. She knew he was sorry for the way things had happened and yet, her anger would not lie. If they spoke, she would not be able to contain the rage that pulsed through her. Wiping a thin thread of drool from her mouth she stood and listened to the sounds of movement from the hall. Stretching the kinks out of her muscles, she headed to the door.

Justin had spent a long, uncomfortable night in the parlour. He could have managed the stairs to his room, but he could not find the will to do so. Melissa had not returned to the parlour since her hasty exit and he knew why. A familiar self mocking smile inched its way across his lips as he considered the situation. It wasn't as though he hadn't faced this before and yet, he had hoped that Melissa would have been different. Once again he cursed himself for a fool. It was almost inconceivable that she would forgive him. After all, none of the others had. He shifted into a more comfortable position as the dawning sun finally lit the parlour walls in shades of gold. He was still debating whether to face her when the main door banged open and he heard the sounds of people moving into the house. Forcing his muscles to work, he staggered into the hall, picking up a poker as he did so.

"It's alright," Marcus called out, his voice breathless with exertion as he and the coachman hefted the body of Lord Morton across the threshold. The pair manoeuvred the body into the parlour and laid it on the rug. Justin glanced down at the body and then up at Marcus with a raised eyebrow.

"Where's Emily?" Justin asked, the absence of the blonde troubling him.

"She has to keep up appearances," Marcus answered, looking down at Lord Morton with a disturbed gaze. "She sent us here with him and your brooch,"

Justin breathed a sigh of relief and relaxed as he realised his salvation. He also knew Emily would not send him an innocent. "Where?"

"It's in the back of the coach, stuffed between the cushions…" Marcus called as Justin shuffled out of the room towards the hall. "Where's my sister?"

"I'm here," Melissa stepped into the parlour only to stop at the sight of Justin and the body. Justin's mouth twitched at her hesitance. He took half a step forward. Melissa stiffened and brushed past him. She saw the resigned, sad look on Justin's face but she couldn't bring herself to care.

"Are you alright?" She asked Marcus, ignoring Justin as he shuffled past her and out toward the coach.

"I'm fine," Marcus glanced down at his sister and then cast a curious look at Justin's departing back. "Are you?"

Melissa bit her lip and then threw her arms about her brother, tears flowing from her eyes. Marcus said little as she sobbed, feeling helpless against the tide of emotion that was flowing through his sister. "It's alright," he murmured after a few moments. Sniffing as she pulled away from her brother, she sank into one of the chairs. Marcus sat too, waiting for Melissa to speak.

"I just can't stop thinking that if I'd just listened to you, I wouldn't be here," Melissa finally said as she wiped her nose. "And that he should have left me alone," She gave another long sniff and continued. "But I know I was stupid about him… I didn't listen when he told me that he wouldn't court me," Her shoulders shuddered as she tried to contain the tears that were threatening to make a reappearance. "And now I'm like this…. I don't know what I'm going to do…" She lost the battle, and the tears flowed again. She hated that she was crying so much, but she couldn't stop. Bleak desperation mixed with anger fuelled her tears and despite the building headache, the emotion still raged.

"Melly I don't know what to say," Marcus whispered finally. "This is something so new to me that, I can't comprehend it," He cast an involuntary glance across at the body on the floor and winced. "But I'm here for you Melly,"

"But for how long?"

Justin walked back into the hall, his brooch clasped between numb fingers. As he reached the parlour, he heard her sobbing, and he bent his head, wishing with all his heart that he could take back the events of the last few months.

"I'm sorry," Justin stepped into the room and looked at her. "Dear God, I'm sorry," With the shuffling gait he had adopted, he walked to the body on the floor.

"What are you doing?" Melissa asked with a tremulous note to her voice.

"I need to live," Justin answered with brutal simplicity. "Emily sent him for me," He looked at Marcus. "Isn't that right?"

"Yes," Marcus couldn't tear his eyes from the image of Justin's corpse like body. He watched as Justin reached down to turn the man other. "Are you doing that now?"

"Yes," Justin answered. "After all, it's a lesson she needs

to learn and sooner rather than later," He flicked open the locket and gently slapped the face of Lord Morton.

"But you'll kill him," Marcus half rose from his chair and stopped at the venomous look in Justin's eyes.

"I am aware of that," Morton began to stir and Justin held the locket up to his face. "Trust me, if there were any other way I would do it," Loathing laced every syllable of his voice as Lord Morton's picture began to sketch itself into the blank canvas. Morton jerked upright and screamed as his ribs snapped in quick succession. Bruises began to appear on each spare patch of skin and he arched backwards as his shoulder dislocated. Melissa watched the process with a look of shocked horror on her face, unable to move from the chair. Her fingers clasped the chair arms until her knuckles grew white. The screams lessened as the man's struggles grew weaker. Justin's body straightened, the milky film draining from his eyes as his body healed to its former glory. Finally after what seemed like an age, the man stopped screaming. A sigh escaped his lips and he lay still. Justin shut the locket and stepped away, trying not to look at Melissa's face.

Melissa had watched, unable to drag herself from the sight of Morton's violent death. As Justin moved away from the body, she finally took hold of herself and ran. Her legs carried her to the hallway and beyond. She raced outside, fear and horror driving her steps. She passed the coachman as she reached the drive, running as though the devil were following her.

"Why did you do that?" Marcus asked, horror turning

his voice into a whisper. "Why did you show her that?"

"She has to see it," Justin answered with great weariness in his voice. "It's what she'll have to do… I…I had to show her," He closed his eyes and whispered. "I wish I hadn't, but it had to be done," Marcus stared at the man, struck by the deep regret that emanated from him. "I'll find her," He muttered as he walked to the door.

"After what you've just done?" Marcus asked with some shock as Justin crossed the threshold. "Do you think it wise?"

"Not particularly," Justin replied in a shadow of his usual wry tones. "But she needs to hate me for now," He shrugged his shoulders as he continued onto the drive. "It's not as if I haven't had this reaction before," He threw the last comment over his shoulder as he picked up the pace. Leaving the house's shadow, he began to run. His newly regenerated legs caught up with Melissa as she raced for the gate. Marcus made to follow, but the coachman stopped him.

"Let 'em be sir," He muttered in gruff tones. "They need to sort it out,"

Melissa came to a halt as Justin drew level with her. Breathing hard from the sudden exertion, she stared at his newly healed visage and fought back a fresh wave of tears.

"I understand if you hate me," Justin said, his voice whisper soft. "and I know I deserve it…" He considered reaching out to her, but thought better of it. "But please believe that I'm sorry,"

Melissa stared at his new skin and drew several gulping

breaths of air. "I know you are," She answered her voice far away and lost. That handsome visage seemed a mockery, and she couldn't escape the image of Morton dying on the floor. "But I'm like this and I know you didn't mean it but…" Her voice was rising to a shout, and she fought to bring it under control. "It doesn't change anything!"

Justin bowed his head, he knew the words. He had heard them and variants several times over the years. He knew his selfishness had brought another to ruin, that she would never be the same as she was.

"I understand," He whispered, regret implicit in his voice. "And I wish I could stand aside and let you find your own way," Lifting his head he stared straight at her. "But I can't,"

Melissa brushed her tears away and made an effort to stop crying. "Justin please let me go back to…"

"No," He stepped closer to her. "You are meant to be missing and you will not die," He glanced down at her hands. "You have no donor and any injury is life threatening. Dying is not pleasant,"

"I can't just kill innocent people," Melissa snarled back finally, anger beginning to smoulder once more.

"And do you think I find it easy?" Justin snapped back. "Even murdering scum like Morton…" Melissa glanced at him sharply. "Do not deserve what I do to them, but believe me when I say that the alternative is much more unpleasant,"

"But what the hell do I do now?" Melissa shouted back. "This is a death sentence,"

"Only if you're careless," Justin replied, moderating his tone as he tried to convince her. "If you have a minor wound, your donor will take that wound and heal normally. It's only fatal to our donors if we take a fatal wound," He reached out then and cupped her face. "You won't be killing someone every week,"

Melissa stiffened slightly as his hand touched her skin and she jerked away. His fingers were warm and tender, different to the cold mockery of life they had been earlier. Her skin crawled and she stood away from him. Justin stared at her and dropped his arm.

"I can't change things Melissa, but please don't leave,"

"I…" Her eyes darted to the left over his right shoulder towards the house. Comprehension and shock dawned on her face at the sight before her.

"What?" Justin turned and looked, registering the thin plume of smoke that was steadily rising from the back of the house.

CHAPTER 20

Montjoy pulled his decaying body through the woods towards the ruined estate. It had taken him several nights to extract himself from the rough grave in the woods. He had crawled out, ripping his fingernails as he had dug his way free. Once into the open air, he had crawled towards the nearest tree, using its bulk to drag himself upright. His body was uncoordinated and clumsy and he chose to ignore the sensations that were crawling beneath his skin. His eyes provided him little vision and he moved as best he could through the dawn. It had taken some time, but the house had soon come into sight. He reached the edge of the property as the carriage had arrived. Diving out of sight behind a tree, he had watched Melissa leave the library.

With shaky staggering footsteps, he had crossed the space to the house and let himself in. Books lined the room and journals were stacked up on the table. He ignored them as he moved through the room, looking for his brooch. He did not know much of the brooch he now wore, but he knew enough to retrieve it. Stepping into the hall, he heard the conversation of the coachman and, he paused in surprise, Marcus De Vire. A very unpleasant smile inched across his lips and he moved into the parlour, looking for his property. Stepping across the body on the floor, he began to search through the ancient chests, looking for something he recognised. After a short search, he found what he was looking for. With a rough grin, he clasped it in his fingers, feeling elated at its discovery.

"We may as well wait inside, they may be sometime," He heard Marcus' voice from the main doorway and he melted back against the wall, waiting to surprise the upstart as he entered the room.

"So what did you mean about Lord Morton?" Marcus asked as they walked into the hall.

"Sir?" The coachman asked.

"About killing his mistress?"

"He did," The coachman clarified. "Not that anyone would do anything about it," The man gave a derisory snort. "Same with Saint-Clair. He thought all the female servants were his to do with as he pleased. Whether married or no," They stopped in the hallway and Montjoy moved deeper into shadow. "He took my wife and struck her when she refused him, but Lady Saint-Clair saw what he was about,"

172

A note of worship entered his voice. "She stopped him, she may have the devil in her at times, but she's got a good heart," The coachman turned to enter the room. Montjoy lunged forward and slammed the man to the ground. Marcus briefly froze at the sight. Montjoy was barely recognisable, yet he knew him from the vicious smile that twisted his lips. Glancing down, he took in the sight of the brooch that lay within Montjoy's twisted grasp as he raised it to the coachman's eye level and he reacted. He lunged forward, throwing the heavy but lumbering body to the ground in one charge. Montjoy's body was soft and his flesh squished unpleasantly beneath his fingers as he tried to keep him from using the coachman as his donor. Montjoy flicked open the locket one handed and began to raise it. Marcus closed his eyes and seized hold of Montjoy's wrist. There was a tearing sound and Montjoy's skin tore. With a bellow of rage and pain, Montjoy punched with his other hand, knocking Marcus to one side. The coachman picked himself off the floor and went for Montjoy, slamming into his chest and throwing him to the ground.

"Get something to tie him with!" He yelled as he struggled to hold the man down. Marcus pulled down one of the curtains and tore a long strip of fabric free. Montjoy wriggled loose, his rotting flesh becoming hard to hold. He slammed his elbow into the coachman's temple, stunning him for a moment. That moment was all he needed. He brandished the locket before the man's startled eyes. Marcus looked up as the coachman began to screech in pain. Montjoy's wounds had begun to affect him. Without thinking, Marcus launched himself across the room and tore the locket from Montjoy's grasp. As his fingers closed on the smooth enamel, a wave of dizziness swamped him and he fell to the floor in a stupor. Nearby, the coachman continued to shriek, the power of the brooch taking his life. Montjoy waited until the coachman had breathed his last before turning to pick up his brooch from Marcus' grasp. He crossed to the window and stared out across the grounds towards Melissa and Justin. For a moment he wondered about waiting for them to return to the house, but he did not wish to face a healed Justin Lestrade. He passed Marcus' unconscious body with a sneer and left the parlour. With long strides he returned to the library. It took a moment's thought to decide what to do. Justin would not follow if he had a fire to deal with. Pulling the guard away from the fireplace, he shovelled handfuls of paper from the library table onto the embers in the grate. As the fire began to lick the edges of the paper, he left the room through the window. With barely a backward glance, he ran back into the safety of the forest as Justin and Melissa began to head back across the grounds.

"Oh dear God no," Justin raced across the grounds toward the building, galvanised into action by the sight of the smoke that was billowing from the library windows. Reaching the front door, he cleared the steps in one jump and rushed into the house.

"Marcus," Melissa followed Justin into the house and began looking for her brother. The smoke in the air thickened as the fire spread rapidly through the library. "Marcus?" Melissa stepped into the parlour and stopped. Marcus lay in the corner of the room, near the unrecognisable forms of Morton and the coachman. With a cry of grief she rushed forward and knelt down at his side. Turning him over, she stifled a choking gasp of horror as a familiar brooch fell from his hand.

Justin dashed into the library. The flames were burning through the carpet and were now consuming the table. The heat was almost unbearable as he raced to fill a bucket.

"Justin," He turned at Melissa's cry and headed for the parlour, panic suddenly surging through him.

"Oh Christ," He blasphemed as he took in the sight of Marcus De Vire with a black blossom of his own.

"Help me," Justin rushed to Melissa's side and after picking up the brooch from the floor, he helped her to drag her brother from the parlour.

They left the increasingly smoke filled hallway and headed outside and away from the fire that was beginning to consume other parts of the house. "My work," He muttered as he laid Marcus down on the drive. He turned back to the house, to the smoke that was beginning to billow from the front door. He took a step forward, only to be stopped by Melissa. "It's all my work, it's everything I've done," He fought to move past her, but she held firm. "It's all of it," he pleaded as the flames grew stronger. "There are volumes in there that I can't replace," There was a smell of burning meat as the flames reached the body of Morton in the parlour.

"There won't be anything left and you'll be injured

for nothing," Melissa said, practicality winning over the despair. "Please Justin, don't be foolish,"

Justin wrested free and took a few steps closer to the door. Flames filled the hallway and surrounded the door, making passage impossible. Stupefied by the sight, he staggered forward a couple more steps and dropped to his knees. As he watched his home burn for the second time in his life, he felt the resolution within him waver and begin to crack. How could he find a cure when all he had researched was no more?

Melissa stared down at his broken form and some of her anger toward him faded. "We'll think of something," Melissa whispered as she placed her arms about him, too sorry for his pain to think of her own woes. "We will start again,"

He turned and he pulled her to him, hugging her fiercely as the flames began to lick the upper floors of the old edifice. "We will find a cure," She assured him as her brother woke to the same new and cursed life as theirs.

1772

CHAPTER 21

Rain trickled down the end of her nose, but Melissa paid it no mind, fixated as she was on the scene opposite and the box that was being lowered into the ground. Behind her slightly and to the left, Marcus folded his arms across his chest and stared at the coffin containing their father. The mourners did not see them, fixed as they were on the lowering box. A tear slid from beneath her eyelashes and trickled down her face, the warmth flaring briefly before being lost in the chill rain water that dripped from the top of her hood and trailed over her skin. Justin stepped forward, leaving the shadow of the trees as he reached Melissa's side.

"It's..." Her head whipped round to face him and he

took a step back at the barely contained fury that he saw in her gaze.

"Don't tell me that it's going to be alright," She turned her head back to the lowering coffin that contained the body of her father. "I could have spent the last few years with him," Justin winced at the accusation he heard in her voice. "I couldn't even see him as he would not understand," She ran her hand across her face and brushed aside the tears that were beginning to fall. "He's thought I was dead for all these years and I did that to him…" She turned to face him and he stiffened, knowing what was to come next. "And you did that to him,"

Justin stayed still, the familiar feeling of guilt flooding through his bones as her bright eyes pierced him. It had been a tense twenty years, the romance that Emily had so wished to encourage had not transpired, but he had not expected it to. Melissa had been like all the others, distraught in her new life and despising him for it. True, she also had to hate Emily as well but, he gave a small sigh, Emily had spent the last ten years in Spain and away from the trio. He had been lumbered with looking after the siblings as both needed coaching in their new life. And now, as he watched the tears fall down her face, he sorely wished that he could take back the last twenty years of pain. He was about to step forward to comfort her when he glanced across at Marcus and caught the slight shake of his head. He took the warning and stepped back, away from Melissa and her temper.

"Give her time," Marcus murmured in an undertone as

Justin reached his side. "She doesn't really hate you," He walked past Justin and reached his sister's side, wrapping her up in his arms. Justin watched them with a gnawing pain growing within him. They at least had each other. In all of the funerals he had attended over the years, he had been alone, even when the others had been in attendance. He swallowed down the incipient self pity and returned his attention to the lowering coffin

Melissa waited until the last of the mourners had left before finally walking up to the gravesite. She stopped before the mound of freshly dug dirt and knelt down into the mud. Taking deep shuddering breaths, she gave way to the anger and grief that had been raging within her from the moment she had heard about the death of her father.

"I'm so sorry," She sobbed, not bothering to wipe the tears that were streaming down her face. "I wish..." She hugged her arms about herself. "I wish I'd been here," Rain fell in sheets, plastering her hair to her head and soaking her to the skin. Lost in her private grief, she did not notice until Marcus rested his hand on her shoulder.

"Come on Melly, it's time to go," She drew her gaze away from the gravesite and stared up at Marcus.

Melissa nodded and allowed him to pull her upright. With gentle movements, Marcus wrapped a heavy coat about her shoulders and began to lead her from the cemetery. As they reached the gate, Melissa glanced back into the cemetery.

'Where's Justin?" She asked as her eyes drifted across the empty space.

"He's gone back to the coach," Marcus explained carefully, hoping that she wouldn't take it as a personal insult. Ever since they had received news of their father's death, Melissa's bitterness and anger towards Justin had increased ten fold.

"I see," She noted cynically as they moved through the downpour. Melissa knew that she was being unfair but she could not help it. Since the events of twenty years ago, they had left the country and travelled across Europe, looking for copies of the books that Justin had once held in his library. Justin had been gentle and apologetic for all of that time and she had almost accepted that he had not been completely at fault but, she cast a look toward her father's grave, at times like this it was harder to forgive.

They reached the coach and Melissa stopped walking, staring up at Justin as he sat holding the reins.

"You go back," She whispered to her brother as she took a step away.

"Melly?"

"I can't..." She whispered, bitterness thrumming through every syllable. "Not today," Pulling her arm free from her brother, she strode off into the rain.

Marcus watched her leave, knowing that she would not appreciate the company if he went after her. From somewhere behind him there was the sound of squelching footsteps as Justin climbed down from the carriage to join him.

"She's not coming," Marcus said as Justin reached his side. "Do you want to go after her?"

"She needs to mourn," Justin replied as he stared at Melissa's departing back. He turned back to the carriage.

"Justin?" He stopped walking and stared back at Marcus. "Are you alright?"

Justin gave a small snort of derisive laughter. "Of course I'm not alright," He admitted as he began to climb back into the carriage. "I've managed to curse the woman I love," He turned to face Marcus as he sat back on the seat. "Would you be alright?"

Marcus silently shook his head as he climbed up and sat next to Justin. The rain pattered onto the skin of the carriage roof and they sat in silence listening to the sound as they waited for Melissa to return.

Melissa walked towards the church, feeling the rain soak through the cloak that enveloped her. Her feet sloshed as she walked through the increasingly muddy path and her skirt grew heavy with the water that permeated it. The small church was early Norman in design with only a few of the stained glass windows that later churches were known for. Ordinarily she would have wondered at the history of the place, but now, drenched and heartsick as she was, she only wished to find sanctuary. Climbing the steps, she pushed open the wide doors and with a sigh of relief, stepped into the cool, quiet interior. Her footsteps echoed on the flag stoned floor and she stared about the candlelit interior barely taking in any of the details. Taking a deep breath she sat down on a pew and stared up at the stained glass window above the nave, deep in thought. She felt lost and wrung out, tormented by the knowledge that she had left her father to die alone. Alone in the quiet, she desperately mouthed a prayer. For several long moments, she stared up at the glass, hoping that God was listening to the wish that lay deep in her heart. The sound of the rain outside increased as the heavy door swung open and the sound of footsteps echoed across the space. Ignoring the heavy tread, she continued to stare at the stained glass, her grief and pain too raw to engage in polite chit chat.

"I knew you'd be here," A familiar sneering voice assaulted her ears and she turned just in time to see the fist fly towards her face. The blow sent her sprawling to the floor, eyes watering with the pain. She glanced up to see Montjoy walk forward, his fists clenched and face flushed with victory. "After all, you wouldn't miss the funeral of your father," He kicked out, but she rolled free, the pain from the broken nose beginning to ebb as her donor leeched the wound from her. Rolling beneath the narrow pew, she avoided the next kick.

"What the devil do you want?" She called across, anguish replaced by seething rage. Skittering along the dusty floor, she reached the end of the pew and got to her feet. Reaching out, she caught hold of the iron candelabra that stood at the end of the pew and hefted it easily. One of the advantages of their condition was a slight increase in strength and stamina and for once she appreciated the benefit of taking another's life.

"You," Montjoy answered as he walked forward, ignoring the weapon that now lay within her hands. "Really Melissa," Melissa felt her rage burn brighter at the smug dismissal in his gaze. How dare he assume that she would be as easily dispatched as she had been in the past. Tightening her grip on the iron stem of the candelabra, she swung out at him. Her arms jarred with the impact as it connected with his temple and he fell back, dazed by her blow.

"You were saying," She mocked as she stabbed downwards with the candelabra using all of her strength. Montjoy gave a choking cry of pain as the prongs jammed into his side. With a cry of rage, he rolled free, his wounds healing as he did so. Melissa swung again, her blow going wide as he scrambled out of the way. Montjoy got to his feet and rushed at her, tearing the candelabra from her hands. Melissa backed off and dived out of the way, marvelling at the ease of her breathing as she did so. The candelabra narrowly missed her as she dove behind one of the pillars. There was a clang as the iron connected with the stone and she backed off, heading for the door. She was under no illusions, even with the healing afforded by the locket, she was no match for Montjoy. Backing towards the still open door, she dodged the next blow before she turned and prepared to run.

"What's the hurry?" Alistair Lestrade stepped through the door and caught hold of her arms, pinning them to her sides. Melissa struggled as Justin's brother hauled her back into the church and almost threw her into Montjoy's arms. Melissa felt Montjoy's arms tighten about her as Alistair reached forward and began to search through her pockets. She allowed a smug smile to crease her features, safe in the knowledge that her brooch was safely hidden from any tampering.

"Where is it?" Alistair demanded as he finished turning out the pockets of her coat.

"Somewhere safe," She answered, feeling rewarded by the frustrated look that settled over Alistair's features. "Did you think I made a habit of carrying with me?" She glanced at Justin's brother and added. "Oh you did," A mocking, sneering note entered her voice. "Well I guess you were missing the day that brains were handed out," She stopped speaking as Alistair slapped her hard across the face. Her vision blurred for the briefest of instances and she tasted blood. Her lip had split and the warm, coppery flow trickled from her mouth before her donor removed this wound as well. The tender throb of pain that radiated across her skin ebbed and she stared up at Alistair defiantly, almost daring him to strike again.

"It doesn't matter," Montjoy whispered into her ear. "We'll just have to separate you forcibly from your donor," She felt a twinge of fear at his words, unsure of just how much damage it would take to would kill the man who held her life. She stared at Alistair's eagerly grinning face and realised that he wanted to see her afraid. Pushing back the fear that had begun to bubble deep within her, she gritted her teeth but decided to brazen it out. She would not give Montjoy or Alistair the satisfaction of seeing her panic.

"I think you're both extremely stupid," She hissed, allowing her rage to overwhelm her concern and fuel her words. "Alistair, are you so in fear of being second to your brother that you must claim anything connected to him?" She almost grinned at the flash of anger she saw in his eyes. "And you Montjoy," She allowed a snort of laughter to lace her tones. "Spending twenty years wanting me," She aimed the words like weapons, savage mockery her arsenal. "My God what a bore your life must be."

Montjoy answered by wrapping his arm about her throat and beginning to squeeze. The pain rushed through her, too powerful to be immediately healed. Choking as his arm cut off her ability to breathe, Melissa clawed at the solid muscle of his arm. Spots danced before her eyes as she hovered close to the edge of unconsciousness.

"Hold on," Alistair waited until her body began to slump in Montjoy's arms before he finally laid a restraining hand on the other man's shoulder. "Let's not do this here, John wants her alive," Montjoy slowly released his grip and she drew a deep breath of air, the ache to her throat slowly ebbing away with each subsequent breath. The mention of John's name sent a stab of fear through her and she tried not to panic. "Justin and Marcus can't be that far away," Alistair reasoned his voice calm.

Melissa felt her breathing return to normal but she waited, slumped in Montjoy's arms, for a chance to escape.

"Very well," Montjoy relaxed his hold slightly and began to pull her towards the door. "Lead the way," Drawing a hand across her mouth, he followed Alistair out into the rain.

As he dragged her down the church steps, she seized her moment to act. Digging her feet against the church steps, she propelled herself backwards. The back of her head slammed into Montjoy's chin and though pain screamed through her skull, she was rewarded with a yelp of pain from her assailant. More importantly, his hand fell from her lips.

"Justin!" She screamed out as loud as she could, the sound echoing shrilly across the space. Alistair turned and reacted quickly to her attempts at freedom by grabbing hold of her legs and bodily picking her up. As they manhandled her towards a nearby coach, she could see Justin and Marcus start to run in her direction. Montjoy and Alistair threw her into the coach and her head slammed against the wall. Dazed for a moment, Melissa failed to pull herself upright before Montjoy climbed in beside her and slammed the door shut. Alistair clambered on the front of the coach and seized the reins. Snapping the reins briskly against the backs of the horses, he set the vehicle in motion.

Marcus and Justin started running, racing towards the coach as it started to move. Justin was in the lead, breathing easily as he ran through the pouring rain. He swore as he watched the coach pick up speed.

"Get back to the coach," Justin shouted back to the trailing form of Marcus, realising that whilst he may catch up with the departing carriage, Marcus would not. He cursed as his mind identified the two abductors and images of what could happen to Melissa in their care filled his mind. He picked up speed, splashing though the muddy puddles and soaking his trousers as he ran.

Melissa dove to the side, slamming her upper shoulder

into seats as she attempted to evade Montjoy's grasping arms. The sprung upholstery absorbed some of the shock of the fall and she tried to push herself upright. Montjoy caught hold of her, only to let go again as the coach took a corner almost too quickly. Two of the wheels left the road and sent them sprawling to the coach floor.

Montjoy cursed as he tried to pick himself upright as Melissa took advantage of the confusion to reach the other door and throw it open. Taking a deep breath, she pushed herself forward and flung herself out of the coach. She hit the ground hard, the muddy gravel tearing into her clothes and skin as she rolled along the road. Picking herself up from the ground, she ran back towards Justin, the skin on her arms and legs healing as she did so. Alistair continued to drive the coach onwards, either unaware of her escape, or not willing to confront his brother.

"Are you…?" He stopped speaking as her arms wrapped about his neck and she leant against his shoulder. After a moment, he raised his arms and wrapped them about her body, holding her to him as though he were afraid that she would disappear.

"They waited for my father's funeral," He heard her words, bitter and frightened against his neck and he stroked her damp hair, trying to impart some sympathy through his touch. The rain fell about them soaking through their clothes as they stood locked in each other's arms. Justin stayed silent as the chill drops of water slid down his neck, making him shiver. Melissa was shivering in his arms and she nestled closer to the warmth of his body, unwilling it seemed to leave the safety of his embrace.

"Are you coming?" Marcus' voice broke into the quiet and Melissa raised her head to stare at him, realisation settling over her features as she looked up at her brother. With a jolt, she pulled away from Justin's embrace and ran to her brother and the relative dryness of the coach. Clambering aboard, she sat down on the chair and wrapped her arms about her body, angry at herself for seeking the comfort of Justin's arms. It was entirely his fault that they were here yet her first reaction had been to hold him. As Justin climbed into the coach next to her, she said nothing, preferring to stare out of the window at the grey landscape as she tried to decipher her feelings. On the coachman's box, Marcus clicked to the horses, and they set off, the suspension not quite dulling the bone jarring rattle of the coach travelling across rocky terrain. The silence grew longer, sharper with things left unsaid. Toying with the sleeve of her dress, she kept her eyes on the muddy landscape, ignoring the man at her side. For the first time in weeks, she had sought the comfort of Justin's arms. She tried to tell herself that it was purely a reaction to the attempted abduction yet the fact remained that she had felt safer within his embrace, that he been her first refuge in crisis. She closed her hands and tucked them within her sleeves, trying to return some warmth to them.

"Did they say what they wanted?" Justin's voice broke into her thoughts and she looked up, staring at his face as though she had never seen it before. His eyes were guarded and watchful, wary of her emotions and potential response. For a moment she said nothing, taking in the face of the man before her and she felt her anger at him begin to subside.

"No," She answered, feeling the anger begin to burn once more as it shifted focus. Her mind flickered back to images of Montjoy, of Alistair, men who were far more responsible for her current state than Justin. "I have no idea..." She sighed and laid her head back against the chair, weary with the storm of emotions that raged within her. "They were waiting for me," She felt Justin's weight shift beside her and she turned her head to stare at him. "They used my father's funeral as a means to capture me..." Her voice broke as the events of the day finally caught up with her. Justin took a breath and gently laid a hand on her arm. With a choking cry, she fell against his side, allowing him to hold her as she reached out to wrap her arms about his body. "I don't know what they wanted," Justin said nothing as she cried against his shoulder. For what seemed like an age, they sat there, holding onto each other as she began to let go of the hard knot of resentment that had built up around her heart. Justin carefully smoothed the stray strands of hair from her face and waited for her to speak.

"Your brother is working with Montjoy," Melissa mumbled finally, her voice husky from tears and tiredness. "And they're both out to get me,"

"Not necessarily just you," He answered, drawing a blanket about her shoulders as she lay against him. "I think this has John's hand all over it,"

"Why though?" She managed to whisper before her

eyelids drooped, and she fell into a deep slumber.

"That's what I want to know," He whispered as he looked down at Melissa's dozing form. John had to be behind the attack in the church, waiting for such a long time for some nebulous opportunity to attack would not be in his brother's thoughts and he doubted that Montjoy would have thought of it, so, it had to have been John. Melissa sighed, and he shifted his arm allowing her to settle more comfortably. Why had he sent them after Melissa? He rubbed his hand across his chin and gave a small sigh. It could just be another manoeuvre in the petty game they had been playing for the past few decades but, on the other hand... Melissa rolled over, and the blanket drifted free. His fingers tenderly tucked the blanket back beneath her chin, and he relaxed back against the cushions, wondering at Melissa and her state of mind. This was the closest they had been for years, the inevitable anger of Melissa's new situation making it impossible for her to consider anything else. Her willingness to seek some comfort in his arms gave him some pause for hope, but it was slight and fleeting. Brushing a stray strand of hair from her face, he lost himself in thoughts full of regret and pain. Emily's hope for a romantic adventure had failed thus far. If only he could be sure that this sudden thaw in her dealings with him was real. As Marcus drove the coach towards their current home, he thought of Montjoy, Alistair and their master, John.

CHAPTER 22

Melissa woke in her bedroom, minus boots and outerwear and covered with a blanket. Pushing herself upright, she stared about the room as though she could barely recognise it. Decorated in warm tones of wood and crimson, the room was lit with a single lamp and a fire crackled merrily in the hearth. A washbasin lay on the dresser opposite, and a fresh outfit hung over the end of the bed. Climbing out of the bed, she approached the window and stared outside. They were back in London and living in a small residence not too far from Grosvenor Square, although today the streets were nearly devoid of people. Rain pattered the window pane as it cascaded in seemingly unending streams from the sky. A brisk North easterly wind tossed the branches of the trees outside, carrying the occasional leaf in amongst the rain. It was a typically English autumnal day and for once she was glad of it. After several moments of contemplation, she turned away from the window and changed, throwing the dirty and damaged clothing into the basket in the corner of the room. Moving to the door, she flung it open and headed downstairs.

"You can't just go off on your own," She stopped moving as she heard Marcus' voice echo from the hallway. "What do you think Melissa will say?" She straightened her back, listening far more closely.

"I doubt she cares," Justin replied, his voice a tired echo as Melissa felt the shock from his words ripple down her spine. "It's no secret that she's grown to hate me," Her fingers seized hold of the banister and gripped it tightly, emotion flooding through her. "And I'm not going to trail after her like a lost puppy,"

"But leaving..."

"You misunderstand me Marcus," Melissa took a tentative step down the stairs. "I'm going to confirm a lead; I'm not going for good,"

"Then you shouldn't have indicated that you weren't going to return," Marcus' voice crackled with anger and Melissa took another step downstairs, Justin's words burning in her brain as she did so.

I doubt she cares.

"You're the one who assumed that," Justin was angry now. Melissa took another step, her heart lodged securely in her throat as she did so.

"But you said that you had to go alone."

"When has that ever meant leaving forever?"

Marcus mumbled something incoherent as Melissa reached the bottom step and headed to the door.

"Emily is a law unto herself and she lives to make trouble," Justin's exasperated tones snapped back, answering Marcus' muttered words. "You should have learnt something from your decade in her company, take everything she says with a grain of salt,"

"She doesn't always speak false,"

"Of course she doesn't, lies flow better when mixed in with truth."

Melissa could not stand to hear much more of the conversation without intervening. She pushed into the parlour and looked at her brother and Justin.

"What the devil's going on?" She demanded her voice harsher than usual. "Are you leaving us?" She threw the words at Justin, watching him wince at the tone in her voice. "And what do you mean about me 'hating you'?"

"Exactly what it sounds like," Justin answered softly. "Let's not lie and claim that you don't," Melissa stared at him, stricken dumb by his words. He looked at her and sighed. "I'm not blaming you for it, but we shouldn't delude ourselves anymore."

"But I don't," Her voice was a soft whisper, anguish in every note. "I..." She sank back against the wall and chewed her lip, unable to find any adequate denials for his claim.

Justin's face softened as he stared at her. "I'm not leaving," He said, in gentler tones. "One of my contacts has asked me to meet him."

"And I think it's a stupid idea," Marcus interjected, his voice snappish and angry.

"So you've said," Justin turned to face Marcus, irritation apparent in his handsome face. "I'm not a novice at this, and I don't want to have to worry about you two," He reached out for his outdoor coat and shrugged it on. "I won't be long," He reached the front door and pulled it open. Turning back from the rainy outside, he glanced over at Melissa. "We'll talk later," He promised before he headed out into the rain, shutting the door behind him.

"Well Marcus?" Melissa rounded on her brother as soon as the door closed. Marcus gave a shrug and headed into the parlour. Melissa followed him into the room and watched him sit down before the fire. "What started it?"

"I misunderstood," Marcus replied, leaning back against the chair. "Justin was in an odd mood after we returned from the funeral. He'd put you to bed and then he sat there," He pointed across at the chair opposite. «He wasn›t drinking, but he looked pensive," Melissa glanced at the chair before returning her attention to her brother. Marcus sighed and continued. "He wasn't being talkative and I had given up on trying to draw him into conversation when the message arrived,"

"What did it say?" Melissa was only half listening, her thoughts on Justin's words. She didn't hate Justin, certainly she was angry with him but how could he think that she hated him?

"I'm not sure, he didn't read it out," Marcus continued.

"He just said he had to leave and that he had to go alone,"
"Do you think he'll be alright?"
"I don't know," He stood up and stared down at the fire.
"Melly, can you tell me how you feel about him?"

CHAPTER 23

Justin moved along the side street, kicking at the pebbles in his path. He knew and expected the wrath of both Melissa and Marcus, yet he had somehow hoped that for once he would be immune. Melissa's attitude over the last few years had almost destroyed that hope. She remained with him more from habit or fear of the unknown than for any lingering feelings. It was a foolish hope, and he shook his head at his romantic notion. It would have been a miracle for Marcus and Melissa to not become angry at their condition and despite her closeness during the ride back to the house; he was not convinced that her attitude to him had changed. Turning the next corner, he walked along the narrow lane and further into the maze of streets, his eyes looking for the signs that would lead to his contact. Rain soaked through his clothes as muck sloshed beneath his feet and he wrinkled his nose at the smell of rotting food and worse. A rat skittered out from beneath a pile of rags, and he swore, startled by the sudden movement.

"Why does Daventry stay here?" He asked himself in a low tone as he ducked beneath a low hanging beam and crossed the alley. The light grew dimmer as he moved further into the warren and away from the wider streets of the capital. The dregs of society lived in warrens like this, and he grew increasingly wary as he trod deeper into the stinking labyrinth. A single torch flickered at the intersection ahead, and he glanced to his left, looking for the sign that he was looking for. Pushing his hair back from his face, he moved directly beneath the guttering torch and searched the wall. Scratched into the grime, soot-encrusted bricks; a rough depiction of a flower could be seen. He grinned at the small carving and turned to follow the direction of the arrow that was etched beneath it. Moving away from the torch he ducked down the right hand path, more of a gap between two buildings and began to pick up the pace. He easily navigated the twisting narrow tunnel and stopped before a low door in the side of the street. Raising his hand, he rapped sharply on the wood. The door opened and he moved inside.

"Damn it Daventry, why couldn't you bring it to me?" He asked as soon as the door closed behind him. The grey haired man released the door handle and favoured him with a tight-lipped smile as he led him down a long grimy hallway.

"Because I like to see you dance to my tune on occasion," He declared as he led the way into a small, dusty parlour. A tiny fire smoked in the hearth and thick tallow candles burned fitfully on every surface. The room was bright but smoky and tears sprang to Justin's eyes at the irritation.

"I think I have what you've asked for," Daventry sat down on his chair near the fire and picked up a glass of brandy. He took a sip and waited for Justin to sit opposite, neglecting to offer him a drink as he did so.

"You have?" Justin sat on the very edge of the chair and leant forward, trying not to show any signs of impatience. He could have threatened the man before him, but that would only get him so far and then he could forget any future dealings with Daventry. For all his slovenly habits and quirks, he was the best source of tomes and other ephemera.

"Indeed," Daventry delighted in taking a long sip of the brandy, watching with relish as Justin tried to control his impatience. "I had the devil of a job to get it," Justin controlled the incipient huff of frustration with some effort as he waited for Daventry to continue in his own time.

Daventry smiled at the young looking man. While he did not fully understand the story of the man before him, he knew that there was something unnatural going on. Justin had been buying books from him for years and in all that time, he had not appeared to age. The boy's money was good and he made a tidy living from his eagerness to locate old books, but he still preferred to meet the boy here, far away from his real home. He took another sip, happy to make Justin wait just that little bit more before he finally stood and walked over to the cabinet on the other side of the room. Removing a key from a pocket in his sleeve, he opened the cupboard and reached inside.

"I hope this is what you're looking for," He said with a smile as he turned back to Justin. "It has a depiction of that flower on the inside cover," Justin's head snapped up and he stared at the other man, trying hard not to seem too eager. Daventry slowly walked back across the room and stopped several paces away.

"Now... can I have my payment?"

Justin stood and reached into an inside pocket, drawing a heavy velvet pouch free and handing it across the space to Daventry. The other man took hold of the pouch, gauged the weight and nodded. He handed across the book and sat back down to count the guineas that spilled from the dark velvet.

Justin opened the front cover and suppressed the eager grin that crossed his lips at the sign of the lotus emblazoned on the first page. Unwilling to study the text here, he concealed the book beneath his jacket and nodded to the other man. "Thank you," Pulling his coat tightly about his shoulders he headed to the main door.

"I take it you want me to keep looking for more," Daventry called after him as he pulled open the door.

"If you would," Justin called back, holding the door ajar as he did so. "Same rates apply?"

"Agreed," Daventry called, not bothering to leave the

shabby parlour to see him out.

"Good," Justin pulled the collar of his coat up to his chin and dived back out into the rain. It was darker now and shadows crowded uncomfortably in the corners. He moved swiftly down the first alley and was heading towards the wider thoroughfare when a pistol shot slammed into his upper shoulder, sending him stumbling back against the wall. He picked himself up and scanned the alley, looking for his assailant as a grim sensation of dread radiated through him. Another shot echoed through the dark alleys, yet this one went wide as he moved into cover and hopefully out of sight.

"Just hand it over brother," Alistair's voice sounded from ahead. "Or I'll kill you and take it," Justin clasped his hand to the book and cursed himself for his stupidity. His eagerness to return and study the book had blinded him to the possibility of pursuit. He had forgotten that Alistair knew most of his contacts, and now his brother was fully allied with John, they were at risk.

"What on earth do you and John want with this book?" He called back, hoping to stall with conversation.

"That's our business," Alistair's voice sounded from the shadows to the right. "Let's face facts; you're not going to find the cure alone," Justin began to carefully move along the alley, looking for his own set of shadows to hide in. "John knows more about this curse than you do,"

"Do tell," Justin reached the corner and pressed himself against the wall. "I presume he told you how he controls Katherine,"

"How do you..." Alistair broke off the surprised question and began to walk down the alley. "It doesn't matter, John is far better suited to researching our predicament," Justin leant down and picked up a piece of wood from the rain swept gutter. Holding it firmly within his grasp, he waited for Alistair to draw closer.

"How do you know?" Justin called almost conversationally.

"Because he's willing to make sacrifices," Alistair was drawing closer now; Justin could see his shadow on the ground, preceding him.

"Well at least I haven't enslaved people," Justin called as he stepped out from the shadows and swung the piece of wood at Alistair's head. Alistair gave a yelp of surprise and began to bring his pistol to bear. Justin swung again, this time catching him full in the chest. Alistair staggered back as Justin continued the offensive. "Or attempted to abduct women," In the rainy darkness of the alley, Justin gave vent to his rage. "Tell me brother why are you really helping that bastard kidnap Melissa?" He punctuated each word with a blow.

Reeling from the hits, Alistair fired wildly, the shot whistling past Justin's head to strike the wall.

"What has he promised you?"

Alistair ducked beneath another blow and charged at Justin. His shoulder slammed into Justin's midsection, sending him to the floor. They grappled with each other, each unable to gain the upper hand whilst their donors took the damage. Taking a hit to the stomach, Alistair reached into Justin's jacket and grabbed hold of the book.

"No!" A minor tussle broke out as both tried to wrest the book from each others' hands. Justin felt his nose break, and reform as Alistair's elbow smashed into his face.

"Not as easy to take me on is it?" Justin snarled as he caught hold of Alistair's head and slammed it against the wall. Dazed by the blow, Alistair let go of the book. With a shout of triumph, Justin rolled away from the fight and got to his feet. With more than a hint of vindictiveness, he kicked his brother solidly in the face. Backing away from his bleeding sibling, he returned the book to his inside pocket and turned to go.

"You don't think she'll be safe forever do you?" Alistair choked out from behind him. "I can assure you brother that she will never be safe," Justin glanced down, a derisive sneer creasing his lips.

"You seem determined to emulate the worst of John's cruelty," Justin said in a soft voice as he leant down and pushed his brother back to the ground. "Tell me why she's so important,"

Alistair closed his mouth and stared at the wall opposite. With a cluck of annoyance, Justin pulled him upright and held him against the wall.

"I'm losing patience Alistair," He warned. "Tell me what you know,"

"It's too late for that," Alistair replied, an evil smirk crossing his features. "Montjoy and John should be at your house by now," He grinned even wider as he continued. "Just off Grosvenor Square as I recall."

Justin back handed him across the face and took off down the alley, running as quickly as his legs would carry. He should have foreseen this turn of events, should have been ready for Alistair and his new friends. He splashed through puddles of filth, not caring about the stench or state of his clothes. His only thought, as he reached the main street, was getting home before John and Montjoy paid a visit.

CHAPTER 24

Melissa sat before the fire, staring into the blaze without really seeing it. Her thoughts were miles and years away, back twenty years or more, when she was an innocent, thinking herself in love.

"This won't do," Marcus placed a large cup of tea at her right hand and interrupted her chain of thought. "You have to forgive,"

"If he hadn't…" She started to protest, but her brother held up his hand, stopping her in mid flow.

"Not him…" Marcus said softly, his green eyes searching her face. "You…"

"Marcus?" She stared up at him, confused by his words and sudden shift in conversation.

"It's not Justin you're upset with," Marcus did not remove his gaze from her face and she shifted uncomfortably under the intensity of his stare.

"I..." She tried once more to protest, but Marcus broke in again, shattering her words with weighty truths of his own.

"You blame yourself if you hadn't pushed for him to notice you," Marcus' fingers settled on hers, and she swallowed back a burst of emotion. "Tell me I'm wrong,"

Melissa stayed silent, listening to the crackle of the fire in the background as she tried to process her brother's words. Her first instinct was to deny it, to loudly declare that he was wrong, but the words wouldn't come. Her mind was drifting back through the years to her first glimpse of Justin Lestrade.

"You did warn me," She whispered, her voice thick with unshed tears. "You tried to stop me and I didn't listen..." She bowed her head then, tears flowing down her cheeks like a river.

"Melly," He drew her into his arms and held her gently, letting her cry for the second time that day. "You weren't to know and neither was I," He rested his chin against the top of her head and stroked her hair. "So please...please try to forgive..."

"How touching," They pulled apart at the familiar voice and Marcus jumped to his feet, and he stared at the source of the voice with something akin to hatred.

"Montjoy," Marcus pushed Melissa behind him and took a step forward. Melissa wiped the tears from her face and picked up a poker from beside the fire. She moved to stand beside her brother, poker held ready in her hands.

"Get out," Marcus squared his shoulders and walked forward, his face grim. "If you want to keep your looks,"

Montjoy ignored him, staring across at Melissa, his eyes travelling over her form with a suggestive leer. "I believe we were interrupted earlier," He took a step forward, only to be intercepted by Marcus. Grabbing hold of Montjoy's collar, he pushed him back against the wall.

"Do I have to tell you again?"

"I don't think there's any need for that," A new voice echoed through the room and a tall, gaunt looking man walked through the door. "It's good to see you again," He added conversationally as he strode to the centre of the room.

"John," Marcus whispered, feeling his stomach drop at the sight of the man who had attempted to kill him all those years ago. He remembered the gloating amusement on John's face as he slammed his foot into his stomach.

"I'm so glad you remember me," John walked past Marcus and stopped in front of Melissa. "It's a pleasure to finally meet you my dear,"

Melissa set her jaw and nodded, unwilling to be terrified by the man who stood before her. John was soft spoken and seemingly innocuous, yet his reputation preceded him and despite her best efforts, a tremble still flowed down her spine.

"What do you want?" She asked, grateful to note that her voice didn't wobble.

"Such rudeness," John chided lightly, moving forward to tap her lightly on the nose. Melissa jerked back and brandished the poker as Marcus released Montjoy and whirled round, rushing to intercede. "Don't be so foolish," John snapped at Melissa, reaching out with inhuman speed to wrest the poker from her. Weaponless, Melissa hesitated as John reached out for her with his free hand.

"Melly," John ignored the blow from Marcus as he seized hold of Melissa and threw her to the floor. Angry beyond words, Marcus punched out again, only to be stopped in mid stride as Montjoy jumped on his back and knocked him down to the floor. Marcus' face smashed into the floor, dazing him momentarily. Montjoy caught hold of the back of Marcus' head and dashed it against the floor, breaking his nose and sending blood spraying across the rug.

"Marcus," Melissa headed towards her brother, only to be stopped by John as he reached down and pulled her upright.

"You need to learn manners," He murmured in her ear as he pushed her against the chair and placed the poker in the flames. "I won't have my servants display such behaviour."

"We're not your servants," Melissa retorted, transfixed by the sight of Marcus bleeding on the floor.

"Oh... you will be," John replied. He reached for the poker, inspected the tip and thrust it back into the flames. "I think I've left you to your own devices for far too long."

Marcus tried to get up but Montjoy smashed his face

back into the floor before sitting on his back, a smug smirk creasing his features.

John's hand wrapped gently about Melissa's throat, holding her against the chair with the barest suggestion of violence. "You, like your brother, will be mine," He whispered, his voice soft yet filled with menace. "You will renounce Justin, or I will make you suffer."

"No," Melissa's voice shook with fear as she watched him remove the poker from the fire for the second time. Her eyes widened at the sight of the glowing red tip of the metal implement. "I will not," He drew the poker closer to her face and she followed its movements carefully, her mouth dry and heart racing.

"You should," He brought the poker close to her eye and she swallowed nervously, feeling the heat from the poker singe her eyelashes from bare inches away. "Or I'll take your eyes."

"They'll grow back," She attempted Emily's brand of devil may care levity, but her voice shook on the last word, imagining all too well the pain that the poker would cause.

"Not after the second time. Your donor can only heal one set." His voice didn't rise above a whisper as he drew closer. "So do you want to continue with this defiance?"

"Why are you doing this?" She couldn't hold back the fear now, her eyes were fixated on the red hot metal. "What do you want?"

"It's not personal," His hand left her throat and gently stroked her face. "You could tell me a great deal," He gave a small smile. "Now are you going to obey me or do I have to…” He left the words hanging, the poker near her eye emphasising his threat better than any words. Montjoy smashed Marcus' face against the floor again as he tried once more to get to his feet.

“No,” Melissa heard Marcus groan from the floor as she fixed John with a fearful, yet determined stare. “I won’t…”

“No?” She was sure she heard bewilderment in John’s voice. “You’re willing to lose your eyes over misguided loyalty?”

“No…” Her voice still shook, but a measure of accusation drifted through her tones. “I won’t join you because you made him,” She nodded her head towards Montjoy. “And he killed my mother, which means you killed my mother,” In a simple act of defiance, she spat in his face. “I would never work for someone like you…ever. So take my eyes and be damned.”

“Melissa,” She could hear a measure of respect mixed with fear in Marcus' voice as he lifted his head again from the floor. Turning back to face John, she bravely faced him down as she waited for the pain from the poker.

Justin has reached the doorway of the house when he heard her scream. With panic humming through his bones, he threw open the door and charged into the house. Reaching the parlour in record time, he rushed into the room, surprising John in the very act of raising the poker to Melissa’s left eye. In a moment of shocked clarity, the scene burned itself into his vision. Marcus on the floor, held there in a vicelike grip by Montjoy and Melissa, he stared at her in horror. She was slumped against the sofa, tears of salt streaming from her one good eye. In horrified fury, he could see that her other eye was missing, burnt from the socket by the red hot heat of the poker in John's hand. Rage boiled up within him, and he launched himself forward, throwing John to the ground with a wild cry.

Shocked by his sudden appearance, John failed to defend himself, and he crashed to the ground, losing his grip on the poker as he did so. In a fog of anger, Justin slammed his fist again and again into John's body, hoping to put him down with punches alone. Behind him and to the left, Marcus continued to struggle against Montjoy, anger lending him strength.

Melissa lay back against the sofa. Her heart pounded painfully within her chest as the white hot pain began to subside. The pain had been indescribable, the sharp stab of agony sending her into a swoon before the magic had begun to work on her missing eye. Sobbing from remembered pain, she pulled herself upright and stared across the room. Her vision was blurred and watery, yet the pain was slowly subsiding as the damage to the eye healed. Picking herself up from the floor, she glanced over at the tussling forms around her. Justin and John were rolling about on the floor before the fireplace, punching and grappling ineffectually as they both tried to gain the upper hand. On the other side of the room, Marcus was still trying to free himself from Montjoy's grip. Blood now soaked through his shirt as Montjoy continually smashed his face into the floor. Reaching out with shaking fingers, Melissa picked up the discarded poker and walked across the room. With a power that was fuelled by anger and pain, she brought the heavy metal implement down on Montjoy's head.

Montjoy fell to one side, the wound on his head healing as Marcus took advantage of the situation and freed himself. Melissa fixed on the swaying form of Montjoy, rage boiling through her veins as walked forward and swung again, clubbing him to the floor, the still hot tip of the poker searing into his skin. Montjoy shrank away, the healing from his donor repairing the damage as she hit again and again, as though she were beating a carpet. Sobs of rage and pain flowed through her as she continued to strike, as though she were content to beat the man to death.

"Melly," Marcus reached her side as she raised the poker again. "Enough," He reached out a hand and gently took the weapon from her.

"He deserves it," She snarled, her voice barely recognisable as she pointed at the bloody mess that was Montjoy. "He killed mother, he beat you to a pulp and wanted to rape me, you can't tell me he doesn't deserve it."

"I won't tell you he doesn't deserve it, but I think you've made your point. He turned back and pointed at John struggling with Justin. "I think Justin may need some help."

Melissa tore her eyes away from Montjoy and back to Justin on the other side of the room. Blood ran from his nose as he struggled with the tall, uncompromising frame of John. As she rushed forward to help, John managed to land a lucky blow on Justin, dazing him for long enough to slip a knife from his pocket and jab it between his ribs. Melissa and Marcus rushed across the room as John rummaged through the pockets in Justin's coat. Justin began to heal yet John rammed the knife deeper into his body. Marcus lunged forward, poker held high. With what could only be called annoyance, John seized hold of the lapels of Justin's coat and shoved him into Marcus' path, sending them both sprawling to the ground. Melissa scrabbled for the poker as it rolled across the floor.

"Amateur," He commented as he reached once more into Justin's coat and drew forth a slender tome. Removing the knife from Justin's side, he turned and looked at Marcus. "It would appear that I need to hand out more object lessons," He kicked Justin's body out of the way and held the knife to Marcus' throat. "What do you say?"

"Get away from him," Melissa's voice shook as she advanced, poker held in a shaking grip. "And get out," John barely glanced at her as he drew the edge of the blade delicately across Marcus' skin. "I said to get away from him."

"Or?" He glanced over at her, amusement in his cold gaze.

"I'll stop you," She whispered, holding the poker in what she hoped was a menacing gesture.

"I sincerely doubt your ability to do so," John uttered softly as he moved the knife closer to Marcus' throat. "Though by all means you can try. I'll even give you a clean shot," He moved the knife and sat back, leaving Marcus to rub his throat gingerly.

Melissa swung out at him with all the strength she could muster. The poker connecting solidly with his upper arm and she gaped as John reacted to the blow with an amused smile. She drew her arm to strike again. The poker whistled through the air, only for John to catch it in mid swing. With one quick move, he pulled the poker from her hands and threw it to the floor.

"Will you try with your teeth?" He asked, mocking amusement running through his tones. "Or your nails?" He took a step towards her, and she stepped back, fear increasing her heart rate as his cold, cruel gaze settled on her. "Do you wish me to take the other eye?"

"Leave my sister alone," Marcus staggered upright, only to be backhanded back to the ground.

"When will you learn?" John uttered as he walked back to Marcus. With a casual flick of his wrist, he sent the dagger sailing into Marcus' leg. Marcus gave a scream as the blade embedded itself into his thigh. "Consider this my first lesson in the appreciation of pain," He reached down and removed the blade. With deliberately slow steps, he walked across the room toward Melissa, "Now I believe you owe me an eye."

Melissa backed into the wall with a whimper as John reached out for her. His fingers caught hold of her hair and pulled her forward. He raised the blade to her eye, only to be dragged back by a dead, but very angry Justin.

"Get away from her," Despite the stiffness in his limbs, he wrapped his arms about John's throat and began to squeeze. Relief at Justin's arrival seared through Melissa. For the first time that day, she forgot all of her reasons to be angry with him.

John fought back, but Justin held on, determination giving him strength. John's face began to turn red, then blue as he struggled for breath. Unable to break free, John used the last of his strength to throw the tome into the fire.

"No!" Justin shouted as the book fell into the roaring flames, the parchment catching almost immediately. Melissa rushed to the grate and reached for the book, the skin of her hands burning painfully as she pulled the burning book from the flames. Throwing the book to the rug, she grabbed the blanket from the nearby sofa and started to smother the flames. As she beat out the last of the fire, Justin finished strangling John. He let the corpse fall to the floor and moved over to check the damaged tome.

"Bastard," He swore as he stared at the mess of blackened pages. "There's barely anything left," He reached down and flicked through a couple of the pages. A wave of devastating anguish washed over him as he realised that only a few lines of text remained unburnt.

"This was the first thing I've found with this symbol," He whispered, regret and loss swamping the anger. Melissa looked down at the lost, stunned look on his face and her bitterness towards him dissolved. Reaching down, she wrapped her arms about his shoulders, feeling his shoulders shake. "And he destroyed it," He shrugged out of her arms, picked himself up and walked back to where he had left John's body, only to swear once more, when he saw the empty space on the carpet. "I forgot to kill him twice," He said with a rueful note to his voice, before sitting down on the sofa, staring at the burnt mess on the floor.

Melissa watched him for a long moment before she sat down next to him. Reaching out gingerly, she caught hold of his fingers and held them for a moment.

"I'm sorry," She whispered. That book could have held all the answers, and John had destroyed it merely to deny Justin possession of it. Now that she had encountered John, she realised just how misplaced her anger had been. Justin had not wanted to draw her into this, he had tried so hard to stay away from her and prevent John from hurting her. She had been blaming Justin for something John was solely responsible for.

He turned to face her and she was shocked at the bleak desperation she saw on his face. "Sorry for what?" He asked, hopelessness echoing through his tones. She caught her breath, unsure of how to proceed.

"For being so…" She stumbled with the words, the mix of emotions running through her mind like a circus. "So…" She waved her hands helplessly, "Hateful," Some of the bleakness faded from his gaze, but he said nothing. "I've blamed you for things that I shouldn't blame you for," She looked down at her hands, unwilling to stare him fully in the face. "I don't hate you Justin… I was just…" She swallowed back the tears, unwilling to cry.

Justin was silent for a long moment, letting her words sink into his mind. The words were comforting, but he could not forget the pile of burnt paper. The clock ticked loudly in the corner of the room, and the silence grew uncomfortable. He could feel the tension in her rising as the silence continued. Taking a long breath, he raised his eyes to the ceiling and tried to find some calm.

"Justin?" Melissa spoke again, her voice trembling as she wondered if she had gone too far with her accusations.

Turning back to her pale face, he exhaled, forcing his lungs to take in air. "I understand…" He said, his voice soft and even. "I even expected the hostility," He stood and walked to the door. "Now if you will excuse me, I need to kill someone else," And with those words, he headed out of the door.

Melissa bent her head forward, letting the tears flow. "I don't think he'll forgive me," I wish I could stop crying," She muttered, rubbing her arm across her face and brushed away the tears. "That's all I seem to be doing."

"Melly…" Marcus sat down next to her and wrapped an arm about her shoulders. She relaxed into his embrace and closed her eyes. They stayed that way for a few moments whilst Melissa got her emotions under control. "Help me go through the book," She whispered as she opened her eyes, looking at the brittle pile of ash and paper on the floor. "It may help Justin."

Nodding, Marcus followed her down to the floor and they began to gingerly sift through the burnt pages, looking for any that had been spared from the flames.

Justin returned a couple of hours later. He stepped through the hallway of the house, a dark cloud hanging about his shoulders as he thought of the damage to the book. Hanging his cloak over the balustrade, he walked into the parlour and stopped. What remained of the book's pages were carefully laid on the rug, and he was shocked to see just how much had survived. A noise caused his eyes to flick upwards, towards Melissa and Marcus, sat at the table, drinks held in their hands.

"You did this?" He walked forward, warmth dissipating the anger that had been lodged in his chest for most of the night.

"Yes," Melissa laid down her glass and walked forward, slight hesitance in her movements. "We salvaged what we could."

Justin looked down at the collection of paper, a swell of emotion threatening to swamp him.

"I'm sorry for blaming you," She said. "It was wrong of me," She reached his side and caught his arm. "You never meant for this to happen and you tried your hardest to stop it," He looked down at her face, at the tremulous smile that was beginning to form at the corners of her mouth. "It's time I worked with you and not against you."

Justin gave a long, heartfelt sigh and reached out, pulling her into his arms. "Thank you," He whispered, merely wishing to hold her.

Melissa reached her arms about his waist and raised her head. "John did this… not you," She whispered as she reached a hand to his hair and drew his face down to hers. Her lips were hesitant, and the kiss that followed was brief yet full of promise.

From the other side of the room, Marcus cleared his throat and they broke apart. "Not that I'm unhappy that you've made up, but don't you think it's about time we moved?"

Justin drew back from Melissa and nodded, realising the truth of what Marcus said. Staying at the Grosvenor Square house was ill advised now that Montjoy and John knew where they were. "Let's get packing," He said as he moved toward the door.

"And where are we going?" Melissa called as she bent to help Marcus pick up the paper.

"France," The answer drifted down as Justin walked up the stairs, new hope lending a spring to his step.

1793
FRANCE

CHAPTER 25

"Move," Emily's voice barked out the order, and she began to run. Melissa followed as best she could. Her feet skidded on the slick messy cobbles that lined Paris' streets, and she slowed her progress, trying to stay upright.

"What the hell are you stopping for?" The blonde turned to face her, blue eyes angry beneath the large hat and hastily scraped back hair. Dressed in muddy breeches, an oversized shirt and carrying a long bloody dagger at her waist, she was a far cry from the poised, seductive creature she usually portrayed. At Emily's insistence, Melissa had also ditched the long skirts and corsetry and was trying to keep pace with her lithe companion. "Come on," Reaching out a hand, she seized hold of Melissa's wrist and dragged her forward, across the unsteady surface with the grace of a cat. From some distance behind them, they could hear the catcalls and cries of the crowd that milled through the streets. The shouts bounced off ancient stone walls, and the echoes produced amplified the sound so that it appeared to surround and envelop them.

"Why are we running?" Melissa choked out as Emily pulled her along an alley. "We won't die,"

"Because I'd rather not know what decapitation feels like…" Emily's voice was terse as she released Melissa's arm and began to clamber over the wall. "You can stay and find out for me if you like,"

"Don't be ridiculous," Melissa called as she reached up and found the first foothold. Pulling herself up the stone face, she pondered how she had ended up with Emily as her companion for this mad dash through Paris.

"Then don't talk nonsense," Emily's hands reached the top of the wall, and she levered herself to the top. "And get a move on… I don't want to get caught because you have the movement rate of a snail,"

Melissa gritted her teeth and pulled herself upward, her limbs stiff and uncoordinated since the loss of her last donor. Cold trickles of sweat rolled over her skin, and she grunted with the effort of climbing. Emily reached down a hand and pulled her upwards until they straddled the top of the wall. Melissa stopped briefly and stared out across Paris. Fires flickered in the distance as shouts and screams echoed through the air of the ancient city. Emily had no such time for wool gathering as she began to lower herself to street level.

"Tell me something," Melissa hissed as she swung her leg over the top of the wall. "Why are we still in Paris for this insanity?"

"Because…" Emily jumped the last few feet to the floor and waited. "I had to make sure my assets were safe. I may need to come back here and I don't want my fortune missing,"

"I thought…" Melissa steadied herself against the wall and prepared to make the last jump to the floor. "That you had your money in London,"

"Not all of it," Melissa reached the bottom of the wall and gave a yelp of surprise as Emily pulled her into a corner, pressing her fingers against her lips as she did so. From the end of the alley, they could hear the cries of one of the mobs and Melissa stopped struggling. They stood still and silent, pressed together in the filthy corner as the mob rushed past. "Quiet…" Emily's voice whispered unnecessarily against her ear and Melissa flinched as her breath slid over her cheek. Never quite secure in Emily's company, she disliked the necessity that had drawn them together for this mad dash.

Moments passed slowly as they waited in the darkness of the alcove. Emily's body was pressed against the wall and her arm was anchored firmly around Melissa's waist. As they stood, tense and watchful, Melissa felt as though she were in some strange dream. While she didn't actively dislike Emily, she would never count her as a friend and yet here they were, cowered together in the dark. She would have chuckled with the absurdity of it all, had the situation not been so tense. The noise of the crowd began to dissipate as they moved further away into the city. The whoops and jeers grew more distant and slowly the pair relaxed. Emily's hands slipped away from her waist and Melissa stepped forward and out into the alleyway.

"Now what?" Her voice was soft, fearful of attracting further attention. Melissa's green eyes moved away from her companion and ran up and down the alley.

"Now we get you a weapon," Emily murmured as she stepped to the brunette's side. "Then we go after Justin,"

Melissa felt her guts clench slightly at Justin's name. Justin was part of the reason for this mad chase through Paris. Since his arrest the previous evening, Emily and Melissa had spent most of the day trying to reach where he had been incarcerated. Intellectually she knew that the guillotine would not end his life but she wished to avoid that fate for him if possible. Swallowing her fear, she nodded and stepped forward cautiously. As they reached the smoky light on the main street, Emily cast her eyes over Melissa with concern.

"Aren't you missing something?" She asked as her eyes roved over Melissa' overly pale form.

"I don't think…,"

"Your donor," Emily continued, ignoring Melissa's words. "You seem decidedly unwell,"

"I can manage for a time," Melissa pushed past Emily and continued down the street.

"Not if you take any damage…" Emily reached out a

hand and stopped her moving. "Find someone…"

"And do what?" Melissa stared pointedly at Emily's hand, and she slowly removed it. "Tie him up and leave him in the street?" A look of scorn slid over her features as she continued. "We've got nowhere to hold someone."

"Even so…" Emily interrupted. "You are risking death tonight," Her voice was patient and without the hint of condescension that usually marred it. Deep clear eyes held Melissa's and the other woman glanced away, ashamed suddenly of her sarcasm. "If you get injured, fatally or otherwise, you'll slow us down," Melissa did not answer, and Emily pressed the advantage. "You're no good to Justin this way," Her voice altered and the usual mockery was back. "Or rather, you'll be marginally more inept than usual."

"But what do you want me to do?" Melissa chose to ignore the needling digs Emily threw her way, she had known her long enough to realise that the antagonism was practiced and designed to provoke. "We have nowhere to hold someone,"

"Then we'll just have to improvise," Emily continued.

The sound of running feet halted their conversation, and they pressed back against the wall, hiding in the deepest shadows. Emily's arm was back around her waist, as though she feared that Melissa was about to run off. "Find one of the guards at Justin's prison," Emily whispered into her ear as the shouts bounced off the filthy walls of the alley. "Use him and when the fighting happens…"

"He'll take the damage," Melissa finished the thought,

her mind focusing on the fortress which held Justin captive. "What about Marcus?"

"He's safe," Emily replied, her voice ghosting across Melissa' ears as she spoke. "He's outside Paris and waiting to take us to the coast."

"Right," More figures raced past the alley, and Melissa froze, hoping that they didn't look in their direction. As quiet descended once more, Emily's hand moved away from her waist and grabbed hold of her wrist. "Come on," Emily pulled Melissa out into the street, and they began to run.

They hurried along the cobbled streets, muck sliding unpleasantly beneath their feet as they moved. They could hear mobs in the distance, yet they never met them. Emily hurried them through narrow roads that were empty of all but rats. Melissa had never even known that these routes existed, and she was strangely grateful for her guide. In addition, she had thankfully stopped speaking. Though she was extremely capable, her tendency for snide comments rankled and Melissa was glad for the quiet. They rounded a corner and came to a stop. Torches flickered about them concierge, lending a demonic aspect to the place. The former Palais de la Cite, it had been pressed into service as a prison, and its reputation wasn't appealing. It was packed with prisoners awaiting execution, and Justin was with them. She could almost smell the dungeons and the thought of Justin facing the guillotine sent shivers of dread through her.

"He'll be alright," Emily reassured, correctly interpreting

the look on her face. "And when we get his brooch to him, he'll be better than alright,"

"What if they've sentenced him?" Melissa asked, fear making her voice sharper.

"We check the board," Melissa nodded towards the front of the building. "They usually post it fairly early so that the crowds can gather," They headed across the road and rounded the corner to the front of the building. The façade faced the Seine, and two guards stood before the front door.

Melissa nearly stopped walking, but Emily had hold of her arm and kept her moving. Melissa envied her confidence and wondered how many years it would take to be this brazen.

"Bonsoir," She called in cheery French tone. "Ca va?" She smiled as the two men nudged each other, their eyes devouring her figure. They watched as she peered at the execution board. Melissa kept her eyes on the two guards.

After a moment, Emily turned away from the board in satisfaction. Walking away from the building, she reached the river bank and stopped, leaning against the wall with a practised nonchalance. "You too," She reached out and pulled Melissa closer. "Smile," Melissa did so, wondering what she had in mind now. "Show them some leg," Emily muttered as she delivered a dazzlingly seductive smile at the two men on the guard.

"I don't think they'll leave their post?" Melissa argued just as silently as she arranged herself beside Emily.

"Of course they will," Emily replied as she cast a long lingering glance at the guards. "They're men and not very disciplined," She glanced at Melissa and almost snorted. "Or they would come over if you didn't look constipated," Tossing her hair back she continued. "They won't come over just for me and you look suspicious. We'll have to try something else," She hooked her arm about Melissa's waist and they began to leave.

"How about …" Melissa broke away from Emily's side and balled up her fist. "This," With that, she punched Emily in the face. The men watched with alarm as Emily hit the ground, blood pouring from her nose.

"Good plan," Was all that Emily said as she prepared to take the blows, cowering beneath Melissa's foot as though she were scared. As Melissa kicked her in the chest, she began to scream very loudly in French. Her accent wasn't as good as Emily's but after twenty years in the country, she could pass for a native. With each kick to Emily, she screamed out words that would bring the men running. As she rained blows down on the seemingly cowering woman, she ensured that her lotus locket was open and ready in her hand.

"Traitor to the revolution," The words echoed across and reached the guards. After sharing a brief glance, they left their post and rushed over, drawing weapons as they did so. On the floor, Emily prepared, her wounds healing fast as she took careful hold of the sword she carried. The guards reached Melissa and one pulled her away from Emily's prone body. Melissa struggled in the man's grip as the other moved to stare at her.

"That bitch is a noble," Melissa raged as the man slapped her hard across the face. "She had this on her," She flourished the open locket in his face. The man cast his eyes down, the magic of the locket latching on with only the briefest of glances. The man stopped moving at the sight of his face in the locket and as his cry of surprise echoed across the river, Emily reacted. Rolling over, she sliced the long blade across the second guard's hamstring, sending him to the ground with a scream of agony. As he tried to retaliate, Emily reversed the blade and sliced neatly through the artery at the top of his leg. Blood gushed from the open wound as Emily rolled clear. The other man raised his sword and struck at Melissa. She seized hold of the blade, wincing as the sword tore through the skin on her hands. As the healing kicked in, the guard yelped and dropped his sword, staring at his bleeding wounds with disbelief.

"Witchcraft," He whispered, staggering back with shock. Melissa gave a grim smile at his assessment. She did agree with him, but couldn't afford the weakness of sympathy. Reaching down, she picked up his dropped sword and held it at his throat.

"Don't move or make a sound," Melissa threatened in a low voice as she pressed the cold steel of the blade against his neck. "How are you doing?" She called back over her shoulder.

"Absolutely fine," Emily grunted as she tried to lever the now dead body of her assailant over the wall. "I may need some help,"

"Stop playing with the dead and give me a hand with this one?" Melissa snapped, nerves sharpening her tone. "We haven't got long before the next patrol comes round,"

"Alright," Emily left the man slumped against the wall and returned to Melissa's side. "So what do want to do? We can't tie him up and leave him in the street," She echoed Melissa's words from earlier.

"Very funny," Melissa retorted. "He'll go in with us,"

"Alright, you're the boss," Emily moved to the man's side as Melissa rolled her eyes. "Don't do anything," She whispered to the guard. "You won't damage me and you might make me upset. Put your friend's body into the river and lead the way inside. If you're a good boy, you may live through this,"

The man stared at the two women with shock, unable it seemed, to comprehend what was being said.

"You understand that I've cursed you?" Melissa didn't like taking this route, but they had little choice. "If I get hurt, so do you," She leaned in and softened her tone. "If I don't get hurt and I find my friend with no trouble then we'll let you go,"

The man slowly got to his feet, looking down at his hands in shock. "Put the body into the river," Melissa continued, hating every word that left her lips. The man still did not move. With a hiss of impatience, Emily slashed across Melissa's face with her dagger. There was a screech of pain from the guard as a long bloody gash appeared across his cheek. Melissa turned to glower at her.

"What?" The woman asked as the guard rushed to pick up the body of his friend. "We don't have time to coddle him. There may be people inside wondering why the guard isn't on duty," They watched the man lever the body over the wall and into the Seine.

"You're a heartless bitch," Melissa retorted as the man returned to her side.

"It worked didn't it?" Emily ignored the insult as she waved the sword at the guard. "Get moving,"

The man nodded and led the way across the road. As a group, they climbed the steps to the building and he pushed open the door. The door opened to a long, dimly lit hallway, signs of its previous occupancy showing in the paper on the walls.

"Where's Lavrouche?" Melissa asked, using Justin's current name as they moved into the hallway. "Did he pay for a private room?"

"Yes," The man answered, watching the pair with fear in his eyes. "He's paid till tomorrow,"

"Understandable," Emily muttered as she walked past them. "Madame Guillotine is supposed to meet him in the morn," Emily jerked her head and indicated that he should lead the way. "You'd better hope we don't meet resistance," She uttered as he walked past. "Melissa here will be fine…"

"I think he understands," Melissa broke into the conversation. "Take us to Justin and you might get out alive,"

The man swallowed and led them through the corridors, leading them through empty halls until he reached one of the staircases. They took the stairs, two at a time and reached the second floor. The door leading from the landing was closed, and they could hear a murmur of voices from beyond the portal. Emily glanced at Melissa and raised her eyebrows.

"Would you like me to go?" She muttered, her voice low. "Your swordplay is woefully inadequate, and you'll want to keep..." She jerked her head at the shaking man beside them. "This one alive as long as possible,"

Melissa gave a slight roll of her eyes and indicated the door with a sweep of her hand. Emily gave a brief smile and pushed open the door. In the hallway beyond, three guards turned to face the door.

"Good evening boys," Emily carolled in soft, kittenish tones. She walked forward, the blade held lightly at her side. "Want some company?"

"Who the hell are you?" The lead guard walked forward, eyes cold and voice harsh. "What are you doing here?" His eyes swept past Emily to fix on the guard behind her. "Jacques, what are you...?" he did not finish the sentence. Emily, moving faster than he anticipated, attacked almost as the words left his mouth. Her sword sliced across his throat sending him to the floor in one fluid motion. After a moment of frozen shock, his companions reacted. The closest guard attacked Emily, swift, sure strokes slicing through the air. Emily parried the first two strikes, her arm shaking from each blow. On the third strike, she dodged, before answering the attacks with some of her own. As the guard backed away, the third man moved in, attempting to flank her.

"You'd better drop that sword bitch," The second guard brought his sword down as though he were wielding an axe, driving Emily's blade to the floor in one heavy blow. "Whores like you should only play with one kind of blade," Emily gave a bored yawn as the first guard levelled the sword to her throat. Ignoring the sharp edge close to her neck, Emily lifted her sword and struck at the guard again. The guard's sword sliced into her throat and her warm blood sprayed across his face. His cry of satisfaction turned to one of horror as she kept moving forward. Emily felt the flesh on her throat knit together as she stabbed the guard through the shoulder. As he fell to his knees, the second guard dropped his sword and tried to run. Emily moved and sliced the back of his kneecaps, sending him to the ground in agony. "What are you playing at Jacques?" He shouted as Emily kicked his sword away from his grasp and moved closer to him. "Shut up," Emily said with a grim note to her voice. He flailed out with his arms, striking her across the face, yet nothing kept her away. Leaning forward, an almost tender look on her face, Emily opened her locket. From the doorway, Melissa looked away from the resulting carnage, a sick look on her face. She hadn't yet managed to attain Emily's cavalier attitude toward the lives of others. Indeed, since her experience with John twenty years before, she had tried hard to remain completely undamaged, unwilling to expose her donors to more pain than necessary.

"Don't say a word," Emily warned the remaining guard. "Or what's just happened here," She nodded down at the blood drenched body. "Will be pleasant compared to what I can do," She looked over her shoulder and called at Melissa, "Well, get the body moved," She spoke in sharp tones. "Don't stand there like an idiot," Stunned into action by Emily's anger, Melissa walked forward and began to drag the body across the floor. As Melissa shoved the body out of sight, Emily showed the locket to the remaining guard. "Be very good," She warned as the man watched his likeness appear with a face the colour of parchment.

Melissa and Jacques pushed the guard out of sight and returned to the hall. Emily glanced down at her new donor and continued to speak. "Where's Justin Lavrouche?"

With nervous, shaking hands, the guard pointed along the hall and to the left.

"Thank you," Emily nodded with a sweet smile. "Lead the way,"

CHAPTER 26

Justin leant back against the wall and pondered his situation. He could say that he had been in worst places, but he had not yet faced beheading. He had considered making a break for freedom, but the door before him was far too solidly constructed and several guards patrolled the hallways behind it. A check of the window had revealed a solid set of newly constructed iron bars, and it was these, more than the fall on the other side, that had prevented his escape. He was grateful that he had managed to hide his brooch before they had come for him. The only irritation was the loss of the book. He looked down at the floor and scowled, that book was the reason he had not left Paris, and he was certain that he would not locate it again. Since the loss of his library in England, he had been trying to replenish the lost tomes as well as locate new ones. It was proving to be a near impossible task. Many of the books were hard to replace and some were rare to the point of legend. The scraps of parchment that they had salvaged from the book burnt by John had indicated that it had been the second in a trilogy. Following the clues from the book which led them to Paris, he had spent the last five years looking at every book dealer and merchant he could find. Since the start of the revolution, he had managed to avoid the worst of the mobs. Using years of practice, he had evaded most of the trouble until the previous night.

Monsieur Corbeaux had been a merchant, not particularly wealthy, but with past connections to the aristocracy, so he had eventually been sought by the revolution. It was Justin's misfortune that he had been there when Corbeaux had been arrested. In the moments before they broke down the door, Justin had shoved the brooch deep into the embers of the fire. From his many experiments, he knew that the brooch would remain safe and that his notes to Emily and Melissa would lead them to the address. Since his last fight with John, he had made sure that Emily, Melissa and Marcus knew where he would hide his brooch if he were in trouble. The burning heart of a fire was deemed to be safe as no normal person would touch it until it was cold ash. He thrust the brooch into the flames, the heat blistering the skin from his hand as he buried the brooch deep into the white hot ash. Soon after that, they had dragged him outside. He had offered no resistance, unwilling to deal with the pain that a savage beating would bring. Pushing himself away from the wall, he returned to the door and listened. The guards outside were talking, betting on how he would act on his trip to the guillotine. For a moment, he mentally joined in. He thought he would remain stoically silent as they placed him beneath the blade. A snort of amusement escaped his lips at the thought. Not that he had to worry about death, but he did worry about the after effect of a still living corpse on a Paris mob. He fancied they would start burning him, and he had never much cared for the feel or smell of burning flesh.

Returning to the window, he tried the bars again, annoyed that the mortar seemed particularly strong. Had it been old and dry, he could have chipped it away and fallen to freedom out of the window. Broken limbs were easier to manage than fatalities. Turning away, he settled back on the bed. There was luxury here. The condemned nobles spent the last of their money in order to remain in comfort before the stinking cart drew them to death. He was grateful for the solitary room as rescuers would find it easier to locate him. He drifted into an uneasy doze.

He woke at the sounds of combat and smiled. It looked as though the cavalry had arrived. Pulling himself from the bed, he began to drag on his outer clothing and boots, waiting for the door to open. He didn't have to wait long. The door swung open to reveal Melissa and Emily, a guard held hostage between them. He took a moment to drink in their appearance. Both were dressed in breeches and shirts, swords held loosely in their hands. They looked fearsome, powerful and eminently desirable. As his eyes swiftly roved over the bodies of his rescuers, Emily gave him an amused wink, understanding the train of his thoughts in an instant.

"Justin," With a relieved cry, Melissa rushed past Emily and flung herself into his arms. Her warm body fitted snugly against his, and he closed his eyes, relaxing into her embrace with a mixture of relief and desire. Melissa lifted her head and welcomed the pressure of his lips as he bent his head and kissed her. Her arms reached around his back, and her fingers slid into his hair. For a moment, Justin forgot that they still in danger as all his focus shifted to Melissa, to the feel of her lips against his and her searching fingers against his scalp.

Emily cleared her throat, and they pulled apart. The blonde sauntered into the room as calmly as though she were at a ball. Blood dripped from the slender sword she carried and spotted the expensive carpet as she forced the hapless guard further into the room. He obeyed without comment, stunned by the sorcery that he had just witnessed. With a sly smile dancing across her features, Emily walked forward and caught hold of Justin's arm, sidling in close to the couple.

"Don't I get my turn?" She asked softly, winking at Justin as she spoke. "I've missed your kisses," Justin glanced away guiltily as Melissa turned to glare at her. Emily smiled broadly, amused by the angry gleam in Melissa's eyes. "Oh Melissa, stop taking everything so seriously," She joked, grinning even more as Melissa's hands began to clench into fists.

"Hadn't we better go," Justin suggested, attempting to forestall the inevitable argument as he tried to extricate himself from Emily's grasp. "The guards will be coming,"

"Yes, we shouldn't waste time," Melissa turned away from Emily's smug grin and headed back through the door. Justin followed, stopping only to glower at Emily's exquisite features as he moved past. He did not understand why she did this. They had never been more than casual lovers, and she certainly did not care for him, so why did she feel the need to rub their past relationship in Melissa's face?

Emily gave a small smile as she watched the others head through the door.

"You'd better come with us," She announced to the ashen faced guard. "And remember, any damage taken will be borne by yourself, so…"

"I know, stay quiet and lead you outside," Jacques whispered, terrified beyond reason. He had seen the flesh close on the other girl's arm and a fatal wound heal to nothing. He didn't understand it, but he believed that he was now in the company of devils and his only hope of survival was to obey. He followed the woman out of the room and began to run, keeping pace with the small group.

At the head of the party, Melissa moved past the bodies of the dead guards and headed for to the stairs, trying to focus on their current flight. She did not know why she let Emily's digs get to her. Possibly she was jealous of her easy relationship with Justin, considering her own relationship with him was more rocky than rosy. It had taken far too long for her to reconcile what had been done to her and the resulting recrimination had almost destroyed them. Yet, she had tried to get past it, even when her father had died alone, crushed by the loss of both his children.

"Left," Emily snapped from somewhere behind her and Melissa veered down the corridor towards the empty staircase. She glanced across at Justin, he was pale and a fine sheen of sweat coated his skin.

"You'd better find someone," She announced as they moved down the stairs, heading for the main corridor.

"I know," He replied as they took the steps two at a time. The loss of a donor was always uncomfortable and the sensations of sickness would grow as each hour passed. In a past experiment, he had managed to survive a week before the symptoms became unbearable.

"Here's your brooch," She drew the black enamelled locket free and handed it back to him. He received the brooch without comment as they reached the bottom of the stairs. Retrieving the object of his damnation was always a mixed blessing.

"Through there," The guard pointed, at a door on the left. "That leads to the street."

"Wait," Justin said, drawing to a halt before the door. "I'm going to need to find a victim and so do you," He nodded in Emily's direction. "I fancy we'll find better candidates in here than outside."

"You want us to draw more attention to ourselves?" Emily asked with some concern. "We've killed three people and kidnapped a fourth, I sincerely doubt our luck will hold for any more."

"Then what do you suggest?" Justin asked, "Wandering the streets looking for people,"

"Yes," Emily retaliated with a definite sneer to her voice. "Those streets aren't quiet, neither are they full of innocents."

"Much as I hate to say it," Melissa interjected reluctantly, "but she's right. There's too much risk in there."

"You're siding with her?" Justin said with some confusion.

Melissa gave a brief roll of the eyes and nodded. Emily glanced at the other woman and a broad grin split her features. "Oh Melissa I'm so proud of you," Melissa looked away, annoyed by Emily's sarcastic tones. "You're finally getting a mind of your own,"

"And this is why I don't like you," Melissa grumbled as she walked to the door. "Yes I think you have a point, there's no need for the insults,"

"Of course, I'm so sorry," Emily reached out and gave Melissa an awkward hug. "You know we should stick together,"

"Aren't we going?" Discomforted by Emily's effusive hug and words, Melissa pulled away from her side and began to walk quickly toward the door.

Justin looked at Emily and shook his head. "Why can't you be gracious?"

"I can be very gracious, I just don't choose to be," Emily replied as she grabbed hold of Jacques' upper arm and pulled him after Melissa. "Well, are you joining us?"

Melissa reached the door and depressed the handle. She could hear Emily speaking from somewhere behind her, but she paid it no mind. She could never figure the blonde out, infuriating and patronising that she was, Emily was also loyal and generous. When Melissa had told her of Justin's capture, she had immediately offered to assist. Of course that may have been inspired by personal reasons, but it still made an impression. Melissa pushed open the door and walked through. The night was drawing on, and the sky was lightening in the east. Dawn was not very far away. The noise from the mobs was noticeable yet distant, and the scent of smoke hung in the air.

"Where now?" Justin asked as they headed along one of the alleys.

"Outside of Paris," Melissa replied. "Marcus is waiting for us,"

"We'll find someone on route," Emily replied, the sarcasm absent for the first time that evening. "We shouldn't have any trouble now."

CHAPTER 27

Marcus sat outside the burnt out shell of a small inn on the outskirts of Paris. Like the others, he had shed the clothing that marked him as a noble and was now dressed in the garb of a revolutionary. Garb that had belonged to the man now sealed in the cellar of the building behind him. His new donor had been raping a woman when Marcus had found him. Going to the woman's aid, Marcus had rendered the man unconscious and had stolen his clothes before forcing him to stare at the locket in his hand. That had been several hours ago and there was still no sign of the others. When it had become apparent that Paris was becoming far too dangerous, they had agreed to leave and meet outside of the city. In the general confusion of yet another riot, they had become separated. Marcus had fled the city on foot, hoping that the others had reached safety before him, but had been disappointed. Once again, Marcus got to his feet and stared out at the city before him. Lights from multiple fires burned in the darkness, and he paced up and down the road, trying to quell the urge to return to the city and look for his sister. The sound of approaching hooves drifted from somewhere ahead, and he craned his head towards Paris, hope burning in his chest. The sound drew nearer and he craned his head to look, only to be disappointed as a laden cart rolled past him.

"Goddamn it Melissa, where the devil are you?" He left the roadside edge and settled back against the wall of the inn, making certain that he was away from the temptation of returning to Paris. In the past forty years, he had still not lost the desire to protect his sister. Even though permanent harm would come to neither of them, he still worried when they were apart. He leant back against the side of the inn and pondered Melissa. It had been forty years since he had joined this select 'club', forty years since the fire that had destroyed most of Justin's research into the curse that blighted them. In his naiveté, he had offered to help Justin with discovering the cure for their affliction. He had stupidly thought with a fresh pair of eyes, they would uncover the reasons for this living hell in no time; however that had not proven to be the case. He could understand the jaded natures of the others now.

More time passed and another set of hooves clattered on the roughly paved road. He slowly got to his feet and moved deeper into the shadows as the horses slowed to a halt.

"Marcus?" He breathed a sigh of relief as Melissa' voice sounded from the road.

"I'm here," He called as he left the shadow of the inn. His sister dismounted and rushed toward him. He opened his arms, and she fell into them. Relieved that she was safe, he wrapped his arms around her and gave her a hug. "What took you so long?" He asked, looking across the top of Melissa's head towards Justin.

"I got captured by the Revolutionaries," Justin supplied as he pushed a human shaped bundle off his horse and onto the ground. "I also lost the damn book,"

"You nearly lost your head over that damn book," Emily snapped back as she lithely dropped from the back of the horse and landed lightly on the ground. "What was so special about it?"

"It doesn't matter now," Justin uttered as he joined the others. "Marcus," He nodded at the other man as he stretched his stiff muscles.

"What do you mean it's not important?" Emily retorted, advancing on Justin, fire sparking in her eyes. "You risked capture and decapitation for it, so don't tell me you didn't think it important,"

"Well it's hardly likely to matter now," Justin answered leaning against the trunk of a nearby tree. "The book's gone,"

"It may," Melissa turned and joined in the conversation. "Why did you want it so badly? Was it just a replacement?"

She stepped forward, thinking of the tattered and burnt pages from Grosvenor Square. "Was it the second book in the series?"

Justin sighed and closed his eyes, the trunk of the tree pressing into his back as he struggled to find the words for his disappointment.

"Justin?" Emily asked a warning note in her voice.

"Alright," He answered, opening his eyes to stare at the rest of the group. "It wasn't a replacement. One of my contacts informed me that they had seen an illustration of a chest that looked remarkably like my father's in this book," He pushed a hand through his hair in agitation. "I took that to mean that he had the second book,"

Emily's full attention was on Justin now. Her back was rigid with shock or anger as she processed his words.

"You're telling me that you're found the explanation for the chest?" Her voice was soft, but there was condemnation behind it. "And you only just tell us this now?"

"I did say it was important," Justin answered, his voice taut with pent up emotion.

"No you let us believe that it was purely part of your library," Emily's voice had risen in volume, and Justin winced. "If you had said what book it was, we would have helped you. Damn it Justin this is not your personal crusade," She walked forward, raising her hand as she did so. Melissa stepped in front of her. "Get out of the way," She ordered, fury in her gaze. "Do you even understand what this may mean?"

"I understand that it was a chance and only that,"

Melissa retorted as she stared across at Emily's furious features. "If Justin had thought there was any more to it, he wouldn't have left Paris,"

"Oh dear God you're so naïve," Emily shouted, flinging up her arms in disbelief. "Of course he would leave Paris because you wanted to leave Paris," Anger thrummed through her voice, rendering her tone harsh. "He still thinks you are a delicate flower that needs protecting," She advanced on Melissa, face ugly with frustrated fury. "I knew I was being far too optimistic regarding his desire to cure you,"

"Why are you making it my fault?" Melissa now stood toe to toe with the blonde. Marcus and Justin exchanged glances, not willing to witness another fight between Melissa and Emily.

"Because you have him wrapped about your little finger…," Emily's voice was rising. "You're the one who…"

"Em…" Marcus stepped forward and caught hold of her arm. "Calm down…" Melissa took a step away as her brother moved in to defuse the situation. She could understand some of Emily's anger, but she didn't understand the hostility towards her. She could understand if Emily did indeed love Justin, but that did not seem to be the case. They flirted like lovers, but they hadn't been in years. If Emily had wanted more from Justin, why had she been cursed? It was a puzzle that Hugh could have helped her to understand. He would have some insight into Emily's motivations, or at the very least, he could have distracted her. Unfortunately Hugh had gone to America and there was no sign of him returning.

"Don't you bloody tell me to calm down…" Emily answered, but some of the heat had gone out of her voice. Melissa wondered at the change in tone. This was another curiosity about Emily, if she loved Justin, then why did it seem as thought she had feelings for Marcus? Disliking that chain of thought, she stopped her attempt to understand Emily's foibles as the woman continued to speak. "Don't you understand?"

"I do understand…" Justin reached forward and laid his hands on her shoulders, staring into her face steadily. "I know what it means to all of us and if yes I could have kept looking but…" Emily took a deep breath as she listened to Justin's calm voice. "I never saw the book, it was just a rumour…"

Emily reached up a hand and rubbed her eyes. Justin watched the disappointment settle over her face as she turned and threw her arms about Marcus. He glanced up at Melissa' brother and raised an eyebrow as Marcus gingerly hugged the volatile blonde. For a long moment, no one said anything as Emily hugged Marcus. Melissa thought she was crying, yet her eyes were dry when she stepped away.

"Where can I put these?" She asked, pointing at the three human shaped sacks on the floor.

"In the basement of the inn," Marcus replied. "I'll help you,"

As they moved into the building, Melissa reached Justin's side and slid her arms about him.

"So what now?"

Justin said nothing; his eyes were fixed on Paris and the prize he had lost. There had been no guarantee it had been anything but a woodcut in a book, but it still could have been useful and been some clue towards the cure. Even a line giving the location of where it had been created would have been something. He wished he had seized the book and ran when they had stormed the house. The book was probably a pile of ash now. He balled up his fist and slammed it into the tree trunk. Damn Emily for cutting right to the heart of the matter, he could have done something. They could have returned to the house and checked, but he had wanted to leave Paris.

"It's not your fault," Melissa said, catching his hand and preventing him from striking the tree a second time. "Like you said; it may have been a rumour,"

"True," Justin turned and looked down at the newly healed skin on his hands. "It could have been nothing, but it could have been something, and it's not as though we need to worry about dying," He let his head fall back, and he stared up at the sky. "We could have gone back, we could have checked,"

"Then let's do it," Melissa stated so calmly and decisively that he had to look at her to make sure that she hadn't turned into Emily in those few moments. "We go now,"

"The guards?"

"As you've said, we need not fear dying," She was watching his face, watching as the hopeless pessimism of a few moments ago was replaced but a thin gleam of hope.

"If they handle the merchant like any other, the house will have been locked and guarded. Nothing would have been removed from it yet," She stepped forward and rested her hand against his chest. "It won't be left for long, but we can check,"

Justin felt a smile stretch across his lips, and he reached forward to pull her against his chest.

"Have I told you today how much I love you?" He murmured against her hair as she reached her arms around his back.

"Not today no," Melissa murmured as he lifted her chin and began to softly trail kisses across her face.

"Then I'll have to remind you later," He promised between kisses as Melissa closed her eyes and melted beneath the pressure of his lips.

"That's still my sister you're molesting," Marcus' voice sounded from the edge of the inn, and they jumped apart, looking at him with something akin to hate. "Hate me all you want, but that's one thing I'd rather not witness,"

"So what's happening?" Emily asked as she began to drag the next body toward the inn's interior.

"We're going back to Paris," Justin announced. "We need to check the house, maybe we'll find the clue after all,"

CHAPTER 28

Paris during the day was almost calm. There were still mobs roaming the streets, but most of them seemed to be following carts of nobles to the guillotine and clad in their torn and dirty clothing, the quartet had no trouble roaming the streets. They had heard tales of the breakout from the prison the night before, but no one had managed to circulate a decent description of the escapee Lavrouche. They had some difficulty entering the city, calls for papers which actually translated as a request for bribes almost stopped their progress, but thankfully the captain in charge of the post was a true believer in the revolution and they were allowed to pass unmolested.

"We'll have to move a bit more carefully from here on

in," Justin warned the group as they began to walk in the more upmarket regions of Paris. "It's not as though we'll stand out as nobles, but they still won't want us breaking into the house,"

"Couldn't we just convince them that we've been given the job of clearing it?" Emily asked as they passed a small group of men drinking on the corner.

"We could but we don't have the right papers," Justin retorted as they reached the end of the street where the house lay. "Right that's the one at the end of the row,"

"It's guarded," Marcus noted, his sharp eye picking out the two men watching the house from the other side of the road. "Can you get in round the back?"

"Could try," Justin answered as they moved out of sight and moved down the next side street. Moving through the alleyway, they reached the street that ran parallel to the other. "So far so good," He muttered as they walked along the nearly empty street. Many of the houses were empty of tenants, their windows and doors covered with boards in an effort to deny entry. "Though we're standing out like a prostitute in a nunnery,"

"Such a lovely allusion," Emily muttered as they reached their destination. "Well that's why they haven't set guards at the back," She hissed, disappointment thrumming through her tones at the sight of the high wall surrounding the rear of the house. At least ten feet tall and probably closer to twelve, the wall was certainly a deterrance.

"We're going to have to find a way in somehow," Justin muttered as he looked at the large obstacle in their path.

"Does that mean Melissa and I will be on distraction duty?" Melissa glanced at Emily but said nothing. She wasn't very good at Emily's kind of distraction. Despite the amount of time she had been given to practice, she had not yet mastered the ability to lie like Lucifer. Given time, Emily could charm and seduce angels, but Melissa had not yet developed the knack. Uncomfortable with flirtation, she always felt as though she were being unfaithful to Justin, even though there was no intention of anything unsavoury happening. As a consequence, she was unable to relax enough for the lie to succeed.

"Don't include me," Melissa replied. "You've seen how bad I am at that kind of distraction."

"That's the truth," Emily agreed as they walked past the house and onto the next alley. Moving into the shadows, she leant against the wall, addressing the group with matter of fact frankness. "Well, why don't we stick with the old, climb the wall while people keep watch plan?"

Justin glanced up at the wall and raised an eyebrow. "My climbing's not that good," He uttered with resignation in his voice. "Falling off it will hurt,"

"Well it won't be permanent," Melissa interjected as Emily glanced at her with some admiration. "And we need to do this,"

"Alright," Justin replied with a sigh, eyeing the wall with dislike. "Marcus?" He asked as he headed back towards the wall. Marcus waited a moment and followed him across the street. "Give me a leg up,"

Emily and Melissa moved to either ends of the street to

keep watch as Marcus cupped his hands for Justin to use as a footrest. Justin placed his foot in Marcus' hands, and the other man pushed him upwards. Justin scrabbled for a handhold as he stepped onto Marcus' shoulder to gain more height. His hands met rough, moss covered stone and then air. He felt around and gripped the top of the wall with his fingers. With Marcus' hands pushing him higher, he found a firmer hold and began to pull himself up. His muscles burned with the exertion and not for the first time, he was grateful for the curses ability to move pain elsewhere. A stone sliced across his thumb, it healed immediately, but the added slickness of blood made his grip more tenuous than before,

"That's about all I can give you," Marcus grunted with the effort of holding Justin in place. "For God's sake get over that wall,"

Justin gritted his teeth as his muscles screamed with the effort and he vaulted on to the top of the wall. Marcus gave a sigh of relief and moved to where Emily was standing.

"I've just thought of a problem," Emily glanced at him. "How's he going to get back?"

Justin dropped to the ground, jarring the bones in his ankles as he landed. For a few moments, he stayed still as he waited for the healing from the locket to remove the pain. As he waited, he stared about at the small garden he found himself in. A small vegetable patch lay in one corner, and several rose bushes grew wild and tangled in the other. The entire garden had the feeling of neglect and abandonment and though he chastised himself for the flight of fancy, he had to admit that the impression was true. The roses were thick with greenfly and slugs had decimated the lettuce. Stepping away from the wall, he approached the back of the house. The door was a solid wood affair that he fancied would be extremely resistant to one man's boot, yet he had other methods of breaking into properties, quieter methods than smashing the door down. He reached into a pocket and drew a long pin. After several minutes and some very quiet swearing, he walked into the kitchen of the house and began to make his search.

He moved through the hall and walked into the parlour, remembering the night he had been asked to meet with Monsieur Corbeaux. He looked at the destruction already wrought by the revolutionaries and anger began to burn within him. Why had Corbeaux been taken? He had only the slightest connection with the aristocracy, and even that was grudging. Who could have thought that this inoffensive book merchant needed to die? He moved aside several papers from the desk and began to search in earnest. He had only seen the cover of the book before the soldiers had arrived; Corbeaux had hidden it when they had begun to smash down the door.

Moving to the bookcase he kept looking, the tome was bound in green leather with a brass clasp. He had taken note of the colours before the hammering on the door had begun in earnest. Corbeaux had been on this side of the room, so it could be held either in the drawers or the bookcase. He lifted some more ledgers from the shelves and began to rifle through, hoping that the book had been hidden from the soldiers but not so hidden that he would not find it.

After ten minutes, he had exhausted the bookcase and the desk, both drawers and shelves were completely bare, and he had sunk into the parlour chair in the throes of frustrated anger. What could Corbeaux have done with it? He wouldn't have burnt it, that would have been anathema to his book dealer's brain. So he must have hidden it. Justin took a deep breath and closed his eyes, it was entirely possible that he was looking too hard. It would be typical if the book was out in plain sight and he had missed it under the impression that it should have been hidden away. He opened his eyes and looked again at the bookcase and the desk. The sun's rays filtered weakly through the boards on the windows, and he stared into the shadows. As he settled his seething mind, something drew his attention. His eyes drifted to the side of the bookcase and the panelling that covered the walls of the room. Something about the panelling didn't appear right. Almost in a daze, he stood up and walked toward the wall, his breath catching in his throat as he stared at the only panel that was not as flush with the walls as the other. Stepping closer he finally noticed the secret compartment. A smile lit his features as he looked around for the button to open it.

Outside the house, Marcus, Emily and Melissa stood together at the end of the alley staring across at the guards that sat opposite the house.

"He's going to have to come out of the front door," Marcus noted for what must have been the fourth time.

"I know," Melissa replied, looking at the group of men with some concern. "If they spot him, they'll drag him off for looting,"

Emily leant back against the wall of the alley and sighed. "So what do you want us to do?"

Marcus chewed his lip and stared back at the guards, ideas forming and reforming in his mind. "Look, he may try to climb the wall,"

"He can fall from it," Emily noted, "But he had to have your help to climb it. It won't have lost height on the other side of the garden,"

"But possibly he'll find something to climb on," Melissa suggested with an optimistic tone of voice. "After all, it's a high wall, but maybe he can stand on something?"

"That's not the way our luck runs," Emily countered with a matter of fact note to her voice. "In fact I think we should operate under the assumption that he can't climb the wall," She glanced up at Marcus and was gratified to see that he nodded his head. "That way if he can climb the wall then it's good, but at least we have a back up if he can't,"

Melissa nodded and joined Emily in leaning against the wall. "So what do we do? I think we've established that I'm useless at distraction,"

"What about a fire?" Marcus asked, looking across at Emily. "We set fire to one of the empty houses along the street, it draws them away and gives Justin enough time to escape,"

"I don't know Marcus, fire can be problematic. " Emily hedged, remembering the Great Fire of London with a shudder.

"You don't have to start a fire," Melissa added. "Just the smoke,"

"That's actually a good idea," Emily conceded with some reluctance. "All we need to do is set some green twigs on fire in a metal bucket, push it into the hallway of an empty property and raise the alarm."

"Enough smoke should definitely get their attention and if we make enough noise, they should leave that doorway long enough for Justin to leave,"

Emily gave a smile that was pure mischief. "I think this is going to work,"

"The only issue will be warning Justin," Melissa continued, glancing at the other girl with a grin.

"Don't worry about that," Emily replied. "Justin has had more than enough experience with improvising," Pushing away from the wall, she turned to face Melissa. "Let's get on with it then,"

Melissa had to admit to a certain level of excitement as they hurried down the Paris streets. In her old life, she would never have become involved in something like this. Despite Emily's constant sneers, she was glad for her company. The blonde had proven herself to be extremely capable, and she was a natural liar. She glanced over at Emily's face and thought once more about the woman's mercurial nature. Most of the slurs that left Emily's lips were not as serious as she made out and, she was almost sure that the woman retreated behind insults in a way to hide.

"What?" Emily caught her staring. Melissa muttered an apology and turned her face to the front. One thing was sure, Emily cared about Justin. Not that she would admit to it and not that it was love, but Melissa was sure she did. It was a relationship that had concerned Melissa for the first ten years. That Justin and Emily had been lovers was not in doubt, yet they had not been so for some time. But Melissa still compared herself to the vivacious blonde. In addition to stunning looks, Emily had a confident personality with a mile wide ruthless streak. In comparison to her, Melissa felt bland and uninspiring, and she wondered what Justin saw when he glanced her way. Not that she thought she was a total loss but next to Emily she was almost as dull as dishwater.

"Hey," Emily's voice dragged her from her thoughts. "Stop wool gathering and pay attention," Melissa glanced up and stared down the street. A patrol of guards in the distance were walking towards her. Glancing quickly to the side, she looked for her companions, annoyed that her brother had failed to drag her into hiding.

"Over here idiot," Emily's voice sounded to her right, and she stared down the nearby alleyway. Marcus leaned out from behind cover and waved her closer.

"You could have said. " Melissa grumbled as she moving into hiding next to her brother.

"We did," Marcus replied with a chuckle as Melissa glowered at him.

"Traitor," She grumbled. "You're supposed to be on my side,"

"I am," Marcus replied. "But when you're wrong, I'm neutral." She thought about slapping him, but Emily hissed at them to be quiet. They stayed hidden in the shadows as the guards moved past their position.

"Now you can babble," Emily noted with a grouchy tone to her voice. "Have you never had to stay silent for any length of time before?"

Melissa and Marcus glanced at each other but said nothing. Emily sighed and threw up her hands in exasperation. "Fine... Keep talking, bring the wrath of the local judiciary down on our heads. It'll only mean decapitation and burial,"

"We aren't making the noise now," Melissa noted, a slight smug look on her face.

Marcus sighed and looked heavenward. Emily and Melissa seemed to delight in baiting each other and though he loved his sister, he wasn't blind to her faults. Emily on the other hand, he glanced across at her and stepped forward, interceding before things escalated.

"I think we should get going. "

"Quite right," Marcus started as Emily reached forward and took hold of his arm. "Justin is depending on us," Emily's fingers were warm as they curled possessively about his upper arm. Marcus stared down at the delicate digits, making no effort to remove them as a pleasant thrill rippled through his body at her touch. From Melissa's outraged expression he knew he ought to pull away, but he didn't particularly want to. Emily fascinated him, despite her transparent efforts to irritate his sister.

"Are we going? Melissa uttered through gritted teeth. She wasn't sure what upset her more, the sight of Emily dangling from her brother's arm, or the fact that Marcus didn't seem to mind.

"Yes," Emily said as she began walking toward the end of the alley with Marcus in tow. Marcus glanced over his shoulder at her grim, unsmiling visage and mouthed 'Sorry' as Emily pulled him with her into the street.

"Yes, very sincere, brother dearest'" Melissa grumbled to herself as she followed them onto the main street. "Like you made any effort to get away from her."

"What was that?" Marcus' voice drifted from up ahead.

"Absolutely nothing," Melissa called back, unwilling to give Emily the satisfaction of seeing how much her appropriation of Marcus hurt her. "Though if you hurt him," she whispered to the back of her head. "I'll rip your throat out."

They progressed along the street. The riots and looting had left debris along every pathway and each of the grand homes were empty with boards covering their windows. Melissa shuddered as a chill breeze whispered through her hair and sent shivers down her back.

"We're here," Emily announced as she drew to a stop before one of the smaller timber framed buildings. "Time to set a fire,"

Justin managed to pry open the panel and stared into the small space beyond. The book that Corbeaux had been so proud to show him was jammed inside, the battered leather cover curling slightly at the edges. Barely drawing a breath, he drew the thick, bound tome free. As the heavy book was drawn into the light, something fell from its pages and landed on the carpet. Justin bent forward and picked up the scrap of parchment. The surface of the paper was rough, and the freshly scratched words were uneven and blotted.

Our Lady of Reims....

He glanced at the rough writing in puzzlement before turning the paper over to stare at the back. A small image, faint with age, caught his attention. It was a woodcut and the details, while indistinct, caught his attention like nothing else. It was a picture of a stained glass window and in the centre of the image as clear as a bell, the motif of the black lotus flower stood out proudly. A wild exultant thrill thrummed through his body as he stared at the small piece of paper. This could be the break though he had been looking for. This small scrap of parchment represented the best hope he'd had in two hundred years and a buzz of excitement thrummed through his body as he stared at the thin and fragile slip in his fingers. With careful movements he placed the paper securely within the pages of the book and then he looked down at the battered leather cover, itching to find out the secrets it held. He did not know how long he stood there in the ruins of Corbeaux's parlour, the small book clutched gingerly to his chest. He wanted to open the cracked leather cover, wanted desperately to read what lay in the yellowing pages, yet he could not. It was not safe, not here where enemies could break in at any time. With some reluctance he pushed the book into an inside pocket on his coat and out of sight. After he checked for anything he may have missed, he walked back to the kitchen. A glance out of the rear windows revealed that there was no way of scaling the wall from this side and there was no other exit from the house aside from the front door. He was on his third pass though the house when he heard the call of fire from the street. A small smile flickered across his lips as he rushed to the window. He would be willing to bet that Emily was behind the distraction. Moving to the boarded window, he pressed his eye against one of the cracks and stared out.

The guards that had been stood opposite the house were gone, running, he presumed, along the street toward the cry of fire. He waited a few more moments before quietly opening the main door and slipping out into the street. Reaching the road, he quickly checked in both directions, looking for the smoke that he was certain was there. He would expect Emily to provide a physical blaze rather than just scream 'Fire'. With a knowing grin, he caught sight of the column of smoke and with casual, unhurried steps, he moved away from the house and back towards the centre of Paris.

The green wood provided plenty of dark smoke. The metal bucket was placed in the upper floor window of one of the more derelict buildings, the height ensuring that the smoke could be seen from further away. As soon as they had lit the branches, the small group had left the scene as rapidly as possible, moving out of the area without waiting to see what the guards would do.

"What if they don't come to check out the flames?"

Melissa asked as they moved through the alleys and away.

"They will," Emily assured. "People always come to check out a fire," She spoke with the assurance of experience.

As a group they moved through the alleys, avoiding the wide open streets and possible discovery. Like much of the rest of Paris, the streets were filled with hurrying fear filled people and the sign of revolution was proudly displayed on every corner. Emily led the way in silence, her assured steps leading them through the rabbit warren of streets. Hurrying after her, Melissa slipped on the slick cobblestones and almost fell.

"I've got you," Marcus caught hold of her arm and arrested her fall before she slammed painfully into the floor.

"Do you think he found something?" Melissa whispered as they prepared to move again. "Do you think this book has the key?" The quaver in her voice betrayed a painful sense of hope.

"Don't count on it," Emily warned without glancing over her shoulder. "When you've been with Justin as long as I have, you'll know how to deal with these bursts of false hope," Bitterness laced her tones and Melissa glanced at her sharply. "Don't give me that look," Emily snapped at her with an irritation that she could not fully understand. "Wait until you've lived through several of these..." The sound of approaching footsteps stilled her tongue and as one they crouched back into the shadows, hardly daring to breathe. The silhouettes of a small group of men moved past the end of the alley and stopped.

"Ah, hell," Emily whispered.

Melissa shrank back against the wall of the alley and closed her eyes. Intellectually she knew that she couldn't be hurt permanently, but she still feel the pain and her donor would take the scars. A hollow feeling burned within her chest as she thought about the guard trapped in the cellar. He did not deserve what was to happen to him, and she would spare him if she could. Memories of losing her eye to John twenty years ago still tormented her. Though she had been able to see again, her donor had almost died from shock, and she had no desire to inflict such torment again. Even though she tried to choose her victims from the more unpleasant members of society, she still thought of herself as a murderer. At times, she wished she had the strength to stop siphoning the life from others, yet each time she had tried, the pain had been unbearable. Luckily she had not taken enough wounds to actually die, despite Emily's assurance that she would.

"All clear," Her eyes snapped open, and she followed the others across the main road and into another alley, thoughts buzzing through her head like angry flies. Resigned as she was to this life, she grasped hold of any chance for a better outcome. Hope, even false hope, was her only chance of staying sane.

The small group walked back into the more populous areas of Paris and slowly relaxed as the walked through the swelling crowds towards their rendezvous spot on one of the bridges overlooking the Seine. Settling down on the river bank, they watched the flow of humanity with detached silence, waiting for the last of their number to arrive. The sun was warm and a light breeze pleasantly blew across their faces, banishing the fear for a brief time.

"So where are we going after this?" Melissa asked after several moments of silence.

"Stuttgart?" Emily suggested with a lazy wave.

"My German is awful," Melissa retaliated. "How about Madrid or Barcelona?"

"I hate Spain," Emily responded, dismissing the suggestion with and airy wave. "And I don't own any property or have any assets out there, and I don't think Justin has either,"

"We're going to Reims," They turned as Justin came into view. A broad smile lit Melissa's face and she rushed into his arms. Relief flooded through her as he pulled her into a solid, comforting embrace. "Don't say you were concerned?" He whispered as he looked down at her, gentle mockery in his tones.

"Not a bit," Melissa replied in lightly joking tones. She pulled back and stared him full in the face, trying to hide the emotion surging through her.

"Before you two get diverted," Emily interrupted as she moved to stand next to them. "Why are we going to Reims?"

Justin turned to face her with a joyous smile. "Because Emily, I've finally found something,"

CHAPTER 29

"Are you going to let me go?" The former prison guard stared up at Melissa's face, his face pale in the dim cellar light. "Please?" Melissa bit her lip as the plaintive plea tore at her heart. Guilt and regret warred raged through her as she looked at the bound man who was to be her donor. Behind her and to the left, lay the donors for her brother and Justin, both men who had committed the most heinous of crimes. She felt only slight pity for them, yet this man laid at her feet was different to those others. He was no rapist or murderer. A soldier? Yes. A killer certainly, but cruel? She looked down at his broken face, wrigglings of pity twisting through her thoughts. He did not appear to be cruel. He was undeserving of the pain and wretched death that was sure to greet him. And yet, she knew he couldn't be allowed to walk free, he could not be allowed to draw attention to them.

"I...I can't," She stammered out finally, looking away from the man's face as she destroyed his hopes. "I can't,"

"I won't tell anyone about you," He reached out as best he could and tried to catch hold of her wrist, yet his bound frame sent him crashing to the floor before he could reach her. "Please?" His voice was quiet, pleading, she tried to close her ears and heart to him, yet thoughts of remorse echoed deep within her. The desire to free this one innocent man from the horror that she was about to visit on him, burned so brightly that it almost hurt. The man sank back to the floor, quietly sobbing. Melissa watched for a few moments longer before finally glancing down at the locket clasped within her hand. With the man's broken sobs echoing loudly in her ears, she opened the locket and tore her nail through the man's picture held within. As her fingernail ripped the image, the cold snap of the breaking connection rushed through her. She staggered back, gooseflesh breaking out across her skin as the achingly familiar nausea welled up from within. She returned the lotus to the depths of her pocket as she turned to face the man on the floor.

Tne man looked up, his sobs ceased by wonderment as he looked at the dark haired woman sway crazily before him. Taking several deep shuddering breaths, she looked down at the bound figure and whispered. "I'm going to untie you and let you go..." Comprehension drifted into his gaze as he watched her approach and a hopeful, eager gleam lit his eyes. She hunkered down beside him and reached for the knotted ropes with trembling hands. In silence, she released the bonds, red weals laced his skin and he sighed with relief, slumping forward as the blood rushed back into his numb hands. The man began to flex his wrists, watching Melissa as she bent down to untie his legs. She had undone one knot when the man moved. She felt his muscles tense a moment before it happened. As she untied the last of the bonds on his legs, her former captive launched himself toward her, drawing back his fist in a fast, hard strike to her face. Stunned by the speed of the attack, Melissa felt her nose break as the blow snapped her head back and sent her to the floor. Hitting the ground in a dazed heap, she looked up and through a haze of pain and tears, watched him approach. The man's face was twisted with rage and she cursed her stupidity as he reached her side and slammed his foot into her side. A choking cough escaped her lips as the right side of her body exploded into pain from the kick.

"Bitch," Even seething with rage, the man was clever enough not to scream at her and draw the attention of the others. She would have appreciated his swiftness of thought, had he not been in the process of beating her. His foot slammed into her side again and she rolled over, trying to reach her pocket and the brooch. "Oh no you don't," He hissed as he reached down and pulled her upright, wrapping his hands about her throat. The calloused fingers pressed hard against the skin of her neck and she felt the pressure building. She was struggling to breathe, the air her lungs so desperately needed denied by the unrelenting torment of his fingers. Her vision started to fade and blur as she felt herself falling into a deep impenetrable darkness.

The man threw her limp body to the floor and bent down, looking for the object of his enslavement. He had barely begun to search through her pockets before the noise of footsteps from the room beyond distracted him. Leaving the dead body on the floor, he rushed to the low cellar window and pushed it open. As the door to the room opened, he scrambled through the small gap, panic and fear driving him on.

"Wait here a minute, I'll get her," Emily's voice drifted through from the doorway as the man frantically squeezed himself through the narrow gap. Emily's footsteps sounded on the cellar steps as he pulled his legs through the window. Turning back to the window, he gently drew it closed as he watched the other woman descend the stairs into the dimly lit room.

"Come on Melissa, it's time to go," She announced, taking the last few steps two at a time. "We need to get started if we want to get to Reims in good..." The man didn't wait to see any more. The blonde had just spotted the body and he didn't have long. Resisting every urge to run headlong away from the building, he moved back away as quietly as he could, hoping to sneak away before they went after him. He could only hope that he made it to a village before they caught up.

"You bloody fool," He heard the blonde's snarling

words and he moved faster. He hoped that they would be too caught up in the woman's death to follow him straightaway.

"Marcus, Justin!" Emily calls back up the stairs as she bent over Melissa's prone body and slapped her face twice.

"What?" Justin poked his head around the door.

"Get Marcus," Emily rapped out the instructions with the air of a sergeant major. "We have an escapee," Justin started to walk down the stairs, but she waved him back impatiently. "Find him first then worry about the love of your life. I really don't want to be running from an angry mob now,"

Justin's mouth twitched in a rueful smile. "Whatever you say," He called back as he walked back into the parlour, looking for Melissa's brother.

Emily listened to his fading footsteps move away from the cellar door before she returned to Melissa's side. "Wake up you bloody idiot," She slapped her lifeless body once more as she waited for her to wake.

The sensation of dying was distinctly unpleasant, Melissa concluded as she slowly began to rise from the fog that surrounded her. She could feel and hear Emily stood beside her but the sensations were muted as though she were wrapped in a suffocating blanket of wool. With some effort, she managed to open her eyes, blinking at the strange mist that clouded her vision. As Emily bent over her, she tried to push herself upright, but her arms struggled to work. It was as though she had become an observer trapped in a solid, unmoving form of flesh, which if she had to guess, she had. She tried once again, forcing her dead muscles to obey the commands she was screaming at them. Slowly, torturously, her body began to move. Emily watched her struggle with no comment and no assistance. As she pulled herself into a sitting position, Melissa wondered why Justin had not come to sit with her, for this, her first death. She would have shuddered at the thought but normal bodily responses did not seem to function as they should.

"Serve you right," Emily finally spoke as Melissa finished dragging herself into an upright position.

"I..." Melissa stopped speaking, stunned at the ruined sound of her voice.

Emily hunkered down beside her. "I know," She said in a falsely bright tone. "You took one look at his poor lost soul face and decided to let him go,"

If she could have slapped Emily's smug little face just then, she would have done. After a few experimental attempts to make her voice work, she finally spoke "He wasn't a bad man... He hadn't done anything to deserve this,"

"No he hadn't," Emily conceded. "But you're going to have to kill him anyway," She continued to talk, oblivious to the look of shock on Melissa's face. "You're now dead and you can't continue to be dead, so rather than keep the poor sod tied up but alive, you're now going to have to kill him,"

"Couldn't we have just let him go?" Melissa pleaded after a long moment of silence. Despite what he had done to her, despite the wounds, she still did not wish to cause his death.

"Are you really this naive?" Emily asked, anger fuelling her words. "No. We can't just let him go," She waved a hand at Melissa's useless body. "And you're the perfect example as to why," Sinking to her knees, she caught hold of Melissa's hand and waved it slowly through the air while Melissa struggled to regain control of her limbs. "He tried to kill you, which means he's going to be heading out to the nearest town and sending people our way," She sank back into a crouch and continued. "He only has to tell them that we're aristocrats or enemies of the revolution, and that's it. Do you think we can move fast with them?" She indicated the tied and unconscious bodies behind them. "You'd better hope that Justin and Marcus pick him up before he runs into others,"

Melissa looked down, guilt gnawing at her as she listened to Emily's words. She watched a beetle crawl across the packed mud floor through the strange film that now covered her vision. Emily was right, but then when wasn't she? A flare of anger spiked through her as she turned her head away from the black chitin clad creature and back towards her companion. Emily sighed and sat down, her blue eyes searching Melissa's face. "I understand why you did it," She said in a softer, gentler tone. "We've all had to wrestle with our conscience over the years," With a gentle flick of her fingers she knocked the beetle away from Melissa's legs before re-focusing on the reclining woman before her. "I would like nothing better than to stop hurting people, but this curse won't let us. I've tried not to drain others but the pain is…" She closed her eyes as she focused on old memories. "Too much," Melissa opened her mouth to speak, as Emily held up her hand to silence her. "I've even tried standing in the middle of a pyre, hoping to end this," She gave a humourless laugh. "I stood there in agony whilst the flesh peeled from my skin to the bone, but still I lived. I had to find someone to take that death," Melissa thought about placing a hand on her shoulder, but she was not sure how she would take it. In the forty years she had known the woman, she had never heard her talk like this. "I daresay I could have gone to live in a cave but that gets awfully lonely. As long as you take care of yourself, there is no reason to kill your donors," A short laugh escaped her lips. "Hell you could even have them be your donor and not realise it. Such is the power of laudanum and alcohol,"

"I didn't know," Melissa uttered softly, her tortured vocal chords rendering any amount of volume difficult.

"Yes you did," Emily disagreed almost pleasantly with her. "You just didn't understand properly," She gave a groan and stood up. "Now you do," She reached down a hand and dragged Melissa to her feet. "You will do what you have to in order to survive. You can find those most deserving of this fate but you can't let one loose as it threatens us all," She helped Melissa into the remains of a chair and leant back against one of the walls of the cellar. "How did he overpower you?"

"He struck me," Melissa answered, puzzled by the almost comforting tone of the conversation. "Kicked me and then throttled me.”

“Hmm,” Emily thought for a moment before speaking. “Has Justin taught you how to fight?”

“No,” Melissa replied. “Should he have?”

“Certainly,” The blonde continued. “I daresay he doesn’t think you’ll ever be without his protection,” She said the last with a mocking sneer. “I think he’s a fool and that you should know how to defend yourself,”

“I’ll ask him,” Melissa replied, annoyed with Emily’s sneering attitude. Yes she would like to know how to fight and whilst Justin was protective, she was sure he would accomodate her request.

“You could,” Emily said. “Or you could let me teach you,”

“You?” Melissa responded with some outrage. “You hate me,”

“I don’t hate you,” Emily pushed herself away from the wall and walked closer to Melissa. “I think you’re naive and a little simple but I don’t hate you,”

“Thank you I think,” Melissa tried once again to stand but her limbs responded with the speed of treacle, and she stopped. “So why do you want to teach me?”

“Because I can teach you the moves that Justin can’t,” Emily said, becoming bored with the whole conversation. “And I think you should know how to defend yourself. Don’t expect us to be the best of friends, but I will make sure you’re ready,” She pushed herself away from the wall and looked down at Melissa. “Fair enough?”

Melissa thought for a moment. Justin would teach her,

of that she was sure, but he wouldn't push her as strongly as Emily would. He would always be aware that he could hurt her, and he would pull back. On the other hand, Emily would have no compunction about damaging her, if she thought Melissa would learn something. The only negative was dealing with Emily's attitude, and she was sure she could put up with that for a short time.

"Alright," She said, resigning herself to spending more time in her company. "Teach me,"

Emily smiled and held out a hand. 'The first lesson," She said as she caught hold of Melissa's hand. "Is how to move your body when it's like this,"

Justin dragged the unconscious body of the guard back through the ruins of the tavern door and stopped. Sounds of laughter drifted up from the cellar door, and he raised an eyebrow, confused by the noise.

"What's wrong?" Marcus called from behind as he let go of the man's feet.

"Listen," Justin answered as he continued to drag the heavy man through the hall and into the taproom. At the doorway, Marcus took two steps forward and stopped, a puzzled look chasing across his features.

"Is that?" He glanced over at Justin, incredulity in his gaze.

"I do believe it is," Justin dropped his burden to the floor and crossed the room to the cellar steps. He pushed the cellar door open a little more and the sounds of female laughter drifted up to greet them. Justin let the door close and turned to face Marcus. "I don't believe I'm ready to face that," He walked past the other man and back into the taproom.

"Coward," Marcus gave a chuckle as he opened the door to the cellar and began to walk down the steps.

"I should say so," Justin called after him. "That's my current and ex lover giggling in there. I'll lay you any odds; I'm the subject of that conversation,"

Marcus suppressed his laughter as he walked down the steps and towards the dim light of the cellar. The sound of laughter diminished slightly as he moved closer and leant over the banister, checking out the situation before he stepped any further.

Emily and Melissa were stood in the middle of the room. Emily's arms were wrapped about Melissa's waist, holding her upright as she tried to walk. It was a decidedly surreal sight, considering that the two women could usually barely stand each other. A rueful smile touched his lips as he waited for an appropriate moment to descend the stairs.

"I can't believe Justin did that," Melissa's voice drifted up to him and he stared to descend the rickety steps.

"He did," Emily finished with a chuckle. "I doubt you'll have that problem," Marcus moved closer as Emily continued. "Try again," Marcus stopped and leant over the bannister, curiosity overriding manners. Emily's voice was encouraging, almost helpful. Resting his chin on the balustrade, he continued to watch. "Force of will is paramount here," Emily continued. "You have to assert yourself a little more. Command your body to move the way you want,"

"You mean it won't move unless I think about it?" Melissa tried following her advice and focused on her legs. She felt silly, thinking about walking but Emily was being quite insistent.

"Quite correct," Emily replied. She stepped away from Melissa, releasing the hold she had on her waist. As she removed her support, Melissa staggered and almost fell. "Remember you have control of your own body," Emily encouraged as she watched Melissa tottered forward. "Just focus on your limbs,"

Melissa tried to nod, but her head lolled to one side and flopped forward. With a sigh of irritation, she concentrated on looking up. It was difficult, as though she were controlling a puppet with half its strings cut. Slowly, agonisingly slowly, her head lifted, and she stared at her destination as she willed her legs to move. The feeling of disconnection had not lessened, yet she focused on forcing herself forward. With each footfall, she found it easier to command her limbs to move, yet the strange swaddled sensation persisted. Slowly with lumbering, jerking motions she walked forward.

"Better," Emily commented as she watched Melissa lumber towards the wall. "So when do you think your brother is going to join us?" She turned her gaze to the staircase and fixed Marcus with a challenging glare. "Don't you know its rude to eavesdrop,"

"You seemed busy, I didn't want to interrupt," Marcus noted as he stepped back from the rail and continued to walk down the stairs. "We got him,"

"I should hope so," Emily replied with a tiny roll of her eyes. "Even you two couldn't be so inept as to lose someone who only had a minute head start,"

"Oh give it a rest," Melissa croaked as she moved towards them. "I guess I'll have to..." She couldn't finish the sentence, guilt and shame flooding through her at the thought.

"Unless of course you want to run round like a corpse," Emily countered brightly, all trace of friendliness gone from her voice.

"Of course not," Melissa retaliated, managing to manifest some annoyance through the ruins of her windpipe. "I'm just not too happy about being a murderer,"

"If it makes you feel any better you can call it suicide," Emily returned brightly. "He strangled you himself,"

"That doesn't help," Marcus finally broke into the conversation, hoping to head off another argument. "Don't you have any sympathy at all?"

Emily gave a huff of impatience and walked past him toward the stairs. "Sympathy yes," She called out over her shoulder as she mounted the stairs. "The desire to mollycoddle?" She stopped at the basement exit. "No," And with that she left the dank dark of the cellar.

"I think you upset her," Melissa uttered, her words barely audible

"I'm not sure if you can upset her," Marcus replied with a smile. "Come on let's get you upstairs,"

"I don't know if I want to," Melissa whispered.

Marcus stopped moving and placed his arm around his

sister's shoulders. "Come on Melly, we'll get this out of the way and then go to Reims. With any luck, we'll find a cure,"

Allowing Marcus to lead her from the dark of the basement, Melissa focused on the trip to come. She did not think she could continue like this. How had any of the others managed over the years? Not for the first time, she wished she had never set eyes on Justin Lestrade. While she would not want to lose the love and freedom that she had longed for, she could quite do without it if she no longer had to live like the leech she now was.

CHAPTER 30

The cart rattled into Reims just as the sun was setting. Marcus and Justin sat on top of the cart, leaving the two girls to ride within. Despite the increased military presence on the roads, it had been a relatively easy trip from the outskirts of Paris. With each mile they travelled, Justin's enthusiasm had grown and he was positively buoyant with good humour as they drove through the darkening streets. Marcus was driving the cart as Justin made the most of the dwindling light and read some more of the book he had retrieved.

"Have you discovered anything?" Marcus asked as he slowed down to a crawl along the packed roads.

"Possibly," Justin closed the book and stowed it out

of sight. He did not wish to draw any undue attention to their cart by reading. People shuffled past them on the street, eyes blank and weary; here and there he could see revolutionaries, bold in manner and dress. They could not afford to attract further attention, not with the cargo they carried. He looked ahead, the cathedral loomed before him, its stained glass windows glimmering amber with the rays of the dying sun. "Better not go there tonight," Justin continued as he began hunting for a local inn. "With all that Reims stood for, I'm surprised it's still standing,"

"What do we do about...?" Marcus indicated the three sacks that were lying prone on the floor of the cart.

"We'll find something," Justin assured. "We've had a fair bit of practice at this," Justin turned round in his seat and called across to Emily. "Time to go to work," Emily snapped upright from her light doze and glared at him.

"And what about Melissa?" She snapped back. "I'm not doing all the bloody work,"

"Oh for the love of all that's holy..." Justin hissed in exasperation. "Can't you just do what I ask?"

"I'll go," Melissa volunteered, stepping in before Emily could speak. "What do we need?"

"I'm not sure you're up to it yet," Melissa froze as the words left his mouth, she recalled Emily's jibes from earlier and anger at his cavalier dismissal of her worth seared her. Her lips pursed into an obstinate line and she stood.

"Then it's time I learnt," Justin winced at her curt manner as she clambered over the side of the cart and dropped to the ground. He opened his mouth but Marcus shook his head, familiar with his sister's moods and temperament. Justin settled back in the coachman's seat as Melissa asked. "So... what do we need?"

"We need some storage space," Emily called out. "Preferably somewhere quiet with escape routes,"

"Alright," Melissa agreed quickly. "I'll find something,"

"I'll go with you," Marcus offered, preparing to step down.

"No," Melissa held up her hand, halting his progress. "It's time I learnt to do this on my own," She backed away from the cart as she spoke. "Stay near the market, I'll find you,"

"Melissa," She glanced up at Justin and he bowed his head beneath the weight of her stare. "Good luck," He finally said, cowed by the challenge in her gaze.

"Thank you," Melissa walked away from the cart and into the crowd. It wouldn't take her long to find somewhere for them to hide, but that was not the only reason for leaving the group.

She ducked through an alley and out of sight, allowing her anger to carry her. It had been forty years and he still treated her as a fragile piece of glass. She kicked at pebbles as she strode along the cobbled street, ignoring the filth that choked the gutters. It burned her that Emily was right to some degree. She envied the blonde's easy freedom, the way she made her own way through life. Taking a deep breath she moved out of the alley and onto a wider concourse, keeping her eyes peeled for somewhere to stop. Ahead she saw the looming bulk of the cathedral, it buttresses bronzed by the light of the setting sun and she came to a stop. This was where they had to go. There was some information held within its stained glass. Raising her hand, she rubbed her chin in thought, debating her options. She could wait with the others and go in the morning, or she could take the initiative and go now. It was something that Emily would do. She couldn't see her waiting for permission or assistance, in fact she would laugh at the idea.

Time to go to work.

Justin's words burned in her mind, reminding her that he deferred to Emily, that he expected more of her. Emily was considered capable in Justin's eyes and what did that mean for her? Was she only a fragile ornament, decorative and useless? Decision already made, she pressed on, heading for the cathedral, determined to do something useful for once. The crowds thinned out as she reached the stone edifice. It loomed above her, casting a long shadow over her as the light dwindled. She approached the door, looking at the windows set above as she walked closer. As the windows became harder to see, she looked ahead. The door was open and the small figures carved on either sides of the entrance had been vandalised, each one was missing its head. Hoping that the destruction wrought by the revolutionaries did not continue inside, she squared her shoulders and walked through the open doors to the dim, cool interior. Ruddy light poured through the rose window behind her, casting the nave and the heavy wooden pews in fading multicoloured light. She turned back to face the entrance, staring at the ornate stained glass in the large rose windows. The scale of the windows awed her and she felt her heart sink. How could she be expected to find just one image amongst the myriad that must be here?

"May I help you miss?" She started at the noise. A wizened old priest shuffled forward, taper held in his aged hands.

"Yes," She took a half pace forward. "I'm looking for a design in one of the stained glass windows,"

"At this time?" The priest lit one of the candelabras as he spoke. "The stained glass here is quite exquisite but there is little daylight left, you would not be able to appreciate it fully this evening,"

"I know," Melissa bowed her head and continued. "I've only just arrived and we're moving on tomorrow so..." She shrugged. "I won't get much of a chance to see this in daylight,"

"Very well," The priest lit another candelabrum and turned to face her. "So which window captures your interest? The Rose window is exquisite,"

"I can see," Melissa replied, remembering to smile as she spoke. "And I would love to investigate it further, however, today I'm looking for one of the smaller windows," She looked away from the main window, struggling to recall the few details that Justin had told them. For a moment, she regretted running off on her own. But she was here now, and she kept going, determined to discover something without the help of Justin or the irritating blonde. "I was informed that one of the windows showed a design of a lotus flower,"

The priest pursed his lips and thought for a moment. Rubbing his gnarled hands across his chin, he nodded towards the apse. "This way,"

Elated, Melissa followed his slow moving form across the flagstones. The sound of her steps echoed across the space, and she looked down, reading the dedications that were carved into the floor.

"What's that?" She asked as they stepped across a defaced piece of floor. Unlike the damage at the door, this act of vandalism seemed older.

"There was the image of a labyrinth there," He informed her after a brief glance over his shoulder. "It was removed about ten or so years ago,"

"Ahh," Melissa looked down at the ruined floor and wondered why the image had been removed. A strange hot feeling coursed over her skin as she looked at the damaged stone. Something nagged at the edge of her thoughts, but she couldn't quite grasp what it was.

"Here," The priest stopped before a set of stained glass windows. The altar stood directly behind her, yet these windows were dirty and unkempt, the light barely highlighting the details of the glass. She peered at the windows, heart pounding as she focused on the detailed images before her. Through the grime that smeared each panel of glass she could see what she had come for. Directly before her and set dead centre in old faded colour was a representation of the brooch she held in her pocket. As though in a dream she walked forward, raising her hand to reach the images that were above her.

"Do you..." She turned back to the priest, her voice thick with emotion. "Do you know anything about this?"

"In what way?" The priest answered carefully, looking at Melissa with concern.

"Who designed it?" Melissa asked, trying to contain her eagerness. "Are there any stories attached to it?" She glanced up at the ceiling. "What's it meant to represent?"

"I'm not entirely sure I can help," The priest replied. "I can certainly tell you what I know,"

"Oh would you?" Melissa simpered. She took one last look at the panel and followed the priest into a small ante chamber. The priest sat down and gestured at her to sit opposite. Backlit by the light of the dying sun, the priest's face was in shadow as he leant forward to speak.

"Well there isn't much I can tell you about the creator of that pane of glass," Melissa sagged, her enthusiasm and hope vanishing as he spoke. "But," The priest held up his finger, forestalling any questions. "That doesn't mean, I don't have any knowledge of it or indeed any tales of its construction,"

Melissa tried not to shuffle with impatience as the priest began a meandering story concerning the re-creation of the cathedral following an earlier fire. The sun set as the priest droned on and he lit the candles on the desk. As the priest continued to speak, Melissa began to tune out, his voice almost sending her to sleep.

"Now the story goes," Jolting back to the conversation, Melissa waited with fresh eagerness for whatever information that the man could impart. "That particular piece of glass was a special commission. I don't know who designed it, I just know that someone offered a great deal of money for its inclusion,"

"Do you know why?" She asked, trying hard to keep desperation out of her voice.

"Well the tale goes that it is part of the quest for the Grail," Melissa managed, with some difficulty, to keep from rolling her eyes. A grail quest, was that all he could tell her? Disappointment, sour and galling rose in her gut and she swallowed, trying to prevent the feeling of defeat from showing on her face.

"In what way?" She forced herself to ask the question, hoping that there was some information that she could use from this standard story.

"I'm glad you asked," The priest seemed eager to speak now, the supposed interest of his audience spurring him on. "The story goes, a young knight returning from the crusades paid for the construction of the window in the hope that the path to eternity could be undone,"

Melissa tilted her head to one side and considered. It did sound like the beginnings of any standard grail quest, but the path to eternity could also refer to the brooches. A little more intrigued now, she focused once more on the old man and urged him to continue.

"Well, he gave the exact design of the window, paid enough for it and left the words..." The priest cleared his throat and intoned the next words as though he were in a play. "Follow the sunlight on the petals till the way is hidden, then descend into the dark for the next," He finished his speech and sank back against the chair, clearly tired by the recent bout of excitement.

"Follow the sunlight on the petals..." Melissa mused quietly, thinking about the words. It was possible that she would have to wait until daybreak in order to continue unless...She looked up at the priest and asked. "Are there any sunrays or sun depicted on the glass?"

"Yes..." The priest answered. "Of course people have tried to search for the grail before now, but none has succeeded," Holding in a bark of derisive laughter, Melissa tried to focus on the problem in hand. It were possible that early hunters could have already found the second clue, the hint wasn't entirely cryptic and if she could decipher it the others could as well.

"Can I take another look at the glass?"

"Of course," The priest smiled and stood up. Leading her back into the main body of the cathedral, he looked at the deepening shadows and frowned. "I need to finish lighting the candles in the nave," He glanced across at Melissa and continued. "Will you be alright on your own?"

"I will thank you," Relief flooded her as she heard the priest's words. She could now examine the window in relative privacy. She watched the old man walk away before she headed to the window.

The glass was filthy, centuries of muck and grime hiding the full image from her. Reaching down, she pulled free the flask of wine from her belt and soaked a small strip of fabric that she tore from her petticoat. Holding the wine soaked rag in her fingers, she clambered onto a small ledge jutting out from the wall beneath the window. Balancing herself precariously on the lip of stone, she reached up and wiped as much of the dirt from the window as she could. Bit by bit and aided by the alcohol in the wine, the true image of the glass slowly revealed itself. The glass lotus was as dark as the one she held within her pocket and so detailed that she could almost see the design of a hinge on the left-hand side. She took a breath as she wiped further, revealing a design of sunrays against an azure sky. She stopped cleaning to stare at the design with some interest. Several of the rays seemed more prominent than the others, and she mentally repeated the priest's words as she pondered the design. Stuck for inspiration, she decided to continue cleaning the window and there, tucked away in the corner of the window, a tiny compass stood out proudly from the grime. Glancing between the compass and the rays, she deciphered the direction they were pointing. Determining that the rays pointed Northeast, she was about to leave when she looked closer. Beneath the design of the lotus and almost indistinct, was the image of a double-headed gryphon. Leaning back from the window, she stepped off the ledge and looked at the newly cleaned window. Now that the images stood out, she could clearly make out a thin line linking the images of the lotus and the gryphon. The significance of the Gryphon image eluded her and she leant back against a pillar to ponder the problem.

"Are you done Miss?" The priest approached, finally finished with lighting the cathedral. The soft warm glow of candles dispelled the deep shadows about the nave, the light lending a cheery glow to the place.

"Yes thank you," She took one last look at the window. The lotus loomed in the corner of the window, chilling her skin. "The stained glass is wonderful," She uttered as she turned away, hoping to keep the priest's attention from the window. The lotus was a signpost to her and those who shared her curse, it would not do to bring attention to it.

"Yes we are very proud of the stained glass here," The priest agreed as Melissa joined him. "Reims is the finest cathedral in France," They began to walk away from the window. "Of course it was even more splendid before..." he stopped and gave a rueful smile. "But that was the past," He fell silent as they reached the nave and the regimented rows of pews.

"I'm just going to pray for a few moments," She said in what she hoped was a pious voice.

"Of course my child," He turned away from her and returned to the altar, busying himself with the candles and goblets. Melissa sat for a few moments, head bowed as she thought about the stained glass window. She should sort out the accommodation and then inform the others. Yet that thought rankled, she had done most of the work on this and she certainly didn't want Emily to take the glory from her. She closed her eyes, imagining the look on Justin's face when she brought him the next step towards a cure. In that instant, she made up her mind. She would leave the cathedral and follow the clues that the window had laid out for her. Standing, she headed towards the exit.

Leaving the cathedral, she turned right and retraced her

steps to the window. She knew that the door faced west, so finding Northeast was reasonably easy. She ignored the little voice that insisted she return to the others and gather help. Louder than the voice of caution was the desire to beat the blonde in matters of daring. If Emily could manage such feats on her own then so could she. Taking stock of the design from the other side of the glass, she turned and followed the first set of directions.

Lamps were being lit as she moved along the dark streets, but beyond being grateful for the light, she barely noticed. Her eyes looked everywhere; to the floor, to sides of buildings and even to the roofs. The mass of humanity passed by ignored as she trod the streets in contemplation. The direct northeast route took her through narrow streets and down dark alleyways, the guttering torches casting long shadows across the rough and lost denizens of such places. She had visited many such alleys during the last forty years, here she had found the hopeless, the wicked and depraved. She stepped over a pair of legs as she remembered those lives she had drained and what she would give to never do it again. Moving over the muck-encrusted cobbles, she turned her mind back to the legend. Part of her rejoiced for the discovery, yet another part, the small pessimistic part, insisted that she was mistaken. Weighed down with thoughts that declared it another wild goose chase, she was about to give up when an ancient stone wall loomed up out of the darkness before her, halting her progress.

"Follow until your way is hidden," She whispered as she began to search about her. The wall and cobbles here were old, possibly as old as the cathedral itself. In the dark however, it was near impossible to see anything. "Descend into the dark…" She began looking at the ground, at anything which could lead her below ground. After minutes of fruitless searching, she threw up her hands in despair and leant back against the wall. It was hopeless, she would have to wait till morning and bring the others with her. It wasn't something she relished, Emily would only steal her thunder. She pushed her hair back from her face and looked up. The veil of cloud released the shining face of a full moon bathing the alley in silvery light. She almost laughed in relief. The bright shimmer of moonlight lit almost as well as daylight. In the ghostly light, she continued to search, hoping to find something, anything. She looked at the wall again, a small mark capturing her attention. Carved into a loose brick was a small design. Leaning in close she traced the image of a double-headed gryphon with her fingers With a growing sense of hope, she began to pull on the brick, hoping to find something hidden beyond it. For several moments, she stood there trying to remove the block. It remained steadfastly embedded in the wall, and she pulled back with a sigh. The brick was definitely loose, but it wouldn't come free. She paced up and down before the wall before deciding to push the brick further in. Nibbling her lip with nerves, she pushed the block into the wall. There was a click and a whole segment of wall opened before her. The hole only reached her hip; she would have to crawl through the opening. Looking into the crawl space beyond, she noted that it angled downhill. Stepping back from the opening, she wondered if she should locate the others, but the entrance was there, and she didn't know how long it would stay open or even if she could close it. Heading back to the main street, she reached up and pulled one of the torches free from the main thoroughfare. Returning to the crawl space, she hunkered down and began to crawl along the narrow corridor. She had gone ten or so paces when her knee pressed something on the floor and the hatchway closed behind her. She stopped moving and backed up, removing her weight from the button. Nothing happened. A sickening sense of dread began to build in her chest. She was alone in a crawlspace, her only light the guttering, ruddy glow of the torch she was holding. Trying hard to control the mounting panic, she moved forward, hoping to reset the button by kneeling on it once more. Her heart sank as there was no click or opening of the entrance. Fear surged through her, and she crawled back to the wall, hoping to prise it open from this side. She hammered uselessly against the stone, the torch smoke making her choke as it guttered close to her face. Fighting back the desire to panic, she glanced back down into the darkness of the crawl space. Crawling down to the unknown darkness with nowhere to escape to was not the most appealing option, but it was the only one she had. Steeling her nerves, she began to crawl again. The torch only lit the next few feet of rough-hewn stone, and its light played havoc with her night vision, but she could not let the torch go. She kept crawling, her hands sustaining cuts and bruises from the jagged floor.

It took an age to crawl from street level and had it not been for her donor she would have been exhausted long before. She was approaching the depths of despair when she finally reached the end of the crawlspace. The tunnel led out into a small room. Dragging herself across out of the small space, she had barely cleared the tunnel before there was a click and the wall sealed up behind her.

"No," She slammed her fists into the wall, the bruises faded as soon as they formed. "No..." She whimpered, collapsing against the now solid wall, tears running down her face as she pounded the wall with her fists. The blows did nothing to the unyielding stone and eventually she stopped, taking deep lungfuls of air as she tried to regain control of herself. Drawing back from the wall, she stared at the button on the floor that she had crawled over. That too was set in the ground and unmoving. She sat back on the floor and rested her head in her hands. After wallowing in self-pity, she shook herself upright and picked up the torch. Standing, she began to explore the space.

The room was square and featureless, the stone wall rough cut and veined with moss. She paced the room with increasing fear as her torch revealed no sign of an exit. The light stole across the floor, highlighting bare stone, blank wall and more moss. It crept into the corners of the room, the ruddy light now moving over shreds of fabric and bone. She covered her cry of alarm with her fist as her torch slowly highlighted two skeletons crumpled on the floor. They lay in the corners of the room, scraps of mouldy fabric still wrapped about their forms. With tentative steps she approached the bones, the sight bringing bile to the back of her throat. Her gaze travelled up the body, the images burning themselves into her mind. Leg bones were still loosely wrapped in rotted scraps of leather, and both ribcages were open to the air. She swallowed back the bitter taste of nausea as the eye holes of the first skeleton stared blankly at her. The stark portrayal of death haunted her and visions of dying of starvation lost and alone burned through her mind, and that was not the worst that tormented her. She would become one of those rag wrapped bundles of bones, but she wouldn't lie still and at peace, for her, there would be starvation and then death followed by years of fully aware decomposition. Blind panic raged through her mind, and she raced back to the walls, hammering on every inch of the cold stone looking for a way free. Her nails tore and reformed as she pulled at every likely crevice in the stone. Exhausted by her bout of terror, she sank back to the floor, sobbing uncontrollably. Long minutes passed until the tears ceased and she sat back, her head sore from the emotion. Pushing unruly tendrils of hair from her face, Melissa stood and began to examine the rest of the room. Moving away from the walls with her torch held high, she soon located something she had not noticed in her haste to find an exit in the walls. In the centre of the room, a short square pedestal of stone lay.

Raising the torch high, she crossed the room to stand before it. The pedestal was built into the floor, and the top had been fashioned into a stone casket. Hope flared into life within her, this could deliver a way out or at least a clue to one. Unlike the rest of the room or indeed the route here, the casket shape was exquisitely carved. She leant closer looking at the carvings with growing anticipation. On closer inspection, each of the four sides depicted lotus flower in many forms. Relief and excitement sang through her bones as she traced each carving with her fingers. After examining the sides, she finally drew her eyes to the top of the casket. There was no visible hinges or lock on the lid, for she could see a fine line where the lid began but set into a small stone disc was a carved shape designed for some small object. Drawing the torch closer to the stone shape, she fixed on the familiar shape with growing exultation. The depression was in the exact shape of the lotus locket that she held within her pocket. With trembling hands she drew forth her brooch and pressed it into the stone space. Whispering a prayer, she turned the locket clockwise. There was a click, and the lid popped open. She held the torch high and gazed within, a hiss of surprise escaping her lips as she stared down at the contents of the stone box. Resting within the aged stone casket was a brooch in the shape of an orchid, blood red and beautifully fashioned from gold and enamel; it lay in the stone glimmering lightly in the torchlight. Conscious of the lotus flower clasped in her hand, she was loath to pick up the small but masterfully carved piece of jewellery. Placing the lotus back into her pocket, she allowed the lid of the casket to fall back. An inscription was carved into the stone. Written in middle English, the phrase took some time to be deciphered. After running it through her head several times, Melissa was finally confident of the meaning.

"Hold the bloom in your hand and close the casket. The symbol of death will lead the way,"

Careful not to touch the enamelled orchid with bare hands, she wrapped her skirt about her fingers and gingerly picked up the brooch. As she lifted the brooch free, a small disc popped up from the bottom of the case. The orchid felt heavier than the lotus; cast in solid gold and decorated in deep jewel colours, it was a thing of beauty. With a surge of excitement, she noted its similarity to the lotus flower. Reaching forward with the tips of her fingers she closed the casket. As the stone lid settled back into place, there was a click from somewhere else in the room. Turning rapidly to face the direction of the sound, she began to search the room for the source. The torchlight threw strange shadows as she moved back and forth, looking anxiously for something new. After another ten minutes of searching, she located what she was looking for. In the corner of the room and close to the floor, a small panel had opened. With a sigh of relief, she looked down into the small hole. A small metal box lay in the floor. She carefully lifted the box free, revealing another carved lotus set into the floor. Setting the lotus into the floor, she slowly began to turn it. A clicking noise, as though she were winding a clock, sounded. She continued to turn the flower, listening as a faint rumbling sound joined the clicking noise. The rumbling sound increased until finally, the wall behind her opened, revealing a dark passageway beyond. With a sigh of relief, Melissa moved toward the opening. Tucking the box under her arm as best as possible, she crouched down and to crawl along the tunnel, hoping that this would finally lead her to freedom.

She crawled through the darkness for so seemed like hours. The torch faded and burnt out, leaving her to navigate the narrow, low tunnel in utter darkness. Swallowing down the fear that was threatening to overwhelm her, Melissa kept crawling, desperate to reach the end of the tunnel. With the torch gone, the darkness was like a living thing, suffocating her as she slowly moved the length of the tunnel. The crawlspace seemed to have no end, yet she fancied she could see a light at the far end. With a choking sigh of relief, she sped up, heading for the faint glow with a renewed sense of purpose.

She exited the tunnel into a small cellar. A small lamp sat on a table, it's light barely illuminating the dark corners.

"Now this is a surprise," She started at the voice and stared up into the curious gaze of a tall, well built man. "I was expecting Lestrade,"

CHAPTER 31

"Have you found her?" Marcus asked as Justin finally returned to the side of the cart. Justin shook his head as he looked back at the body of Melissa's donor. The man had stopped whimpering, but his hands still bled freely. Melissa's lateness had been a mild source of irritation, but when the bruises and cuts had started to appear on the man's hands, they had begun to worry. It had been hours, and there was still no sign of her. Both Justin and Emily had headed out into Reims, looking for her. Marcus had wanted to search, but he had been convinced to wait with the cart. He now stared at the injured man, anxiety gnawing in his chest.

"Damn," He uttered, taking a step forward. "Where did

you look?”

“All over Reims,” Justin responded, looking over at the body with an unreadable expression. “And there’s no sign,”

“I went to the cathedral,” Emily’s voice sounded from behind them. “She went there,”

“And?” Justin answered, his voice taut with worry.

“She left after looking at the window,” She stood next to Marcus and laid a comforting hand on his arm. “The priest didn’t know where she went,”

“What the hell is she thinking?” Justin snapped finally, “We were supposed to be going there tomorrow,”

“Possibly she wanted to surprise you,” Emily replied with a shrug. “Either way, the trail went cold after that,”

“What could the priest tell you?” Marcus interjected. “Did she say anything before she went?”

“Not that he said,” Emily leant back against the side of the cart and folded her arms. “I went to the inn and checked if she had registered us but she didn’t arrive,”

Justin felt his heart sink and he stared up at the guttering torches. He hadn’t received much in the way of information. “I don’t know where else to look,” He admitted finally, staring down at the damaged body on the cart. “Unless she went to a house, but I don’t see why she would do that,” He sighed heavily and looked up towards the sky. “I don’t know why she went off on her own,”

Emily gave a choking laugh and stared across at him with mild disbelief. “Really?” She pushed herself away from the cart and came to stand opposite him. “I thought it was fairly plain,” Her eyes darted back and forth across

Justin and Marcus. "What? Neither of you noticed?"

"Emily," Justin warned in low tones. "Stop playing and just tell us,"

"Alright darling," She smiled sweetly. "But I don't think you're going to like it," She raised her eyebrows at the expression on Justin's face and continued to speak. "I'd be willing to bet that she wants to prove something,"

"Why?"

Emily almost choked at the look of non-comprehension of Justin's face. "Why?" She tilted her head back and gave a sharp bark of derisive laughter. "Because, you've been treating her as though she's been made of glass since she joined us," Justin took a small step back as Emily's words pierced him. "It's been forty years since she stopped being the scared innocent she once was, but you still treat her as though she'll break. No one likes to be considered useless and inept,"

"I don't consider her to be useless," Justin protested, trying hard not to see the truth in Emily's words.

"But that's how you treat her," Emily persisted. "Have you ever let her handle things on her own?" She didn't wait for an answer as she waved a hand in Marcus' direction. "You ask Marcus or you ask me, I don't believe you've ever asked Melissa. I've seen the look on her face when you expect me to handle things,"

Justin stayed silent, thinking about Emily's words. It was true, he rarely asked Melissa to handle any of the difficulties that characterised their lives but he hadn't wanted to burden her. "I don't think..." He began, trying to find some justification.

"Justin…" Emily interrupted with exaggerated patience. "You let me handle difficult jobs and I was your lover, Melissa knows this,"

"That still doesn't mean she should have rushed off to do this on her own," Justin finally spoke, angry at Emily's words and implications. "She could have just said," Emily opened her mouth to speak, he raised his hand, and she stayed silent. "But I will take the point, however why she did it is not important right now," He came to stand next to Emily. "Did you discover anything more from the priest?"

"Only that she asked to see the stained glass…" Revelation suddenly shone in her face. "And that she asked about a local legend,"

"You didn't find out what the legend said?" Marcus asked, stepping forward to join their conversation.

"No, unfortunately not,"

"Well I think that'll be our next line of enquiry," Justin glanced at Marcus, Melissa's brother had taken a small step forward and there was determination in his gaze. "Marcus," The other man raised an eyebrow, promising anger if Justin asked him to wait. "You'd better follow the trail," He reached up and took hold of the reins. "And you'd better go with him," He called across to Emily.

"Are you sure?" Emily asked, watching him lead the horses with some concern.

"Of course," He answered, unwilling to voice his desire to search for Melissa with the others. It made sense that her brother would search for her and that Emily should question the priest. Besides, it was entirely possible that she would not want to see him. Thinking back on Emily's words, he was certain that Melissa would view his presence as a problem.

Emily nodded as she slowly turned away from Justin. The trio parted company as two walked to the cathedral and the third headed towards the inn. He covered the bodies on the back of the cart and moved through the dark streets, hoping that he would run into Melissa on route.

Marcus watched Justin move off down the street and glanced across at Emily. "Is he alright?"

"He'll be fine," Emily replied flippantly as she hooked her arm through Marcus' and led him away down the street.

"So where are we going? Marcus thought about removing her hand from his but decided against it. Her fingers were comfortable and warm against his and he felt no desire to remove them.

"Cathedral first," Emily replied carelessly as they travelled through the crowded streets. Despite the darkness, the town was still full of people, yet Emily moved through them with ease. Marcus allowed himself to be dragged along as she led him towards the massive, ornate bulk of Reims cathedral. Raising her fist she knocked on the solid door, the sound seeming small against the size of the cathedral. As they waited, Marcus found his attention wandering; he took in the decapitated heads on either side of the door and wondered who had removed the ornately carved figures. Minutes passed and Emily knocked again.

In the intervening silence, she settled back against the door frame and stared up at him.

"What?" He asked, noting casually that she was nibbling at a long strand of hair. The light of the torches cast her face into shadow, yet he could feel her gaze like something physical. Gooseflesh rippled across his skin, and he swallowed, feeling tension rise between them,"

"I was just wondering," She replied in that infuriating calm voice that she had.

"Hmm?" He stared at her with suspicion in his gaze.

"Marcus, do you realise this is the first time we've been alone together since Paris?" It was a casual question, yet Marcus could hear the currents behind it.

"What about it?" He managed to ask, turning his mind away from the thoughts that had begun to form within his head.

"Nothing," Her reply was frivolous, light and teasing and she stepped forward, running her hand along his upper arm. "I just thought it was an interesting observation," Marcus could not stop the small intake of breath that her touch provoked, and she gave a small smile. "I think we should be alone more often,"

Marcus was spared from answering by the sound of footsteps approaching the door. He stepped back from Emily and adopted a serious expression. The door was unbolted, and it swung open to reveal an elderly priest.

"Yes?" He asked, his eyes running over Marcus with some suspicion.

"Father," Emily stepped forward, her study in breathless

innocence. It was an act that Marcus constantly marvelled at, how she could alter her demeanour at the slightest provocation. "I'm sorry to call so late, but could you tell me the legend?"

"Legend?" The priest looked puzzled for a moment and them he smiled softly. "Of course," He gestured to the church behind him. Emily gave a grateful smile and moved past him into the church. Marcus made to follow, but the priest stood in his way. "And who is this?" He asked, looking at him with some concern.

"This is my betrothed," Emily said brightly, wrapping a hand around Marcus' arm. Marcus shot her a swift look but didn't protest; he merely smiled and hoped that he didn't look too dense. "He wasn't happy with me walking about the town at night,"

"Quite right," The priest conceded as he allowed Marcus and Emily into the church. "So you wish to know about the legend?" He spoke conversationally as he led them along the Nave.

It took barely any time for the legend to be explained to the waiting pair. As the priest finished speaking, Marcus asked the priest to lead them to the stained glass window.

"See." He whispered to Emily, nodding up at the images. "I'm guessing she followed the directions,"

"We'd better follow them too," Emily replied in an undertone before she returned to the priest's side. "Thank you," She gave the old man a small smile and generously donated to the poor box. Taking her cue, Marcus did the same before stepping back into the dark streets. They could hear the sounds of bars being drawn across the doors and they walked away, towards the directions given by the legend.

"So I think we can say that the legend isn't anything to do with the Holy Grail," Marcus stated as they moved through the emptying streets.

"I should say so," Emily replied as she tucked her arm through his. "It's about these damn brooches," She added unnecessarily as they walked through the empty streets.

"Are you certain she followed the directions?" Marcus asked as they moved into the recesses of an alley.

Emily gave him a pitying look. "She's your sister, what do you think?"

Marcus nodded, remembering the stubborn streak that characterised Melissa. He could well imagine that she would traipse off into danger alone, though he hadn't thought she would be this reckless.

"Quite so," Emily interpreted his silence as agreement. "Here we are," They stopped at a blank wall.

"A dead end," Marcus could not keep the disappointment from his voice. "She could not have come this way,"

"I think she did," Emily disagreed as she released his arm and began to examine the wall. "I think she came this way and went beyond," Marcus watched with curiosity as she began to run her hands over the moss covered stones.

Emily felt the old stone beneath the tendrils of greenery, feeling the once solid pieces of stone crumble lightly beneath her fingers. Despite its age, however, the wall was solid, the crumbling face a mere illusion. "There's got to be something here," She muttered to herself as she continued her hunt. "Don't just stand there," She snapped over at Marcus. "Take a look,"

Marcus walked forward and began to examine the wall. He still wasn't sure they would find anything. After several minutes of determined searching, they located a small picture of a gryphon.

"Here," Marcus drew Emily's attention to the small symbol and the block behind it. "What do you think?"

"I think you shouldn't go through there," A new voice called from the end the alley. Marcus and Emily whirled round to face the newcomer, Marcus' raising his fists ready to fight. Stepping out of the shadows and lit by the silvery moonlight, a handsome young man walked in from the street, a gentle smile on his face. The man's blond hair shone white in the moonlight, and Emily relaxed.

"Abbott?" Disbelief echoed through her words as she watched the handsome man walk forward. Marcus glanced across at Emily with some confusion as the other man smiled across at her.

"Good evening," He reached her side and leant forward. "It's been a very long time," He reached forward and placed both hands on her shoulders. "Don't you have a kiss for me?"

"Not really," Emily replied as she stared up at the newcomer.

"Oh?" He cast a look at Marcus and gave a small smile. "Do you think he'll be jealous?"

"Who the devil are you?" Marcus asked, a sudden surge

of anger burning through his mind. Emily drew back as Abbott turned to smile at Marcus.

"I think that's my line," Abbott answered with a chuckle. "I know it's been a few years Emily but when have you started to drag along your paramours?"

"He's one of us," Emily answered, stepping away from Abbott's side. "Quite recently,"

"I should say so," Abbott slouched back against the wall and peered at the pair with interest. "John never mentioned anyone new,"

"You've seen John?" Emily stiffened at the news, and she peered at Abbot with suspicion.

"Fifty years ago," He yawned, seemingly bored with the conversation. "I barely spoke to him," Pushing away from the wall, he caught hold of Emily's arm. "John doesn't interest me but..." He glanced at Marcus. "He does. I thought we were done with adding people to our little group,"

"It's a long story."

"And we have plenty of time," Abbott began to walk back towards the street. "Come on, we have so much catching up to do."

"We're busy at the moment," Emily continued, not moving from her spot.

"I daresay," He stopped and looked back over his shoulder. "But you won't find what you're looking for in there,"

"Abbott?" Emily finally took a step forward, suspicion clouding her features. "What do you know?"

"Not very much at all actually," He said, turning to face her "Only..." He gave a seemingly benign grin. "The girl you're looking for is currently in my house,"

CHAPTER 32

Justin hid the cart and its cargo in a safe spot out of sight before he began to head toward the inn. He would register for rooms and then join the other two in searching for Melissa. Even though the hiding of the cart was a necessity, he wished that he had foregone his responsibility and ventured out into the town to look for her himself. However he knew that Melissa would not appreciate such an action. Emily, God curse her, was right in her assumption of Melissa's frame of mind. Thinking back on the trip from Paris to Reims, he had noted her quiet seething but he had associated it with the death of the man at the inn. When he asked Emily to locate the inn out of habit, he could not understand why Melissa had taken it so personally. He had not touched Emily in the last forty years, and he had never loved her. He kicked a small stone, wondering if he would ever understand women, even with all the additional years he had added to his life. He moved through an alley, taking a short cut towards his destination as his thoughts focused on Melissa and Emily. So focused on his inner turmoil, he failed to notice the figure that marked his progress along the streets.

The last forty years had been strange, the addition of Melissa and her brother to his circle had been somewhat of an intrusion into his ordered existence. He had patterns of behaviour, honed over years of solitude and though he loved the spice she had brought to his life, he still hadn't quite gotten used to her addition to it. He chuckled to himself at the temerity of criticising his change of circumstances when he was responsible for them. Although the first few years had been rocky and there had been many arguments, they had recently settled into an easy relationship. Even after all the time together he still did not fully understand her. He turned the corner at the end of the alley and kept walking, eyes fixed on the cobblestones before him as his thoughts continued to roil inside. He had only wanted to keep her safe, it didn't mean that he thought she was incapable of handling things, even if this incident seemed to indicate otherwise. The inn came into view, and he strode ahead, hoping to deal with this small problem before heading out to sort out the larger one.

"Good evening Justin," Katherine stepped out before him, dressed in revolutionary colours, her chestnut hair forced beneath a cap. "Long time no see,"

Justin gave a sigh of exasperation and stopped. At every turn, Katherine and John seemed to be there; shadowing and thwarting him. It was enough to make him scream; instead, he drew a breath and answered as politely as he could. "It has been a long time,"

"How are you?" Justin did not return her smile. Smiling was for those he was actually happy to see. "Is John with you?" Wasting no time on polite converse, he moved directly to his concern. "I've no time to deal with him now,"

"But he has time to deal with you," Another voice spoke from behind him and he turned to face Alistair.

"Well, well," Justin looked over his brother with disapproval. "I wondered when you would finally let your hatred get the better of you," Glancing back at Katherine, he continued. "Joining John's crusade does not become you brother,"

"Did I ask for your opinion?" Alistair asked as he moved closer. "I don't believe I did," Justin glanced over his shoulder as Katherine began to walk toward him. "I want you to come with us, Justin,"

Justin gave a bark of incredulous laughter. "Do you honestly think that I would come quietly?"

"Not really," Alistair replied with a chuckle. He reached into his coat and drew forth a long bladed knife. Justin spared him an amused smile before launching himself forward and punching Alistair squarely in the face. Alistair staggered backwards and fell to the floor in a heap.

"Don't be a fool," Justin uttered through gritted teeth.

"John's friendship is nothing more than an empty sham," He kept a wary eye on Katherine as he moved to deliver a solid kick to Alistair's side.

Alistair rolled away from the blow and picked himself up. He lunged forward in a staggering charge, catching Justin's upper arm with a clumsy swing of his blade. "Did I ever say it was about friendship?" Twisting his upper body, he swung his fist at Justin's face. "He's going to help me get my freedom," Justin ducked away from the blow, the cut on his arm healing as he moved. "And my revenge," Justin drew back his arm to return the favour, only to have his arm caught and held by Katherine's delicate hands. Alistair took the opportunity and slashed again, slicing into Justin's side as his brother pushed Katherine away. The alley was narrow, making it difficult for them to manoeuvre. Hindered by his two opponents, Justin took more wounds than he would normally and though his skin healed, his clothes were soon decorated with bright crimson blood.

"For God's sake Alistair I'm your brother," Justin ducked a swing from Katherine, only to find himself sailing into the alley wall, courtesy of a heavy swing from Alistair. His head slammed into the dark stone, dazing him. Alistair held him against the wall as Katherine rummaged through his pockets.

"Yes... and you did this," Alistair answered him. "You cursed all of us," He gave a small sneer. "And you need to pay,"

"He doesn't have his brooch," Katherine announced

as she finally removed her hand from his pockets. Justin glanced over her at and grinned.

"How stupid do you think I am?" He returned his eyes to stare at his brother. "Do you think that I make a habit of carrying it with me?" Alistair's face twisted with rage and he pushed Katherine aside, reaching into Justin's pockets himself. "I learnt that the last time I tangled with your master," Alistair raised his fist and backhanded him across the face. Justin worked his jaw until the healing finally eased the pain. "What do you intend to do now?"

Alistair sighed and drew his knife across his brother's throat. He barely waited for the wound to close before he struck again, sending his brother to the floor in a heap. With a snarl of frustration, he kicked out at the body of his brother.

"Now what?" Katherine asked, staring at the body with a mixture of pity and resignation.

"We take him to John and get out of France," Alistair answered, the anger leaving his face as he looked down at his brother. "Those three will be lost without him; we can then deal with them at our leisure,"

Katherine rolled her eyes behind Alistair's back as he reached down to pick up Justin's body.

CHAPTER 33

Melissa sat in a plainly decorated parlour and stared at the small metal box before her. Her 'host' had left some time earlier, with a promise to locate her companions and she was not sorry to see him leave, unnerved by his overly familiar manner. Not that she thought he would harm her, but it was better to be safe. Abbott had identified himself with a cheery smile and generally friendly demeanour, yet beyond acknowledging that he too was a member of their club, he had said little else. He had plied her with refreshments and left, he said, to locate the others. While it was true that she had heard him leave, she did not fully trust him. She had not forgotten that the tunnel had led to the cellar beneath his house. Once she was sure she were alone, she had checked for escape routes. The large parlour windows were locked and so was the parlour door, yet she was not above breaking the window. Satisfied that she could escape if she should need to, she had stayed within the parlour and waited. It was entirely possibly that he could find the others and bring them here, in which case she should wait. Beyond thoughts of reunion, however, she wanted to stay and discover more about this man. While she had heard about Abbott and the other people in their little 'club', she knew very little about them. Justin had perhaps mentioned Abbott once and not in any detail.

As the time passed, her thoughts drifted away from Abbott and his motives and returned to the small chest that lay on the table before her. Plain and slightly rusted with a simple catch, it invited investigation. The fire popped and crackled in the hearth as she focused on the box and wondered about the contents. After several moments of introspection, she reached forward and flipped the lid. The casket was empty save for one piece of parchment. Carefully she reached forward and drew it from the box. Brittle with age, the edges crumbled in her fingers and she swiftly placed it down on the table. Poring over the delicate piece of parchment, her eyes were immediately drawn to the centre of the picture and a faded depiction of the orchid brooch. Around the main picture, several small diagrams begged for attention and one in particular caught her eye. The line drawing showed the back of the brooch and she peered down at it, the tips of her thumb and forefinger slowly rubbing her lips as she took in the information before her.

After several moments of thought, she stood and began to pace the room. The heavy weight of the enamelled orchid banged against her leg, and she reached into her pocket, hand carefully covered with a handkerchief, and drew the brooch free. In the light of the parlour, she could see it more clearly. Carved in the same fashion as the lotus flowers, but without the hinges that they possessed, it seemed to be nothing more than a beautiful piece of jewellery. She sat back down and carefully examined each facet of the brooch before she turned it over. Engraved onto the golden surface were the miniscule letters that she had seen on the drawing. She strained her eyes trying to decipher the tiny writing, but to no avail. Drawing away from the brooch, she began to hunt through the room for a magnifying glass. Pulling open a desk drawer, she pushed aside papers and scraps of parchment before she stopped short, arrested by a larger picture of the orchid brooch. Alongside the diagram of the brooch, in a script written with an elegant hand, was a translation of the minute lettering. The clock in the hallway chimed the quarter hour as she stared down at the drawing, weighing larceny against a desire to know more. The desire for knowledge won and, feeling like a thief, she drew forth the paper with shaking hands and read it through carefully twice. After the second reading, she glanced down at the orchid in her hand and carefully placed it on a table. Putting down the handkerchief that protected her fingers, she gingerly reached forward to grasp the orchid with bare skin.

"NO!" As her fingers closed on the smooth metal, Abbott's anguished cry echoed across the room as Melissa pitched forward onto the floor.

"Ahh hell," Abbott rushed forward, only to be shoved out of the way as Marcus ran to his sister's side.

"What the devil happened to her?" He asked, turning her over, distress in his voice.

"I don't know," Abbott replied with a shrug. Marcus whirled to face him, jabbing an angry finger against his chest.

"I don't believe you," He was breathing easily, yet Abbott could see murderous intent in his face. "You didn't want her to touch it."

"Of course I didn't want her to touch it," Abbott knocked Marcus' finger aside and kicked the small flower away from Melissa's form. "Do you think it's a good idea to pick up an item carved by the same people who carved the lotus we wear?"

The floor fell away the moment her bare skin connected with the cool, smooth surface of the orchid. Darkness shrouded her vision, and she felt herself hit the floor, yet unlike the all-encompassing darkness that the lotus produced, she could still see. Through a grey veil, she saw her brother peer anxiously into her face, and she tried to speak, but the muscles in her face were frozen. Marcus' words washed over her, yet they were distorted and indistinct. He lifted her from the ground and laid her on a couch, continuing an angry conversation with Abbot. Melissa felt herself drift, the voices near her fading as another sound began to supplant them. A bell tone, sweet yet painful, echoed through her mind and blotted out all other sounds. The soft note dominated her thoughts, growing louder and more strident as it continued to sound. It grew in volume and as it did the parlour began to vanish, and another vista rose in its place. The echoes of the note began to die, and the scene before her solidified. She could see trees and buildings before her and behind them a mountain, taller than any she had seen. Several figures walked towards her and captured her attention. She blinked, watching as they approached, they were small, lithe and attractive yet somehow repellent at the same time. Each wore a version of the lotus flower, although theirs were white and silver. As they drew closer, their whispers washed over her, the speech clear and sweet sounding.

"Heretic..." The first voice was ghostly and tinged with hatred. From her frozen position on the floor, she watched as he approached and began to reach out for her.

"A lost one..." Other voices crowded about her and the sweet tones sent shudders along her spine.

"Find her..."

She felt herself panic as they reached her side, their long fingers stretching out to touch her skin. She attempted to back off, to pull away before they could reach her but she was unable to move. The lead figure brushed a cold hand against her cheek and pain seared her skin.

"We have her,"

She jolted upright, a scream echoing across the parlour as she finally regained hold of her senses.

"Melissa?" Marcus knelt at her side, Emily too; she could see the concern in both of their faces as she pulled herself into a sitting position. Behind them and leant nonchalantly against the wall was Abbott, his face fixed in an expression of curiosity and concern.

"What happened?" A note of what she took to be mild concern laced his tones, and he scrutinised her features as he spoke.

"I don't really know," She pressed her hand to her cheek, remembering the blistering feel of that hand against her skin. The chill radiated through her bones and settled in her very marrow. That touch had held the chill of the grave, and she wondered if she would ever be warm again. Marcus placed an arm about her shoulders and she leant into his embrace gratefully. "I saw..." She hesitated, unsure of the reality of her vision.

"What?" Emily asked, moving in to sit next to Marcus, her blue eyes brimming with curiosity.

"I saw a town in the mountains," She spoke slowly, carefully as she attempted to clarify the experience in her mind. "And people," She glanced up at her brother. "They saw me," She shook her head and closed her eyes, trying to hold onto the memories that were slipping from her grasp. "They called me a heretic and said that they were going to find me,"

Emily shot a glance at Abbott, who listened carefully on the other side of the room. "What do you think?" She asked.

"I think she shouldn't have picked it up," Abbott

returned the gaze coolly. His eyes flicked across to Melissa and he continued. "Given what happened the last time an enamel brooch was removed from a case,"

"Then why did you have the translation lying around?" Melissa snapped out, infuriated by his nonchalant manner.

"Knowledge is always useful," He pushed himself from the wall. "And it may come in handy someday," He reached her side and looked down at her. "The more pressing concern is why you felt it necessary to got through my cupboards?"

Melissa bit her lip and bowed her head, ashamed for her snooping.

"How long have you had this knowledge?" Emily interrupted, suspicion making her voice sharp.

"Oh..." Abbott thought for a moment. "Approximately one hundred years,"

"One hundred..." Staggered by the news, Emily stood and looked at him. "You've had access to this..." She waved at the brooch on the floor. "For one hundred years and you never thought to inform us? Why haven't you told us this before?" She faced him down, anger thrumming through every syllable. "And for that matter, if you knew about that secret tunnel, why didn't you inform us?"

"Emily..." Abbott moved closer and placed his hands on her shoulders "My dear sweet Emily," She tossed her head angrily and pulled away "Think a little. Why would I want to tell Justin or yourself any information about the curse? You'd only try to find a cure," Emily went very still as he continued. "And I don't want to be cured,"

Emily felt Melissa rise to her feet, yet she could not take her eyes from Abbott's face. "You don't want the cure?" She disliked repetition, but she wanted to be completely clear about what she had just heard. Marcus had also stood, but her focus was on Abbott and his sudden declaration.

"No," He smiled, amused at her apparent inability to grasp his meaning. "Of course not," He took a step backwards and smiled at the three of them. "Why would I give up the chance to live forever?"

"Abbott?" Emily's voice was an appalled whisper.

"Oh not that I like killing people," Abbott replied as he stepped back and smiled at the group of them. "Far from it," He reached down and picked a flower from a vase on the table. "But I don't want to die. I want to see everything this world can do," He twirled the flower between his fingers and continued. "I never thought I would see the march of progress and this curse has allowed me to do that,"

"But you're killing people to do it," Melissa interjected, her eyes bright with anger. "How can you live with yourself?"

"Quite easily, actually," He responded in a careless tone. "Much the same way you have survived over the years," He sighed at the look of repulsion on her face. "I do feel sorry from time to time," He gave a shrug of his shoulders. "But then I think of the alternative," He turned away from them and headed toward the door. "But all of this is beside the point." He pointed at Melissa. "She's played with the brooch; we need to know more about it and what that vision means,"

"What do you know about it?" Melissa asked, struggling to get her revulsion under control. Abbott gave a small smile, his fingers gently tugging the petals from the flower in his hands as he regarded the group.

Marcus pushed forward now, his patience at his very limit. "Start explaining..."

"Or what?" Abbott retorted as he whirled round to face Marcus. "There is nothing you can threaten me with," With a look of resignation he spoke with exaggerated patience. "We are all very hard to kill unless you mean to divest me of my limbs and..." He glanced across at Melissa and Marcus. "I don't think you're willing to do that,"

"They may be reluctant," Emily replied, "But I'm not," She approached Abbott. "I don't think we need the threats," She softened her tones as she lifted her hand. "Tell me Abbott,"

Abbott leant forward and trailed the remnants of the flower across the skin of her cheek. "If you truly wanted to know," Abbot whispered with a small smile. "You'd kiss me,"

Marcus started forward, only to be stopped by Emily's outstretched hand. "You'd tell us if I kissed you?" Incredulity thrummed through her voice.

"If you're attempting seduction, you shouldn't be surprised when I take you up on it," Abbott retorted with a small snap to his tones. He leant close to her face and whispered. "I'm not Justin," His hand hovered over her breastbone. "If you're offering yourself, I'll take it," He glanced up at Marcus. "It all depends on how much you're willing to give in front of your lover.

"Just stop," Melissa interrupted before Marcus could step in. She glanced across at her brother's face, noticing the rage that had begun to burn behind his eyes. Placing herself between Marcus and Abbott, she seized hold of his shoulder turning him round to face her. "And tell us,"

"What about you?" He turned to Melissa. "Care to trade?" Abbott glanced down at Melissa's pale face, a small smile playing about his lips. "Just one little kiss and I guarantee that you will know all you need.

Melissa stared at him, her mind whirring a mile a minute as she looked at the handsome face leering at her. In that instant, she was transported back forty years and Montjoy's advances. Despite his teasing tones, he was almost as bad as that monster and anger pulsed through her. She lunged forward and thrust her thumb into his eye. Abbott gave a choking cry at the pain and his hand flew to cover his stinging eyeball. "I will happily leave you blind," Her voice was low and threatening. "I want the information Abbot and I want it now," Abbott recovered from the pain as his donor took the wound for him and as he lowered his fingers he glared at the group. Marcus seized hold of Abbott's upper arm and pressed him against the wall. "I'm not feeling particularly patient today," Melissa finished as she slid her dagger out of her pocket and raised it to his face.

"Threats with us are meaningless," Abbott chuckled lightly at the sight of the blade. "You should know that,"

"True..." Melissa said, her green eyes glittering coldly

in the light. "But by the time we've finished, no one will be able to tell what your face used to look like,"

Marcus turned his head to stare at his sister, a worried look on his face at the ugly threats spilling from her mouth.

Abbott stared at her for a long moment before chuckling. "Alright if you insist," He rested his head back against the wall and continued. "I found the trail approximately one hundred years ago; I discovered that where you did," He nodded at the brooch. "I wasn't stupid enough to pick it up bare handed. I'm sure you realise that it is of the same craftsmanship as the lotus brooch?" Melissa nodded, her face grim. "I had the devil of the job to get out of there; you have to take the brooch in order to leave,"

"So what did you do?" Melissa interrupted, remembering the dark, dank room where she had found the brooch.

"I opened the wall and propped it open," Abbott answered as though the answer were incredibly simple. "I took a tracing of the parchment and left everything where I found it,"

"What about the bodies?" Melissa asked, thinking of the skeletons lying lost and broken on the flagstones,"

"Who?" Abbott shrugged, clearly uninterested in the bodies that littered the floor of that chamber. "Like I said, I found the information,"

"You didn't investigate?" Emily interjected, disbelief in her voice.

"Why would I?" Abbott stared directly at the blonde. "It would have led to an end," He nodded across at Melissa. "In all likelihood I would have suffered what happened to her. For all we know, she's slowly dying,"

Marcus' eye flicked across to his sister. "She seems fine,"

"The note states..." Abbott cleared his throat and continued in a mocking tone. "For freedom of the body and spirit, hold the orchid tight against thy skin'," He gave a small chuckle. "I took that to mean death,"

"Well I'm not dead," Melissa retorted, staring down at the orchid on the floor.

"There are worst things than death as I'm sure you know," Abbott replied with a shrug of his shoulders. "Now do you mind leaving, I've told you all I know,"

"Don't lie to me Abbott," Emily stared directly at his face. "You know more."

Abbott smiled at the blonde and whispered. "Maybe I do…" He nodded at Melissa and her brother. "But I'm not saying anything with these two stood here. I'll talk to you alone,"

Melissa and Emily exchanged a pained glance before the brunette gave a curt nod. "Hear him out," Marcus started with surprise at Melissa's pronouncement. Abbott gave a smug smile as Melissa released her hold on Abbott's arm and caught hold of her brother. Marcus started to protest as his sister dragged him across the floor. "She can always tell us later," Melissa whispered as they moved out into the hallway.

Emily waited until Melissa was out of sight before she reached out to embrace the man before her.

"I honestly thought you were going to let her take my eyes," Abbott murmured against her ear as he bent his head to rest on top of hers.

"Oh come now," Her breath whispered across his skin. "You'd have recovered,"

"True," He stroked his fingers across her cheek, and she shuddered. "But it would have been an inconvenience,"

"What did you want to tell me?" She softened her voice.

Abbott hesitated, listening to the sound of clock ticking as he tried to find the words.

"Abbott?" Emily pulled back from the embrace, her voice low with unsaid threats.

"That piece of parchment wasn't the only item in the box," He admitted finally, nodding towards the cabinet in the corner as he did so. "The book's in there,"

Emily stepped away from his side and pulled open the drawer. "You didn't even hide it?" She asked, pointing at the roughly bound tome which sat proudly and alone in the drawer.

"There was no need," Abbott replied. "You'd have to know to look for it,"

"May I?" Emily stretched out her fingers to the book.

"I'd rather you didn't," Abbott replied as he stepped forward and placed his fingers on her shoulder. Emily tilted her face up to his, and he continued. "But you can," Emily gave a small smile and reached out to pick up the book.

"Thank you," Emily's fingers traced the cover with nervous anticipation. "Is the cure in here?"

"No," Abbott responded, dropping his grip on her shoulder. "But you may find the cure through the clues,"

"Then why did you tell me?" Emily flicked open the cover to reveal a detailed drawing of the orchid flower. "If you don't want to lose our supposed immortality, you could have kept quiet,"

"I told you because you are likely to be pragmatic," He reached over her shoulder and turned the delicate pages of the book. "Read that," He pointed to a passage written in spidery writing. Emily read through the text, eyes widening as she did so. As she reached the end of the paragraph, she flicked a questioning gaze at Abbott.

"See," Abbott gave a small shrug. "The others would ignore that and continue, but I don't think you will," Emily shut the book one handed and clasped it to her chest, a small sigh escaping her lips as she did so. "You do understand don't you?" Abbott continued, looking at her troubled face. "Searching for the cure could be the worst thing you could do,"

CHAPTER 34

"What did he tell you?" Melissa asked for the second time as they walked toward the inn. "You said you'd tell us,"

"That was your suggestion," Emily corrected in a bland tone as they reached the inn doorway.

"Emily," Melissa appealed as she pulled open the door and they walked inside. The inn was crowded, the smell of unwashed bodies, vomit and spilled ale almost making them gag. Steeling themselves to the stench they crossed the room, heading for the bar. Stood behind the heavy wooden bench was a heavyset man in his late forties. Melissa and Marcus headed straight to the barman as Emily sat down at an empty table situated by the window.

"We have rooms booked in the name of Dumarche," Marcus spoke for the first time since leaving Abbott's house. The barkeep pulled a register toward him and began to look for the name they usually used when staying at inns. As Marcus searched through his pockets for spare coin, he became aware of Melissa's curious stare. Not that he could blame her. He had remained silent through the walk here, showing little interest in the conversation that Melissa and Emily had engaged in.

Melissa was confused by her brother's silence. Aside from a few sideways glances at the two women during their walk, he had barely interacted with them and now he stood beside her, radiating a sense of tension that she did not understand.

"Are you alright?" Melissa placed a concerned hand on his arm. "You haven't said a word since we left Abbott's home,"

Marcus took a breath and glanced down at his sister, concern on his features. "What you did at Abbott's concerned me," He uttered finally, giving voice to the worries that were running through his head.

"What?" Melissa shook her head and looked down at her feet, remembering her conduct with a mixture of shame and exhilaration. For a moment, she had felt as powerful as Emily. "I wouldn't have hurt...."

"But you did," Marcus interjected softly. "You hurt his donor, not him," He lowered his voice even further. "I didn't think you were capable of that. Not with what happened outside Paris,"

"I..." Melissa struggled for words as she recalled the donor she had freed. It was true that she had lost her temper with Abbott, his sneering attitude to their search for a cure had managed to find her last nerve, but she hadn't meant to go through with her threat. In that moment, she had only thought of answering as though she were Emily, fearless and powerful. She looked up at Marcus' stern face, and shame trickled through her. "I wouldn't have gone through with it,"

"I didn't know that," He stopped speaking as the barman finally looked up from the ledger.

"I'm sorry sir, I don't seem to have a booking in that name," Marcus' eyes glanced straight down at the ledger as he ignored Melissa's shocked gasp.

"Are you certain?" He asked as he reached across the bar to draw the book towards him.

"Positive sir," The barman drew the book further away with a disapproving look on his face. "I haven't got anything listed for that name, perhaps they want to another inn," He turned away from the pair of them and began to serve other patrons.

"Marcus?" Melissa asked, worry thrumming through her voice. Emily reached their side, and they left the inn. Finding a deserted alley, they huddled together.

"He should have arrived by now," Marcus noted unnecessarily. "Something must have happened," He glanced across at Emily. "Check his brooch," Emily reached into a pocket as the trio leaned in. Flipping the brooch open, Melissa stifled a gasp at the blank face where

Justin's donor used to sit.

"Well someone got him;" Emily snapped the brooch closed and leant back against the wall of the alley.

"Abbott?" Marcus asked, his voice humming with suppressed outrage. Melissa shot him a curious look at the traces of anticipation that she detected beneath his anger.

"No," Emily replied, rubbing her fingers across her chin in thought. "Abbott doesn't like Justin, but he wouldn't do that to him,"

"John again?" Melissa asked as she tore her eyes away from the brooch in Emily's hand.

"Who else?" Emily mused, running her fingers across the smooth surface of the lotus as she spoke. "They'll be moving him,"

"Let's go then," Melissa turned towards the street but Emily's hand snaked out to surround her wrist and stopped her from moving.

"Go where?" Emily asked mildly. "We don't know which road they've taken or even if they've left. Where do you want us to look?"

Melissa pulled her arm free and resisted the urge to scream at the other woman. "We search the town,"

"And if he's on the road?" Emily's voice was calm as she voiced questions into the air.

"Then we take to the road," Melissa replied, allowing her anger to rise to the surface.

"By which time, he could be miles away," Marcus answered.

"Then we'd better start looking now," She pulled her

arm free from Emily's grasp and stomped to the mouth of the alley. At this late hour, traffic was light, and she could identify every soul that traipsed through the streets. Taking a steadying breath, she turned to face the others. "Come on," Her voice was sharp with impatience and fear. "Or do you want us to lose him?"

Emily flicked a quick glance across at Marcus. His eyes met hers and he raised an eyebrow, concerned at her reluctance to immediately begin the search. Emily ignored the unspoken question and stepped out into the street. She reached Melissa's side and placed a calming hand on her shoulder.

"We'll look..." Melissa gave a sharp huff of impatience at the non committal answer, shook off Emily's hand and strode away down the street. Emily moved to follow but Marcus caught her arm and turned her to face him.

"Why aren't you more concerned?" He asked his voice low so that Melissa could not hear.

"Oh I am concerned," Emily replied in similar tones. "I just know we're not going to find him," She took her eyes from Melissa's departing form and stared straight into his eyes. "They've had at least an half hour head start, if they took the road," She pushed a strand of blonde hair away from her face and continued. "If they didn't take to the road, they're hiding somewhere in Reims," She made an expansive gesture with her hands. "And Reims isn't small," She nodded at the distant back of Melissa. "If John or Katherine has him, then there's little chance that we'll find them, and all the enthusiasm in the world won't help."

"Maybe," Marcus murmured as he began to pull away. "But that doesn't mean we shouldn't look," He removed his hand. "So come on."

Emily watched Marcus follow his sister for a few moments, her eyes trailing across his lean frame before she shrugged and joined the siblings in their search.

Several hours passed and they had exhausted the hiding places within the town. They stood as a group in the town square, defeated by the enormity of their task.

"I told you," Emily said in mild tones. 'We won't find him,"

"You could have at least tried," Melissa snapped back, angry tears welling in her green eyes.

Emily took a long whistling breath and mentally counted to ten. "What do you think I was doing?" She replied, marching up to Melissa and pressing her face up against hers. "Justin is long gone," She spoke each word carefully, yet rage gave the sounds a snarling edge. "He'll have to find his own way out,"

"Do we need to find him a donor?" Marcus asked quickly, stepping between his sister and Emily and the impending row.

"Maybe," Emily replied. "He'll need the strength to escape,"

"Then let's get on with it," Melissa stormed past Emily and headed back towards the darkened alleyways, letting the rage and frustration carry her forward. The anger was becoming a familiar feeling. It soothed her, brought her comfort and drove her. Her feet sloshed in the muddy puddles that covered the floor of the alley but she did not notice. Emily was lying to them again, of that she was certain, and Justin was missing. She swallowed back a sob and welcomed the anger that chased away the fear.

There

She stopped as a voice echoed through the twisting corners of the alley. Despite the cold light of a full moon, she could see nothing except the shadows. Water lapped against her feet, chill and slimy as she stared into the dim corners, looking for the source of the voice, yet she could see nothing. The voice had seemed to shake her very core, as though the speaker were talking to her very soul. Shaking her head, she dismissed her fears as little more than paranoia and delusion. Turning back to the alley, she walked forward, ignoring the crawling sensation in her skin that suggested she was being watched.

Now

Pain seared through her skull, and she fell, driven to her knees by the pounding sensation that suppressed every though. As her knees hit the muck covered floor, she could barely hear the cries of Marcus and Emily through the shrieking agony that pulsed through her mind. As the pain radiated from her skull to her skin, she jerked forward, landing prone in the large puddle. Foul water rushed up her nose and through her mouth, suffocating her and drowning the whimpers of pain as liquid began to fill her lungs. Yet there was little she could do to prevent it. Her body was frozen in agony.

Is it done?

Words echoed through her head with pinpoint clarity, yet even they did not hold her attention for long. Marcus pulled her up from the puddle and held her to him, she barely felt him. He was mouthing words in her direction, but she could not hear him. There was nothing beyond the pain.

No... she isn't the primary...

Then stop... It's pointless to continue.

Melissa opened her eyes and took a shuddering breath as the pain subsided as quickly as it had come. Marcus held her in his arms, and she could see the concern in his face. Over his shoulder, Emily leant in with worry on her porcelain features. Her breath came in gasps, and she gingerly felt her head for the damage she expected to find. Fingers ran through wet, filthy hair and tears ran tracks through the dirt on her face as she massaged her scalp.

"What happened?" Marcus asked, his arms still encircled her, and she leant against his body, comforted by his closeness and concern. Unable to speak, she removed her hands from her head and stared at the fingers, shocked to see that her skin was free of blood. Her skull still ached with the memory of that wracking pain that had surged through her body and shock sent uncontrollable shivers through her. "It's alright, don't try to move," Marcus whispered as he staggered to his feet, Melissa wrapped protectively in his arms. He looked over at Emily over his sister's head. "I think we should take her back to Abbott's,"

"Are you sure that's wise," Emily looked down at Melissa's crumpled form with an unreadable expression.

"Not really," Marcus conceded with a wry expression. "But there's nowhere else,"

Emily tore her eyes away from Melissa's body and she nodded reluctantly. Melissa was swooning, her eyes closing as she slipped into unconsciousness. The small group moved away from the alley and headed back to the modest house that Abbott called home. They had barely knocked on the peeling door before it swung open.

"That didn't take long," He announced as they passed him. Interest flickered in his eyes as Marcus carried the still form of his sister across the threshold. "What happened?" He asked, fixing his gaze on Emily.

"She collapsed in agony," Marcus replied as he carried her into the parlour. Arranging her carefully on the cushioned love seat, he brushed her hair back from her face before staring up at Abbott. "Now why don't you tell me what you know?"

"I don't know that much more than you," Abbott replied in a smooth, easy tone. "But I would suggest that you don't linger long," Emily raised an eyebrow at his words and he continued. "I don't know why she's like that," He moved away from the group and towards the door.

"Abbott?" Emily spoke softly, and he stopped moving.

"I can't help,"

"Can't or won't?" Marcus stood and faced the pair of them down. "I know we're new to this, but I can tell that you're both lying,"

"Good for you," Abbott replied, leaning back against the door and folding his arms. "But it doesn't change things,"

He fixed Marcus with a piercing stare and continued. "I can't help you," He indicated Melissa with a wave of his hand. "I'll let you stay until she gets better, but after that..."

"You want us to go," Marcus interrupted, disgust clear in his voice. "You know something about this curse and that orchid brooch," He shook his head and tried to control the rage that was beginning to bubble within him. "And you're refusing to tell us," Marcus turned his hazel eyes onto Emily and addressed her. "And you..." Emily froze at the disappointment she heard in his voice. "You're just the same in keeping this from us," He softened his tone and she could hear the hurt behind his words. "I thought you were different,"

"Whatever gave you that idea?" Emily replied in a taut voice, clenching her hands into fists. "I never claimed to be altruistic or moral,"

"No..." Marcus turned away from her icy stare and bent over the form of his sister. "You never did," He confirmed in a flat voice. "You just looked out for yourself and your..." He nodded at Abbott. "Friends," There was a sneering innuendo to his voice. "I guess we were just holding you back," He turned away from her and stared down at Melissa's body. "After all, we are here because of you," Emily nearly took a step backwards at the hate she heard in his voice. "My parents are dead and now my sister is..." He drew his gaze away from the still pale form on the couch. "Like this."

"And you're blaming me?" Emily dug her fingernails into her palms as she controlled her facial expression with some effort. "Perhaps you're right," Abbott glanced at her and marvelled at the control she exerted over her mannerisms. "It is my fault that your precious sister is still alive and not rotting in a grave somewhere," She picked up the cape from the arm of the chair. "With all my crimes, I don't know how you can put up with me," With a light, airy gesture, she tugged her cape about herself and picked up her bag. "So maybe it's time we parted ways?" The heavy leather bag settled into place on her shoulder as she flipped her tousled hair out of her face, "Perhaps we'll meet again in a hundred years,"

Marcus' head snapped up, and anger filled his face at her flippant manner. "Then go," He snapped. "I'm sure we can do without the lying and the trouble,"

"Fine," Emily retorted as she headed for the door. "Enjoy your eternity," She turned to face Abbott and caught hold of his arm, pulling him down for a passionate kiss. Marcus turned away, the sight annoying him more than it should.

"Until the next time," Abbott said as they broke the kiss.

"Indeed," Emily whirled away from Abbott's hold and stalked toward the door. Without a backwards glance, she strode out of the house and into the street.

Silence settled uneasily on the parlour. Marcus remained in place by the door, staring almost stupidly into the blank hallway in the wake of Emily's exit. He took several deep breaths, feeling the fury that had been pulsing through him morph into confusion. He ran his hands through his hair as he tried to process what had just happened. Melissa was still on the couch, her skin deathly pale and cold to the touch.

"Well," Abbott broke the silence and walked forward. "You handled that poorly," Marcus nodded once, too stunned by this evening's events to talk. "After all," Abbott continued, smiling as he reached for the poker by the fireplace. "You do want her," That broke the spell and Marcus launched himself at the other man, slamming his fist into the face that sneered at him. Abbott staggered back and blotted his bloody lip with the tips of his fingers. "Too close to home?" He asked as he reached into a pocket for his handkerchief.

"What do you know about it?" Marcus sucked in a large breath and controlled the urge to punch him again.

"Much," Abbott raised the poker and stirred up the dying embers in the grate. "If you're willing to control yourself for a bit, I may help you,"

Marcus raised an eyebrow. He couldn't quite believe what he was hearing, Abbott clearly shared more with Emily than mere friendship. He had reconciled himself to the fact that she had been Justin's one-time lover, but to discover her affiliation with Abbott was almost more than he could stomach.

"I don't need your advice," He growled the words and immediately wished he could take them back. Melissa was still unconscious, and he could not afford to turn away any offer of assistance.

"Then you're a fool," Abbott announced into the sudden silence. "You desire her," Marcus stilled as Abbott spoke. "It's understandable, she is very beautiful," He was watching Marcus closely, seeing the tension in his shoulders and frame.

"Yes," Marcus replied in the softest of tones and for a brief moment, Abbott felt some tiny pangs of sympathy for the newest member of their little band. Marcus clearly held stronger feelings than plain desire, but who was he to play cupid? With a wicked little idea taking root in his head, he continued to speak.

"It's a shame you'll never have her," Marcus' head snapped up as his gaze swept Abbott's frame. Holding back the temptation to smile, Abbott continued with his cruel game. "Emily has been my lover for years and she's hardly likely to take up with someone as foolish as you,"

Marcus felt as though he had been punched in the gut and he sat back with a heavy sigh. "I see," Abbott almost laughed at the stricken look on the other man's face, surprised at how easy it was to poison the well. The clock chimed the quarter hour and punctuated the oppressive stillness. Marcus could find no more words to answer him. It was true that he had held hopes of pursuing a relationship of Emily but with Abbott's gloating tones sounding in the silence of his mind; he could not help but acknowledge the futility of such fantasies.

Abbott gave him a few moments to wallow in introspection before he crossed the room and bent over Melissa's chill body. She was breathing steadily and seemed only to be asleep. He reached down and wrapped a blanket about her before turning back to face Marcus. "She shows no sign of coming out of it,"

Marcus shook his head and cleared thoughts of Emily from his mind. Stepping to Abbott's side, he stared down at his sister. "What do you know about this?" Abbott turned away from his study of Melissa and rubbed his chin in thought. "Abbott?" Marcus pressed, concern for his sister making his voice sharp.

"I don't know that much really," Marcus gave an exasperated sigh. "But," Abbott decided to tease with the barest smidgeon of truth. "I do know that it won't kill her or damage her further,"

Marcus sat on the arm of the chair and brushed a stray strand of hair away from Melissa's pale face. "Do you think she can hear me?"

"I wouldn't know," Abbott replied in a flippant tone as he leant back against the arm of the chair. He casually reached into a pocket and drew forth a small snuff box. Fashioned in gold, the elegantly carved piece of ornamentation flashed in the candlelight as he flipped open the lid and took a pinch of the powder that lay within. "Snuff?" He asked, holding the small box out to Marcus.

"No," Marcus shook his head, staring down at his sister, worry eating at him like acid. Despite the horrors of the past few decades, he had never felt as scared or helpless as he did now. Whatever these brooches were, they were clearly powerful and not to be messed with.

Abbott gave a small roll of his eyes before snapping the lid of the box closed. "Well I think I've done all I can do," He announced as he got to his feet.

"Do?" Marcus replied with a mocking laugh. "I don't

believe you've done anything,"

"I wouldn't say that," Abbott said, picking up the cape that lay by the door. "I gave you a place to stay, and I told you where your sister was," Shrugging into the dark blue garment, he turned to face the door. "And now, I'm going to bed," He reached the door and picked up the candle that sat by the door. "If you need anything in the night, please don't bother me," And with that he left the room, leaving Marcus to stare after him in consternation. He heard Abbott's heavy footsteps climb the stairs, and he relaxed, settling against the back of the chair with something akin to relief. A different kind of quiet settled over the small parlour, a gentler, calmer silence than what had gone before. He wondered if he would ever get used to the mocking superiority that all of the others seemed to display. Even Justin treated him like an immature child on occasion, and it wasn't a feeling he relished. Melissa moaned softly, and he refocused on her still form. Heart pounding in his chest, he took hold of her hand and leant forward.

"Melly..." His voice was quiet and entreating as he tried to reach his sister. "Please come back," With gentle pressure, he drew her into his arms. "Don't leave me here alone..." Raising his eyes to the ceiling, he blinked away tears that he told himself were the result of tiredness. "Not with him..." he knew he was begging, but he did not care."I sent Emily away and Justin," He gulped. "Justin needs you," IIis voice was growing softer as he pleaded. "Please Melly...come back..."

CHAPTER 35

The fog caressed her skin, leaving gooseflesh in its wake. It suffocated and cradled her. From a distance, she could hear the talk of the others, but it was muted, as though they were underwater. For her, there was only the fog deadening each nerve as it swirled and flowed across her body.

"Abomination," The voice filled her head, sending spikes of pain through her skull. She turned to face the speaker, yet the fog obscured her vision.

"What do you mean?" Melissa called, her voice reedy and plaintive in the abyss that surrounded her. She felt arms pick her up from the floor, but it made little difference. It was as though she were wrapped in tight blankets, insulated from the sensations of the world. Briefly she wondered if she had died and if this was how it felt.

"Heretic,"

The voice echoed this time, as though there were others hiding within the fog. Melissa whirled around to look and gasped. The fog had lifted, and she was stood once again in the dusty portrait filled corridor that had plagued her dreams for the past forty years. This time the pictures were of storm and sunset, yet the horror they usually inspired had not diminished. The dust that coated each surface seemed lighter, less dense and myriad footprints tracked through the dirt on the floor. As always she followed the corridor to its end and the horrifying aspect of the flower she now wore. Stood before the open maw of the lotus, she could see the figures from before, the white lotus bloom standing proudly upon their breasts.

"Cursed one," The lead figure stated, pointing a long tapered finger in her direction.

"I don't..." Her words stilled in her throat as they walked toward her, crowding her vision. "Please..."

A finger traced across her flesh, and she gasped at the burning cold that the touch inspired. "Fallen one..." Another hand settled on her shoulder and pulled her backwards. She tried to stay upright, but her legs were captured by others, and she felt herself being lifted into the air. Fear raged through her as they carried her closer to the giant lotus that dominated the centre of the room.

"Please..." She tried again, but they paid her no attention as they held her body over the grinning maw. She thrashed helplessly in their grip, trying to get free.

"Melly... Please come back," The words washed over

her and the figures stilled. On the edge of her vision, she could see faint tinges of candlelight, the warming glow pulling her away from the cold prison. The hand on her leg fell away, and she kicked out, pushing the figures away from her. As Marcus' voice reverberated through the chill, fog-laden landscape, she pushed back against the hands holding her. Her foot connected with a solid thump, and she dropped to the ground. Pushing herself through the crowd of figures, she reached for the light and Marcus.

"Please Melly....come back," With a gasp she thrust herself free from the last figure and dove into the friendly glow of candles and firelight. Taking a deep shuddering breath she opened her eyes as Marcus pulled her into a crushing hug.

"Thank God," He whispered, hugging her to him as she gratefully wrapped her arms around him, tears beginning to form in her eyes. As she began to sob, he held her tightly, comfortingly, allowing her cry without comment.

"It's alright Melly," He whispered as her sobs began to subside. A couple more tears landed on his shoulder, and she finally drew away, revealing her tear-stained face to him. With a gentle touch, he pushed several strands of hair away from her face and smiled reassuringly. "What happened?"

Melissa gulped back further tears and struggled to find her voice. Her head ached from the rush of emotion, and the lump in her throat threatened to choke her. The memories that assailed her were sharp and crisp and her skin still held the chill of the fog. Reaching into her pocket, she dragged out a handkerchief and blew her nose before hugging her arms about herself.

"There were these figures..." In halting, hushed tones, she relayed what she could recall of the dream and shuddered at the sensation of fear that the memories inspired "They called me a fallen one," She stared at her brother and her eyes gleamed with unshed tears. "I didn't understand, but I could feel them touching me," She shuddered and drew her legs up to her chin. "I then heard your voice and managed to fight back," Her black hair fell forward across her face as she rested her chin on her knees.

"Who were they?" Marcus asked, watching her cradle herself with some concern. Melissa was badly frightened, that much was obvious and he had no idea of what idea of what to do. Again his thoughts flashed to Emily and her calm sense of control. Even in a situation as strange as this, she would have an answer.

"I don't know but..." Looking up from her perch, Melissa scrunched up her face in thought as she tried to understand just what she had seen. "I think they're the people who designed the brooches."

"Well that would make sense," Marcus replied as he reached for the blanket and wrapped it about her shoulders. "It did lay you out."

"But I don't know what it did," Melissa said as she snuggled into the fabric, trying to regain some warmth. Memories of that long dusty corridor plagued her mind and she wondered if she should mention her earlier dreams.

"It's not like the lotus," Marcus reasoned as he picked

up the fallen brooch with his handkerchief. "It didn't duplicate itself,"

"So what do you think?" She was slowly warming up, the woollen blanket bringing heat to her frozen limbs.

Marcus shrugged and moved to the fireplace. Deep in thought, he added several large logs to the hot embers and poked them into life with the poker.

"What does Emily think?" Melissa asked, looking about the room, curious about Emily's absence. Marcus sighed and sat back on his heels at the question, wondering just how he was going to explain. The silence lengthened as he discarded sentence after sentence. "Marcus?" He glanced back at the sofa, Melissa was leaning forward, her green eyes fixed on his as she tried to discern what the issue was.

"She..." He hesitated. "Well... Emily..."

Melissa finally stood up and crossed the room to face him. "Spit it out," She commanded.

"I..." He tried again, feeling the words stick to the roof of his mouth. "Emily left..." He said it quickly, hoping that speed would lessen the impact of his words. "I upset her and she left,"

"Marcus," Melissa's voice whipped across the space between them. "What did you say?" her voice was dangerously calm, and Marcus winced.

"I accused her of lying and only being there for people like Abbott," Marcus admitted, feeling his stomach sink even further under Melissa's scrutiny.

"And?"

"I blamed her for our predicament," Marcus could

barely lift his eyes to look at his sister. "She then left,"

"Oh Marcus," Melissa protested as she stared at her older brother. "We can't afford to lose Emily as well as Justin," Pushing the blanket from her shoulders she stood. "You'd better go and get her," She announced.

"Me?" Marcus asked, a stunned note entering his voice. "Why me?"

"Because you're the one who drove her off," She snapped back at him.

He sighed in assent and reached down to pick up his cape. "I don't think she'll want to see me," He noted as he shrugged the garment over his shoulders.

"And you think she'd want to see me?" Melissa retorted.

Marcus' shoulders drooped as he acknowledged her words. Not that he minded apologising, but he was unsure that Emily would return when he did so. With a rush of anger, he remembered her flippant, almost lazy exit. It felt as though she had been waiting for an excuse. He opened his mouth to speak, but Melissa shushed him with a wave of her hand.

"No Marcus, we need Emily, much as I dislike her, I can't deny that she's a formidable ally,"

"Then why don't you go?"

Melissa rolled her eyes and spoke slowly, distinctly, as though she wear talking to a buffoon. "Because I'm not the one in love with her," Marcus started at her words but she continued as though he hadn't. "And I'm not the one who drove her off," Taking a deep breath, she walked forward and placed a hand on his shoulder. "Go and apologise, I know it'll be hard," Her mouth twisted into a tight line. "God knows she is annoying, but we need her. And she will talk to you, me she'd ignore out of spite," Marcus felt his shoulders dip as he acknowledged the truth of Melissa's words.

"Alright," He conceded with considerable reluctance. "I'll go and apologise. Will you be okay here?" He nodded toward the ceiling, indicating his concern about Abbott with that small gesture.

"I'll be fine," Melissa replied as she stepped back and gave him a small push toward the door. "Now get going before she gets too far away,"

She watched him leave the room before she sat down heavily on the couch, the chill still lingering in her bones. Now that she was awake, the memory of the experience was fuzzy and clouded in uncertainty. Had it not been for the lingering chill in her bones, she could have dismissed it all as a dream, yet the cold and the fear remained. Shuddering, she wrapped her arms across her chest and rubbed the tops of her arms with her hands. She could not explain to Marcus about her dream, for she had been dreaming of that corridor and giant lotus flower for years and had not told him. A creak sounded from upstairs, and her head snapped up, hoping that Abbott would stay in his room; she could not deal with any further drama. Stillness settled on the house, and she tucked her legs beneath her as she reached for the blanket. Huddled in the warm and scratchy wool, she let her mind drift through the events of the day. Justin's disappearance; the arrival of Abbott and the finding of the orchid all clamoured for a place in her thoughts. She glanced over at the scarlet brooch, her mind racing a mile a minute. Had she really contacted the creators of this curse? Taking a deep breath she reached out with a blanket covered hand and picked it up from the table. Bringing it close to her eyes, she began to examine each facet of the gold and enamel creation. Like the lotus she wore, the brooch was exquisitely designed and beautifully detailed. Each petal glowed in rich colour and the engraving on the leaves gave the impression that they were alive. Unlike the lotus, there was no catch or hinges. She turned it over and stared at the writing on the back. For a long time she stared down at the flower, thinking of the words before her. Nibbling her lip, she came to a decision and reached out with bare fingers for the brooch.

CHAPTER 36

A strange crackling sound woke Justin from the depths of a troubled sleep. His arms and legs were bound tightly to the wooden floor of what he could only assume to be a wagon. He could hear the sounds of wheels over cobblestones and his body was jolted uncomfortably as the vehicle rumbled over the uneven ground. Through the film that covered his eyes, he couldn't make out where he was. The strange sound came again, and he twisted his head, trying to identify the direction of the sound.

"Justin?" The voice was soft, a whisper that echoed through his skull with almost painful clarity. He tried to move, to find the speaker, yet he could see no one. The wagon bumped through a pothole and the motion sent his head back to the floor in a sharp, slamming motion. Groaning with the pain and dizziness that reverberated like a gong through his head, Justin closed his eyes.

"Justin?" The voice came again, clearer more distinct than before.

"Melissa?" His eyes snapped open, and he tried hard to look for her. "Where are you?" His limited vision swept over the rough wood and sackcloth with no success.

"I'm..." Her voice petered out, leaving nothing but strange, echoes crackling in his mind. "...are you?" Her voice was back, and he strained to hear the rest of the sentence.

With great effort, he tried to jerk into an upright position, but the rope was lashed securely to the floor. All he achieved for his effort was screaming pain in his joints.

"Justin..." The voice faded out entirely and nothing but silence flooded his mind.

"Melissa!" He called out, hoping to hear her respond. He pulled against his bonds and pain erupted through his trapped limbs. He felt woozy and sick, the pain swamping his body. "Melissa?" He tried again, but there was still no response. With his legs and arms like lead, he struggled to break free of the bonds that held him. The pain was indescribable and after a few moments of attempting to wriggle free, he was sick.

"Justin," Katherine poked her head through the curtain that separated the cab of the wagon from the back. "You're not getting free, you're only going to hurt yourself," Her eyes flickered over the small pool of vomit, and she shook her head. "Just calm down," She clambered into the back and mopped up the stinking puddle. She stowed the rag away and reached down, wiping his face with a clean cloth. "I don't want you to hurt yourself," Gentle movements cleaned up the vomit that had dribbled down his chin, and she handed him a flask of brandy. Taking a swig, he rinsed the taste from his mouth.

"Thank you," He uttered before raising his head to stare at her face. Beneath the fall of chestnut hair, her face was sad, almost regretful as she pushed the strands of hair away from his face. "Please don't make it any harder,"

"How does John control you?" Justin asked through shallow breaths.

Katherine turned away, looking anyway but at Justin's face. "Did Emily tell you?"

"Yes," He would have caught hold of her hand, but his bonds were too restrictive. "Tell me about it?" He had spent some of the last forty years investigating Emily's claims about John's control, but he had found nothing. He had wondered if Katherine was using an excuse to distance herself from her actions but, he glanced up at her face, he wasn't so sure of that now. His eyes focused on her face, the set of her lips and how they twisted with some strong emotion. "I can help," He offered with genuine concern.

"I doubt it," Katherine replied as she sat back on her heels and looked down at him. "You don't even know what he's done, how can you fix it?"

"You can tell me about it,"

Katherine gave a small snort and pulled away from

Justin's side. "Emily asked the same thing," She uttered, moving back to the partition as she spoke. "I'll tell you what I told her. I don't know what he did," She turned back to face him, and he could see the anger on her face. "Do you think I would keep it secret if I had the chance of changing anything?" Tears pricked in her eyes. "I have to do as he tells me to," She jerked her head in the direction of the wagoneers seat. "Your brother may know, but he's not sharing," Loathing thrummed through her voice. "He's fully signed up to John's little crusade, despite the fact that he hates the man,"

"Then help me to help you," Justin pleaded in low tones. "I know you don't want to do this,"

"What I want is immaterial," Katherine replied in low, soft tones. "And you can't help, just hope that it doesn't work on you," She lifted the cloth and left him on the floor of the wagon. Justin tried once more to free himself, to no avail. Taking several deep breaths, he lay back on the floor and closed his eyes, hoping that the others would find him before too long. As the cart rattled across the rough country roads, he cast his mind back to before Katherine's arrival and the sound of Melissa's voice. The words had been as clear as a bell, almost as though she were sat beside him. He kept his eyes closed as he worked on the conundrum. The simplest answer stated that he could not have heard her for if she had been there, she would have attempted to free him. Her hatred of Katherine would have made it impossible for her to wait so, his eyes flickered open, It could have been wishful thinking on his part, a desire to hear her voice?

A cramp in his shoulder sent echoes of pain through his back but he ignored it, focusing on his latest theory left no time for discomfort. Imagination seemed even less likely. He had been in dire situations before, worse scenarios than this in fact, but he had yet to hear things. Staring up at the canopy he ran her voice through his head. It had sounded echoey, distant, as though she were underwater. Despite the clarity of the sound, her voice still sounded as though she were far away. Sighing, he tried to roll over to his side, but his bonds kept him fixed to the floor. As the carriage rumbled on, he lost himself in the strange question of Melissa's voice.

CHAPTER 37

Marcus returned to the house just before dawn. He had spent most of the night roaming the streets of Reims and finding nothing of any consequence. In the steel grey light of predawn, he found himself walking the route back toward Abbott's house with a heavy heart. In the hours he had been searching, he had unable to locate any trace of Justin or Emily and worry ate away at him like acid. Despite the arguments that characterised their relationship, he had not realised just how much he had relied on the experience of the older two, and the thought of facing a long questionable future with no help panicked him somewhat. He stopped on a street corner and stared up at the roofs of the houses opposite, trying to stop thinking about his words to Emily.

With a sigh, he pushed his fingers through his hair and tried not to focus on his loss. In the lonely trek though the streets of Reims, he admitted that his feelings for her had become more than platonic in the last few years. He had always known that Emily was attractive but in the wake of her departure he had to admit that Emily had never been too far from his thoughts. He had walked from street to empty street, his thoughts mirroring the empty quiet, as he realised just how much Emily's loss had affected him.

"Christ, I'm an idiot," He muttered as he pushed himself onward, trying not to think about the way Emily smiled or the fact that Abbott had noticed his feelings before he had become to discover them himself. "How could I have said that to her?" Fingers of yellow gold light stole across the sky as he reached the door to the house and pushed it open. He matched his steps to the ticking of the clock as he crossed the threshold and walked towards the parlour.

"Melissa," He crossed the room in a rush and knelt down beside her sprawled body. Blood trickled from her nose, and her eyes were closed. "Melissa?" Her fingers were clasped around the orchid flower, and he tore it from her grasp, throwing it to the floor.

"Marcus?" Melissa heard Marcus' voice from far away as she slowly began to return to consciousness. She felt Marcus lift her from the floor and place her on the cushioned softness of the couch. Her head pounded with the beginnings of an immense headache and she tasted coppery blood within her mouth. Her fingers missed the hard planes of the orchid brooch and she opened her eyes, looking for the gold trinket.

"What the hell were you playing at?" Marcus' voice rasped with anger as he watched her eyes flicker open. "Why were you playing with that thing?" He pushed her hair back from her face and tucked the blanket around her. "You know it's dangerous," Drawing a handkerchief from his pocket, he mopped the trickle of blood from her nose.

Melissa's gaze flashed directly to the locket on the floor as she pushed the blanket away. "I managed to talk to Justin," She announced in shaky tones as she reached out toward the brooch. Wonder tinged her voice as she stretched out to pick up the brooch. It had been a shot in the dark, an effort to follow the inscription on the brooch. She allowed her thoughts to travel back to the moment she had managed to reach her mind out toward Justin. Even though the effort had sent her to the floor, she had managed to reach him. The fragmented, disjointed bits of conversation had sent daggers of pain through her head, but that had not diluted the joyous satisfaction that had soared through her at the sound of his voice. "That's what it does; it lets us communicate to each other,"

"That's crazy,"

"Is it?" Melissa picked the orchid from the floor and stared fixatedly at it. "We can't die, and we drain other peoples' life force," She held the orchid up to the light. "Why can't this one allow us to communicate?"

"Because... because.," Marcus stuttered, unable to find an adequate response. "It can't be possible,"

"It is," Melissa replied, holding the orchid up to the light.

"That inscription," She pointed at the back of the locket. "States that those who have the dark gift could speak at a distance," She hesitated. "I took a chance,"

"Melissa," Marcus sat down beside her with a heavy sigh. "I'm sure you thought you heard him,"

"Oh don't do that Marcus," An angry note entered her voice at his slightly patronising tone. "I know I heard him, that's what knocked me out," Silence settled between the pair of them as Marcus struggled to find something else to say to his sister. "I take it you didn't find Emily," If anything, the silence grew quieter as Marcus bowed his head.

"No," He answered, letting the word hang in the air. The silence lengthened between them and Melissa caught hold of her brother's hand. "I looked for hours and nothing," He shook off her fingers and stood, pacing across the shabby room with nervous, agitated steps.

"And no sign of Justin?"

"I thought you'd spoken to him," Marcus' voice rapped out in mocking notes. He took a breath at the annoyed scowl on his sister's face. "But no, I didn't see any sign of him," He answered in a calmer tone. "It looks like we're on our own,"

Melissa bowed her head and stood up. Reaching for the cape that hung across the chair, she dragged it over her shoulders. "Then let's try and find them," She announced as she headed for the door.

To be continued

Keep reading for a sneak peek at
AMBER SKY,

the first in the
C.O.I.L.S of Copper and Brass Series…

CHAPTER 1

It was November and soot laden fog obscured her progress as Taya walked quickly through the busy street. A chill wind kept the fog moving and froze exposed skin. She was grateful for the shifting whiteness of the fog; it kept curious eyes from her and gave her freedom. The Factory was ahead, belching clouds of smoke and steam into the air as lines of workers queued outside. She averted her eyes and kept going, thoughts of the Factory led to thoughts of the mine and that she could not allow. The work site fell behind her as she began to move uphill, away from the choking smog of the Factory District and towards the Mercantile District. The traffic thinned out as her feet carried her through the cold, whispering quiet of the fog. The traffic was lighter here and better dressed. Several threadbare garments covered her body a moth eaten woollen hat was jammed down on her hair and her boots were held together with twine stuffed with rags to keep the cold out. As she headed into the district, the fog shrouded her from prying eyes and made her progress easier. Moving along the well paved roads of the merchant district with the elusiveness of a wild thing, she avoided the few merchants that braved the cold, speeding up as she reached her destination.

The house was built from white stone that was discoloured from the soot in the atmosphere. On the faded cherry coloured door, a knocker in the shape of a lion warned her off with what she fancied was a contemptuous gaze. For a long moment she stared at the door, wondering at the wisdom of what she was doing. Taking a deep breath, she raised her hand and knocked. For several moments she waited on the doorstop, shifting uneasily from one foot to the other, nervous beyond thought.

The door creaked open and a maid stared down at her with unconcealed distaste.

"No beggars," She announced as she moved to close the door.

"No wait," She placed her foot in the door and leant forward. "I need to speak to Darius...Please," The woman stared down at her with disbelief, sure that the master's son would not want to see a scruffy urchin.

"I don't think so," The woman began pushing the door, physically moving her fragile frame with her weight. Taya held her ground, trying to keep the door open.

"Please…" She pleaded, her voice loud in the hallway. "I need to see him,"

"What's going on?" A male voice echoed across the space and the maid stopped.

"It's this beggar sir," The woman held the door as she turned to face the speaker. "She wishes to talk to you,"

"Let me see," The man walked forward and stared down at Taya, interest sparking in his gaze.

"I need to see you Darius," She appealed directly to him, staring into his ice blue eyes with silent entreaty. "It's important,"

Darius thought for a moment before he nodded. "Let her in," He said to the maid, stepping back along the hall. With a look of shock on her features, the woman stepped away from the door and let Taya into the hall.

Warmth enveloped her as she stepped off the street and followed Darius' beckoning finger to the sitting room. A fire blazed in the hearth, filling the room with warmth. She looked around at the luxuriant surroundings and swallowed nervously.

"Warm yourself up," Darius spoke, indicating the roaring fire and she stepped before it gratefully, feeling the heat radiate across her cold skin. "Emma," He turned to the maid. "Can you find me some old clothes?" With a sour look on her face, the maid agreed. As soon as she had left Darius turned back to the room. "Now that she's gone," He said as he walked forward. "Why don't you tell me what you want?"

Taya bit her lip and fidgeted. What had seemed like a good idea in the safety of her home, now felt like insanity. She glanced at him, noticing the arrogant cast to his features and the surety of his gaze. He was handsome, she realised with a jolt. Beneath a shock of black hair, ice blue eyes stared out at her with disconcerting directness.

"My name's Taya and…" She stopped, wondering how she could continue with her request.

"And?" He encouraged, noticing her hesitation. "I can't help you if you don't ask,"

"My father has just been sent to the mines," She said quickly, watching the realisation cross his face.

"I see," He noted softly, staring at her with interest. "And?"

"He already has a weak heart," She found herself saying. "The mines will kill him,"

"I fancy that's the idea," He uttered reaching for a glass of amber liquid that lay on the mantel and took a sip. "What do you expect me to do about it?"

"You're the son of the overseer," She argued, her voice becoming stronger as she attempted to argue her case. "They say you can get people released,"

"Possibly," He took another sip and regarded her closely. "Who is he?"

Taya swallowed nervously, hoping that her gamble paid off. If she were wrong, he could have the guard here within moments. "Caleb Emerson," She announced, fear rippling through every syllable.

"The saboteur," He whispered, understanding crossing his features. "He's a high profile prisoner,"

"He was set up…"

"I have no doubt," He answered, mockery rippling through his tones.

"It's true," She was angry now. "They pinned it on him because he was protesting at the ration reduction. He would never…." He held up a hand and she stopped speaking, breathing rapidly with the sudden rush of emotion.

"All right I get the point," He fell silent, regarding her closely. For several long moments, he said nothing, his face creased in thought. Tay watched him with increasing impatience.

"Please," She moved to stand before him, her voice pleading as she stared at his face. "He won't survive and the money won't be sent to me and my siblings. We'll all starve,"

"It's not as simple as that," He said finally, looking down at her. "Your father has been sent to the mines to die, you must know that," She glanced away from his gaze, unwilling to see the truth she saw reflected there. "If I manage to get him released, my head is on the block,"

"Then get him transferred," She pleaded, trying not to let tears flow. "Put him on a lighter duty, anything that will keep him alive,"

"It's a big risk,"

"Please,"

"Alright…" He said finally, "I'll see what I can do,"

"Thank you,"

"Just one thing," She turned back to face him. "What are you offering for my help?"

Tay stopped, panic flowing through her. "I thought,"

"You thought I did this out of the goodness of my heart?" He gave a short mirthless laugh. "Not a bit of it, this is going to be dangerous for me. What are you offering for my help?"